indeep

indeep

Erotic Stories

simonsheppard

alyson books
los angeles

MANUFACTURED IN THE UNITED STATES OF AMERICA.

THIS TRADE PAPERBACK ORIGINAL IS PUBLISHED BY ALYSON PUBLICATIONS,
P.O. BOX 4371, LOS ANGELES, CALIFORNIA 90078-4371.
DISTRIBUTION IN THE UNITED KINGDOM BY TURNAROUND PUBLISHER SERVICES LTD.,
UNIT 3 OLYMPIA TRADING ESTATE, COBURG ROAD, WOOD GREEN,
LONDON N22 6TZ ENGLAND.

FIRST EDITION: SEPTEMBER 2004

04 05 06 07 08 **a** 10 9 8 7 6 5 4 3 2 1

ISBN 1-55583-804-9

LIBRARY OF CONGRESS CATALOGING-IN-PUBLICATION DATA
SHEPPARD, SIMON (SIMON H.)
    IN DEEP : EROTIC STORIES / SIMON SHEPPARD.—1ST ED.
    ISBN 1-55583-804-9
    I. EROTIC STORIES, AMERICAN. 2. GAY MEN—FICTION. I. TITLE
PS3619.H4615 2004
813'.6—DC22   2004049053

CREDITS
COVER PHOTOGRAPHY BY BODY IMAGE PRODUCTIONS.
COVER DESIGN BY MATT SAMS.

For Nick Street, a real mensch.
And for William, a great cuddler.

Contents

"That means you think it could be a hit," said Sammy.
"It's very difficult to fail at pornography," Deasey said.

—Michael Chabon, *The Amazing Adventures of Kavalier & Clay*

acknowledgments

I owe many thanks to a great number of folks who've offered aid, comfort, and the occasional salutary short, sharp shock. I've said it before: porn writers are, by and large, the nicest bunch of folks you (or John Ashcroft, for that matter) could hope to meet. My love and appreciation go out to a whole bunch of them.

In the interest of brevity, though, I'll keep things focused. I'd like to thank three guys at Alyson: Nick, Dan, and Scott. And to hereby acknowledge the folks who've helped midwife (midhusband?) some of the stories in this book: Alan Bell, Gary Bowen, Scott Brassart, M. Christian, Jim Ericson, Greg Herren, Richard Labonte, Michael Luongo, Peter Millar, Mary Ann Mohanraj, Bill Noble, Alec Wagner, and Greg Wharton. A tip of the hat goes to Winston Leyland, from whose book *Out in the Castro* "A QBJ at JB" is reprinted.

Lastly, I'd like to humbly thank the many queer men who, in one way or another, served as the inspiration for these stories. Whether I observed you, desired you, or got in your pants, you guys were—each and every one—more beautiful than my fallible prose can possibly convey.

foreword

Why I Still Love to Write Porn

I confess: I love to worship at the Altar of Dick. And surely the last couple of years—say, since I put together my first short story collection, *Hotter Than Hell*—have been an interesting time for those of us guys who like to get down on our knees.

For one thing, the ancient and honorable practice of sodomy is now legal in all 50 of the United States of America, bringing the country kicking and screaming—and a little late—into the 20th century. And, not so suddenly, gay has gone, in a lot of ways, mainstream. It's a mixed blessing, as most blessings are. On the one hand, straight America has gotten kind of used to the idea that we queers are everywhere, and that we aren't going back in no damn closet.

But—and here's the big "but"—male-male sex is still wildly under dispute. Is it okay for us to redecorate straights' houses? Sure. Get married? Maybe. Fuck one another vigorously up the butt? Well, um, uh...

So here am I, still writing stories about guys getting it on with one another. And I still really love doing it. Yes, writing *Kinkorama*, a nonfiction book celebrating perversion, was great fun (if harrowing at times). But creating erotica, especially stories of male lust, is somehow special. I've rarely shied away from pretension, so let me

foreword

say it right out: I think writing queer porn is a privilege. More: I think it's a sacred trust.

Yes, battling for queer rights is vitally important, but let's not forget what's up below the belt. No matter how many sitcom characters are gay, no matter how widespread domestic-partnership laws become, even if in the years ahead there's legalized gay marriage—hell, even a gay president—there's something irreducibly, uniquely wonderful about what happens when a man wants a man. And it's even cooler when a man *gets* a man.

No, not everyone thinks so. Some people hate us for what we are, for what we do. Christ on a bicycle! Why do some folks get their knickers in such a twist over what other people do with their own bodies? It's a bit of an unpleasant mystery, huh?

Back in 1972, French queer theorist Guy Hocquenhem wrote (and I promise this'll be the last bit of pretentious intellectualism...at least for a while), "If the homosexual image contains a complex knot of dread and desire, if the homosexual fantasy is more obscene than any other and at the same time more exciting, if it is impossible to appear anywhere as a self-confessed homosexual without upsetting families...then the reason must be that for us 20th century Westerners there is a close connection between desire and homosexuality. Homosexuality expresses something—some aspect of desire—which appears nowhere else, and that something is not merely the accomplishment of the sexual act with a person of the same sex." And if some really smart French guy said that, who the hell am I to disagree?

So if I can do my bit for the shock troops of sodomy—if I can celebrate, in all its complex thorniness and simple glory, homo-sex—then buddy, I think that's time and effort well spent.

Over the years, more than a few people have asked me why I don't try writing straight porn, or non-sexual queer lit, or mysteries or science fiction or something, anything, else. Okay, maybe it's a bit of laziness; maybe it's fear of failure. But most of all—thoroughly, transcendently most of all—I write queer porn because I adore male homosexuality. Just adore it: in a Walt Whitman sense; in a porn video sense; in terms of boy-meets-boy romance; in terms of getting down on your knees and sucking a stranger's hard cock. In a world of compromise, disappointment, mortality, I celebrate the way men look and feel and smell and taste because that's what can bring me closer to whatever provisional Heaven is out there; stick my face in a sweaty man's smelly armpit and I see God.. Dear and patient and horny reader, I repeat: I love, really love, to worship at the Altar of Dick. No apologies.

So if I can keep writing about all that—the finely modulated dances of desire; hot holes waiting to be filled; the pleasures of the penis; big, spurting gobs of jizz—I'll be happy. And it's my fondest hope that it will make you happy, too.

—Simon Sheppard

adamandsteve

In the beginning, God created Adam and Steve.

Needless to say, they loved each other a lot, quite a lot. And when they came home from toiling in the fields, they'd gleefully strip off their clothes and jump right into bed. Steve really loved it when Adam got on all fours, naked ass in the air, the line of dark blond hair in his crack inviting a friendly visit from Steve's cock. Adam, meanwhile, enjoyed Steve's prodigious oral talents; it seemed to Adam that no one had ever given head better than his lover...which was quite literally the case. Steve had an uncanny knack of gulping the head of his lover's nicely curved dick all the way down his gullet, using his throat muscles to milk salty-sweet drops of precum out of Adam's piss slit. At moments like that, when Adam felt he was surely going to shoot his wad, he'd gasp out, "Fuck me." And Steve would happily oblige.

While Steve was quite a conventional hunk—tall, dark, well-muscled, with a chiseled face out of a magazine—Adam looked less "male model" than strictly working class. He was built like a fire-plug, with big, powerful thighs, just the hint of a belly, and a shaved head that made him look a bit like rough trade. Which was fine with Steve. Whenever he woke before Adam and looked over at his still peacefully sleeping boyfriend, he'd think something along the lines of *What a hunk* and his dick would begin to swell. He'd rub his hard-on against Adam's meaty butt and lean over and kiss his lover's lips. Adam would open his eyes and smile, and within moments, Steve's big, hard cock would be inside him, pumping away. Adam, lying on his back, legs in the air, would look up at his boyfriend's beautiful, sweaty face and push his ass upward, impaling himself on every inch of Steve. Then he'd reach down, muscular forearm brushing his belly, and stroke himself with his calloused hand. It wouldn't take long till he shot a big, salty load—if he'd had a belly button, there would have been a little pool of jizz there. If Steve hadn't shot off yet, Adam would reach up and pinch Steve's prominent nipples, pretty hard, till he felt Steve's cock pulsing out sperm inside his ass. And then they'd wipe up and go make the morning coffee.

It was love, all right. They were in paradise.

And so things went, year after happy year, in their little house somewhere west of Nod. So it might have gone forever, peaceful and unruffled, if the stranger hadn't come to town. The stranger was narrow-hipped, his tongue kept flicking out over his thin lips, and he acted like he knew what he was talking about.

"Understand ye not," the stranger said, after he'd shown up uninvited at their door, "that what ye doest is wrong?"

"Actually, no," said Adam. "Now get lost."

"Wrong," said the stranger. "Wrong, wrong, wrong."

Adam shut the door in his face.

Steve looked doubtful. "Maybe we should have heard him out," he said.

"Guy's an asshole," Adam said, playfully reaching for his boyfriend's crotch.

And there matters might have rested had the stranger not shown up again the next night. When Adam opened the door, he muttered "Oh, shit," but the stranger just barged right inside, like he had something to sell.

"I tell ye both," the skinny stranger intoned, "that unless ye change your ways, verily thou art doomed."

"Didn't I tell you yesterday to fuck off?" Adam said. But Steve kind of cleared his throat, and when Adam looked over, his boyfriend had a funny expression on his face, one he'd never seen there before. It looked a lot like guilt.

"Adam, maybe we should hear what he has to say?"

"Of course we shouldn't. What the fuck is wrong with you, Steve?" Adam said. And then, to the stranger, "Get the hell out of our house, mister." He held up a reddened, meaty fist. "Or else."

The stranger turned tail and fled, looking back over his shoulder for one parting shot. "Verily, there art no place thou canst hide from thine own sin," he hissed.

"Sin? What the fuck is that?" Adam said. But Steve still had that look on his face, as though he wanted to cry, and it worried Adam. The rest of the day seemed strained. When Adam whipped out his hardening prick, expecting that Steve would, as usual, get down on his knees and start licking, his boyfriend demurred. "Not now, okay?" Adam was left to jack off alone, spilling his seed into a hankie.

And after they'd finished dinner, Steve said, "You mind doing the dishes by yourself this one time? I want to go for a walk."

"But it's dark out."

"There's a full moon," Steve said, and headed out the door.

When Steve got back, hours later, he seemed like a stranger.

"You saw him, didn't you?" Adam said. "He talked to you."

But Steve just said, "Listen, I'm going to sleep on the couch tonight, okay?"

The next morning, Adam was woken not by his lover's gentle touch, the insistent throb of Steve's hard dick, but by the rattling of pots and pans. He struggled to consciousness.

"Steve?" he called.

"Yeah?"

"Whatcha doing out there?"

"Packing up."

"Packing up?"

"Adam, listen, I need to get a place of my own. Just for a while. I need to be by myself, to sort things out."

"*Steve!*" Adam leapt out of bed. His boyfriend was in the kitchen, stowing cookware into a bundle.

"I'm going to leave most of our stuff with you, okay? I just need to get away for a while."

"Steve, what the fuck are you doing?"

Steve looked at Adam's stocky, naked body, the flesh he knew so well, the pendulous cock still half-hard with morning wood. But no...he'd made his mind up. "It's just for a while, okay? I think."

And all of Adam's tears and pleas could not make Steve change his mind. By sundown, he was gone.

If Adam thought he loved Steve before, now he was more than certain. The days without him were long, the nights longer. He was glad that the stranger never showed his face again; Adam was not a violent man, but some provocations are too great. And nothing could be worse, Adam thought, than trying to destroy love.

Soon things went from bad to worse. Adam ran into his friend Lud, who told him he'd heard that Steve was engaged to be married. "To this girl Traci, from over near Gomorrah."

"Well, that was quick," said Adam, feigning a devil-may-care attitude. But he was all torn up inside.

Day after day, week after week, he dragged himself through life, missing Steve, cursing the stranger and his vicious meddling. He began to drink, a little at first, then to excess, sometimes waking up in a pool of his own vomit. It was past pathetic, but he missed his boyfriend with a pain that pierced his heart.

Then one weary night, while Adam was preparing a mess of pottage, there was a knock, gentle but insistent, on the door. He opened it slowly, hesitant to hope. But there stood Steve; with the setting sun behind him lighting up his shock of hair, he looked like an angel. The two men stood speechless, face-to-face.

Finally, Steve dropped to his knees. "I'm so sorry, Adam," he said. "So very, very sorry. You were right. The guy was an asshole, and I was wrong to listen to him. Loving you could never be wrong."

Adam felt hot tears running down his cheeks. "And Traci?" he asked.

"It was all a mistake. But now I understand who I am. I'm the man who loves you, and only you." He looked up. "I know you probably can't forgive me, but..."

Adam reached down and stroked Steve's beautiful face. "Of course I can." He helped Steve to his feet and threw his arms around him. "Baby," he said, holding Steve tight. "My baby." He felt his lover's cock swelling up against his own.

"I love you," said Steve, "and I'll love you forever. And I want to fuck your brains out."

Without another word, Adam stripped off his clothes and got down on all fours. The light of the full moon made his naked flesh glow. Steve got naked, too, and knelt behind his lover. "God, I missed you so much," he said, and bent over his lover, licking the small of Adam's back, then moving his tongue down to his tailbone, to the top of his ass crack. He spread his boyfriend's chunky butt cheeks, then moved his mouth further down the hairy cleft. Adam's asshole radiated heat, a heat that Steve's tongue sought and found, zeroing in on the soft flesh of the hole, working its way inside. Adam moaned and opened up, and his lover's tongue entered him deeper.

"Oh, fuck, fuck yeah," the first man on Earth said. "That feels so fucking good. So good."

Steve slurped at the tender flesh inside Adam a while longer, then reared back to a kneeling position. His dick was rock-hard and drooling precum like a motherfucker.

"Adam," he said, his cock head rubbing up against his partner's wet, twitching hole.

"Steve," Adam answered back, moving his ass backward till he felt the big, swollen head of his lover's prick enter him, pushing its way in past the ring of muscle. He relaxed and let Steve slip his cock all the way in, gasping as he felt the slightly painful pleasure of getting fucked.

Steve's strokes deepened as he felt Adam's miraculous ass open up for him. He stroked his boyfriend's muscular butt, his big, furry thighs. *There's no way in hell,* he thought, *this can possibly be wrong.* And to Adam he said, "Let's get you on your back, sexy. I want to be able to look into your eyes."

When Adam was on his back, his big legs over his lover's shoulders, Steve positioned his cock up against Adam's pleading hole, then shoved his way inside again. Adam grunted and smiled. Steve thought he'd never seen anything—not the birds of the air nor the flowers in the fields—anywhere near as lovely as his boyfriend's sweaty face.

"Fuck me harder," Adam said, and so Steve did, his strokes almost brutal now, pounding against Adam's prostate until milky fluid dribbled from Adam's slit. Adam closed his eyes and opened his mouth, and Steve let a stream of spit flow from his lips into Adam's mouth. Adam gulped it down like it was honey.

As Adam and Steve neared their orgasms, a hush came over the room, nothing to be heard but the holy sound of flesh entering flesh. The light of the full moon brightened, and when Adam opened his eyes and looked into Steve's beautiful face, he would have sworn he could see angels from the corner of his eye.

And there were in fact angels in the room, hovering over the forms of the two naked men in love. The light in Adam and Steve's little home was almost supernaturally bright now, moving in swirls in time with the beating of the angels' wings. Adam's ass was aflame with desire. Steve's cock was bursting-full of cum. Steve bent over and planted his mouth on Adam's and their tongues met, an electric spark, and refused to part. Neither could hold back any longer. They both found release, Steve deep within Adam, Adam all over his own belly, and as they shot their loads, the light in the room flashed into brightness, dissolving everything—the angels, the men on the floor, even time and space itself—for one long, sacred moment.

And God, in His wisdom, smiled down.

indeep

Utila's just a flyspeck on the map of the world. It lies right off the Honduran coast, one of the Bay Islands, a place settled by pirates who braved the seas for gold.

These days the island's wealth arrives with young divers who come to explore the coral reef. Visitors don't arrive by frigate anymore; they fly in from La Ceiba on small planes, planes with warning signs written in Russian, decommissioned junkers from Aeroflot or someplace. Every time a plane dips its wings toward the Caribbean's blue, the passengers hold their breaths and pray. I know I did. Except for the praying part.

I'd been to Guatemala already, spent a full-moon night amongst the pyramids of Tikal, communing with ghosts, getting over a love affair I never should have allowed to drag me down. I'd submerged myself in Kate, her desires and her life and most of all her needs. And after two years of misery, I'd discovered it was a mistake. She was a mistake, my job was a mistake, my life was going nowhere. I decided to skip the worst of a Philadelphia winter and head to Central America to lick my wounds.

The flimsy little plane managed to touch down on Utila's grassy airstrip, just beside a crystal-blue harbor. It was only a short walk to the main street. Quaint as hell, wooden buildings, tropical paradise. Dive shops. Restaurants. Lots of small hotels. Hotels without a single room for rent.

Semi-exhausted from dragging my backpack up and down the street in a fruitless search for a place to stay, I collapsed into

indeep

a tattered wicker chair in the lobby of Lucie's Hotel.

"Hey. You look exhausted."

I looked up. He was dark and slightly stocky, Greek background maybe, or Israeli, wearing shorts, flip-flops, and a raggedy T-shirt.

"I am. You know of any place to stay? I'll be damned if I can find a vacant room."

"You should have caught the earlier flight over."

"Now you tell me." I grimaced.

"Listen. There's a second bed in my room. If you don't snore, you'd be welcome to spend the night. I'll just have to check it out with the management."

"Lucie?" I asked.

"There is no Lucie. Never has been, I hear." He extended his hand. "My name's Aaron."

"Thom," I said. "Pleased to meet you. How long you been here?"

"A while. Great place to dive."

"So I hear."

"Water's so clear you can always see the bottom. All the way down."

I spent the afternoon settling in, exploring the little town. Half the families in town had the same surname, Harrison. And half the businesses were dive shops.

It was a great place for scuba, all right. Or at least a bargain; pre-purchasing 10 boat dives brought the price down to a third of what it would have cost stateside. I found a likely looking dive shop, the Neptune, checked it out, and paid for 10 dives, enough to keep me busy during my planned week on the island.

I was at the far end of the main street when the sky began dumping rain. Everything was getting that wet-tropics smell as I jogged back toward the hotel.

I made it back soaked to the skin and went to my new room and changed my clothes. I was sitting on the porch overlooking the harbor, listening to the rain hammering on the corrugated metal roof, when a blonde woman came up the stairs. She wasn't bad looking—a little plump, maybe, but she had nice breasts, and her nipples showed through her rain-damp T-shirt.

"Hello," she said, her accent Scandinavian. "You just arrived?"

"Yeah, this morning." I was thinking about how one of those nipples would feel in my mouth. I hadn't had a woman since Kate left me.

"You stay at this hotel?"

"Yes," I said, "I'm doubling up with a man named Aaron."

She made a strange face.

"Anything wrong?"

"No, it's just that I've heard..." Another mysterious look. "Never mind."

We chatted for a while about approximately nothing, the way that strangers on the road do. I kept glancing at her tits, I guess.

I finally decided to pop the question. "Are you doing anything tonight? Want to go for a drink?"

"I should tell you," she said, "that I am a lesbian."

And that was that.

That night I went for dinner at a restaurant down the road, the food tasty but served at a snail's pace. It was Saturday, so the town's two discos were cranking up their sound systems, blatting bad music into the balmy tropical night. I popped into one and by the time I'd finished my first rum-and-Coke had decided it really wasn't my scene.

I headed back to the hotel and curled up in bed. I'd had to get up early to make the trip from the mainland of Honduras, so I drifted off quick.

Something woke me up.

I looked around. In the dim blue moonlight, I could see that my roommate Aaron had returned. He was sprawled on his back in the other bed, a few feet away in the small room. The sheets were tangled around his feet. His hairy body was naked, and he was jerking off.

I hadn't watched guys jack off since Boy Scouts, and I was kind of curious. Careful not to draw his attention, I watched Aaron as he stroked and squeezed his dick. His technique, I noticed, was very different from mine; I tend to really pound away. He was more poetic, slow, like it was happening underwater.

I felt, to my surprise, my own cock getting hard. No embarrassment, no shame, just surprise. I would have reached down to my crotch, but I was afraid he'd see me. So I lay there scarcely breathing for three, four, five minutes as he played with himself. Every once in a while he'd take his hand away to get more spit, and I could see his cock was very hard, not very big, and gleaming wet.

Eventually he started writhing and arching his back, moaning loudly enough to wake me up, if I'd been asleep. With a muffled groan, he oozed a big load of cum on his belly, then wiped it up with his hand and licked it off his palm. He pulled the covers up, rolled over with his back toward me, and seemed to go to sleep.

The next morning I woke up in a sticky little puddle. I hadn't jacked off the night before, but my cum had made an escape anyway.

Aaron was already gone. I was up early enough to go on a morning boat dive. I grabbed a cup of coffee and a slice of coconut bread at a nearby bakery. I thought about the night before, then tried not to. I figured it wouldn't happen again. I slurped down the last of the coffee and headed for the Neptune Diver Shop.

Even without reservations I had no trouble getting a place on the morning boat. I pulled on the rented dive gear, the wet suit tightly hugging my body, grabbed my two full tanks, and headed for the dock. There were four other customers on the boat: a Canadian married couple, and a dreadlocked blond surfer from Southern California and his purple-haired girlfriend. The divemaster, Berndt, briefed us as we headed southwest of the island to Stingray Point.

The Canadians had just been PADI certified, so we took it fairly easy on the first dive, only heading down to 30 feet or so. The water was glorious, the coral beautiful, the reef fish streaking colorfully around our group.

It had been months since I'd last been diving, and now I remembered why I loved it so: the astonishing peace of the liquid world, the feeling of being where people weren't meant to go, the cold isolation of breathing the air of life through a mouthpiece gripped between my teeth, the beauty of the reef system, which in Honduras is pretty damn overwhelming. Lettuce coral, brain coral, pillar coral, elkhorn and star. And the schools of angelfish, parrot fish, chromis. The second dive, at Jack Neil Point, was just as nice, even nicer as big sea turtles swam among our little group. When Berndt led us back to the boat, I was sorry to leave the water. I was sorry to get back to life.

But it was time to head back to shore.

Two dives a day are usually plenty for me. I had a lunch of fried fish at a little place run by two sisters, then went back to sit on the hotel porch, and read and caught up on writing postcards. People came and went, sometimes making small talk. I wondered where the Scandinavian lesbian was; I would have liked to ask her more about my roommate, but she never appeared.

It was late afternoon before I saw Aaron. He headed up the stairs and climbed into the hammock suspended from the porch.

"Having fun?" he asked.

"Yeah, went on a couple of dives this morning."

"Explored the island yet? Out by Pumpkin Hill?"

"Nah," I said. "I figure there'll be plenty of time for that. I'm feeling really lazy today."

"We should go out there sometime," Aaron said, "you and I."

"Uh, okay," I agreed.

"Thought about dinner yet?"

"It's early."

"Yeah, but the service is so slow. And sometimes if you don't get to a restaurant early, they run out of whatever you want."

I looked out at the Caribbean, ripples glistening in sunlight. "That's the thing about coming to a place like this. You gotta remain flexible. How long you been here?"

"I'm going to go lie down in the room. Come get me when you're starting to get hungry. After dinner we can go get drunk at the Bucket of Blood."

Dinner was good, the conch soup excellent, though, as Aaron had warned me, the service was glacially slow, even worse than the evening before. By the time we'd paid the check, it was well into the night. Over at the Bucket of Blood we drank rum-and-Cokes till I had trouble seeing straight. The dreadlocked surfer boy was there, looking glum. I wondered where his purple-haired girlfriend had gotten to. For someone who'd been on the island a while, Aaron didn't seem to know anyone there. Which was okay; he was friendly enough, friendlier as the night wore on and we grew drunker. I kind of liked him.

When I'd had enough of cheap rum, strangers, and endless replays of *Bob Marley's Greatest Hits,* I suggested we turn in.

We staggered down the street, among lots of other soused tourists and a few semi-sober locals, and stumbled up the stairs to our room. Aaron threw himself onto his bed.

"Oh, man," he said. He pulled his T-shirt over his head. "I'm ready to pass out," he said. His torso was fleshy, generously covered with dark hair. He began to unzip his khaki shorts.

"Want me to turn out the light?" I asked. "So you can get some sleep?"

"No, leave it on." He was down to his briefs now. He began rubbing his crotch through the white cotton. I just lay there watching him as he peeled off his underwear and started stroking his cock. He'd thrown his near leg over the edge of the bed so I had a view of his balls and the hair between his legs.

"Oh, man," he repeated. His dick was hard.

And so was mine.

I looked him in the face. He looked back with deep, dark eyes and nodded.

I reached down and unzipped my shorts. I wasn't wearing underwear; the flesh of my swelling cock was hot to the touch. I pulled my shorts down and my shirt up, grabbed my dick, and started playing with the foreskin.

We lay there side by side, a couple of feet apart, two almost-strangers, masturbating.

I kept glancing from his eyes to his cock, then back to his face again. As interesting as it was to see him jacking his dick, it was more intense to watch his face. I'd seen women get off, of course, but I'd never watched another man while he had sex. I submerged myself in his eyes as he slowly brought himself close to orgasm.

I wanted to touch him, to feel what another man's cock was like, but I couldn't bring myself to do it. And I was half-afraid and half-hoping he'd get up, come over to me, touch me. But he didn't. So we just lay there, hands working our own hard-ons, until he nodded and said, "Now?"

"Now," I said.

He looked so beautiful when he came. I wondered if I looked

that way too. I glanced down; the hair on his belly was strewn with ropes of cum.

"Good night," he said.

"I've...I'm...gonna go clean up, take a shower."

"Don't move," he said. He swiveled himself out of bed, knelt beside me on the floor. He leaned over my torso and gently lapped up my cum, his tongue moving over my belly and chest. I wanted to grab his head, part of me did, and guide him down to my dick. But I didn't.

When he was done, he wordlessly got into his bed and curled up under the thin bedcover, his back toward me.

After a while he spoke. "You can turn out the light now."

The first thing Aaron said to me when I woke up was, "Fuck the boat dives. Let's go snorkeling out by the airport."

"Sure," I heard myself saying. We slipped into Speedos and T-shirts and, grabbing our fins and masks, headed out.

It was a shortish way down the street to the landing field. As Aaron and I wordlessly walked side by side in the morning sun, I kept thinking back to the night before, the sight of his cock, the feeling of his mouth on my flesh. I looked over at his face, then down to his hairy legs. Despite myself, I was getting hard. I shifted the fins to in front of my crotch, but Aaron caught on and chuckled.

"Don't worry about it," he said. "Happens to the best of us."

Beyond the rocky shoreline, the warm Caribbean stretched forever. Nobody else was around. We adjusted our masks and snorkels, pulled on our fins, and walked backwards into the gently lapping waves.

Even in the shallows, the waters were alive with riotously colored fish. Careful not to cut ourselves on coral, we swam a little ways out, breathing through our little plastic tubes. The ocean bottom receded with every stroke. Sea anemones wavered in the currents, feeding on things too tiny to see.

I felt Aaron's hand stroking my side. For a second, I wanted to push it away. Instead I hung there, floating on the surface of another world while his touch explored my flesh. His fingers moved down to the waistband of my Speedos, then over my ass. Kate had never touched me that way, no woman had. He slipped his fingers beneath the thin fabric, stroked the flesh of my butt. His fingertips moved toward my ass crack. With a kick of my fins, I jetted myself away from him.

I wanted not to be feeling those things. I wanted my cock not to be throbbing in my bathing suit. I wanted to look at the pretty coral and the pretty fish and forget that I'd ever known Aaron. Instead, I floated in the crystal-clear embrace of the water until he caught up with me. I let him touch me again, touch my chest, my belly, run his hand across my crotch, my hard cock, peel down the front of my suit, grab me, my flesh, my dick. He tugged my suit down to around my thighs and dove down beneath me. He pulled at my feet till I was vertical in the water, then surfaced for a breath and dove down again. Looking down I saw him spit out the mouthpiece of his snorkel. Exhaling a trail of bubbles, he wrapped his mouth around my dick, his tongue even wetter than the water. The vagaries of buoyancy dragged us upward till I was on my back, Aaron floating between my thighs, his face now above the waterline. He breathed through his nose, his mouth still in possession of my cock.

"Jesus, Aaron, somebody might see us," I said, and as if on cue, the drone of the morning plane came over the horizon.

He took his mouth from my hard-on, which flopped onto my belly, little waves lapping at my dick flesh.

"Let's go back to the hotel room, then. Unless you're afraid."

"Let's just go back. Go back and do nothing," I said. "Give me time. I've gotta think."

The walk back was awkward. When we got to the hotel Aaron kept on walking down the street. I went up to our room, took a cold shower, then went out to stare at the sea.

As I sat on the porch the Scandinavian girl came up to me.

"You've been spending time with him?"

"Aaron?" I asked.

"*Ja*," she said.

"Just what do you have against him, anyway?" I was sure she could see into me, my dirty secret. I was sure she *knew*.

"He's no good. Dangerous."

"How the hell would you know?"

"He used to be my boyfriend." Her voice was tired, resigned.

"But you're a *lesbian!*"

"Yes, mostly, but Aaron and I lived together in Chicago. We came here to Central America together last month. He used to be my boyfriend."

"Until?" I asked.

"You'll see," she said.

I was lying on my bed beneath an open window. There must have been a power failure. The electricity didn't work. The fan didn't move. Even with the window open it was hot and stifling. I didn't care. I lay there thinking about the shipwreck of my life.

Aaron still hadn't returned when the wind picked up, blowing dark clouds over the island. And then, with that suddenness of tropical rainstorms, it was pouring, coming down in sheets. I could have reached up and shut the window. I didn't.

The rain blew in, soaking me, my clothes, the bed. I didn't care, I didn't give a fuck about anything. I didn't have Kate, I hated my job, I hated my life. I was forced to admit it: The only thing that had given me real pleasure for a long while—well, maybe not pleasure, but it was interesting at least—was Aaron, being with Aaron.

"Enough time?"

Aaron was standing in the open doorway, sopping wet.

"Huh?" I said.

"You had enough time to think about things, to *decide?*" There was the slightest trace of a sneer.

I nodded. He walked over to my bed, stood in front of me, and pulled down his wet Speedos. His dick wasn't hard, not yet, and somehow that made it all the nicer. I could understand now how a woman could see a threat in a hard-on. I could understand how nothing matters, really. I reached for him.

Our wet bodies slid over each other. His dick was hard now, and mine was too. We kissed—the first time I'd ever kissed a man—our tongues like dolphins, our breaths intertwined. When our faces parted I asked a question. "Now what?"

Aaron slid down over the rain-soaked sheets as thunder drummed outside. I expected him to suck my cock. But he pushed my legs up and slid his face down to my ass. His tongue dove inside me. I was ashamed. But my penis was stiff.

Am I a faggot now? I wondered, as he licked my ass, kissing, tonguing, like some strange fish swimming where it didn't belong. I heard a moan—my own—above the thunder. And then lightning. And his mouth moved to my balls, licking, sucking till I began to ache.

"My cock, please. My cock," I begged him.

"Suck me," Aaron said.

"Me suck you?"

"Who else?"

"Yes," I said. "I will." Then I was sorry I'd spoken. But he was already moving over me, twisting his body so his crotch was against my face. The head of his cock, a deep, angry pink, darker than mine, was inches from my mouth. What the hell. I opened wide.

It wasn't bad, sucking cock. A little strange, maybe, but then it got good. I was hungry for Aaron, for his small, hard cock jutting from a bush of curly black hair. I was hungry for him and I gulped him down, as far down my throat as I could without gagging. He pumped into me, rocking back and forth the smallest bit, never leaving the back of my mouth. I grabbed his ass, held on tight. Rain was hitting my face.

I couldn't breathe. I tried to through my nose, but it wasn't enough. I wondered if anybody had ever choked to death sucking cock.

"Let me loose, Thom. Back off, you fuck," Aaron said.

And he pulled his dick out of my mouth and slid down till he was lying on top of me, two men's bodies, wet, face-to-face, dick-to-dick. He kissed me. Harder, longer than before. I felt his hands go around my neck. If lightning had crashed just then, it would have been too melodramatic. Lightning crashed.

His lips were still on mine as he squeezed down gently on my windpipe, harder on the arteries on the sides of my neck. I should have been scared. He squeezed harder. I was all of 28 years old, maybe about to die, and I didn't mind. I wanted him to keep squeezing. Harder. Harder. He did.

I was straining to breathe. Trapped blood was throbbing in my brain. I was still aware enough to feel our two hard cocks rubbing together, wet. I wanted him to fuck me. He wasn't going to; he was going to choke me. Things looked darkish red, little spots dancing before my eyes. I was out of air. I reached for his wrists, intending to pull his hands away. I grabbed them, all right, but I drew them inward instead. The thunder was close now, rattling everything. I was making little mewling noises, hoarse, tiny gasps. My mouth opened wide for his tongue. I wanted to unhinge my jaw for him, a boa constrictor swallowing poisoned prey.

Things became even darker, dark as night. It was nice. I could feel my eyes bulging out of my skull. I threw my head back, gave my throat to him.

"Oh, yeah," he said. "Oh, *man!*"

I thought of the blonde dyke with the big tits. I had been warned. Everything went black.

When I came to, struggling to the surface of consciousness, Aaron was lying beside me on the wet bed. My belly was spattered with ropes of cum.

"I been unconscious for long?" I asked.

"No, not long."

"And whose cum is this? Yours? Mine?"

"Does it matter?" Aaron asked.

"To me it does, yeah." Though I'm not sure I could have put into words just why it was important.

"Both of ours," said Aaron. "You came while I was strangling you."

"Really?"

"Yeah, and so did I." He didn't quite smile.

I wish he'd have fucked me, I was thinking. *At least then I'd know for sure what it feels like.*

"I guess we should close that window now, let the room dry off," I said.

But my bed was still damp when nighttime came around. When it was time to go to sleep I crawled into Aaron's bed and lay there shivering beside him. He didn't say a word, just wrapped his arm around my neck and gave it a squeeze. My cock got hard.

It was still hard when I woke up.

The previous winter Kate and I had gone cross-country skiing out West. I'd gotten hold of some cocaine and we decided it would be fun to ski while we were buzzed. We skied five or six miles to the rim of a valley; the last few hundred yards to the overlook were an icy mess. On the way back the coke started wearing off. We were in the middle of nowhere when a snowstorm hit. One of my gloves had started coming apart; the snow made its way through the unraveled fingertip, bringing a cold that led to numbness. The storm rose to near-whiteout conditions. I was exhausted and lost, and all I wanted to do was give up. I started to whimper. I told Kate that all I wanted, all I could do, was to sit down in the snowy field and wait to die, to freeze, to melt in the next spring's thaw. But she, unsympathetic, had skied on ahead; I had no choice but to follow. Somehow we made it back to the lodge.

I thought about that ski trip the next morning on the boat. Aaron had decided to come along and dive, and as I looked at him I remembered that snowy, helpless feeling.

The boat was heading to the north side of Utila, to the dive site near Blackish Point. The seas were a little rough, so to take my mind off the sway of the boat, I decided it was time to ask.

"I was talking to this blonde girl, says she's your girlfriend. Is she?" Aaron's handsome face darkened. "She's a bitch. A crazy cunt." I kept quiet after that.

We reached the point and the boat dropped anchor. The other divers on the boat weren't very experienced, so Aaron and I had talked the divemaster into letting us go off on our own. We double-checked each other's equipment, let some air into our BCD vests, held our hands over our masks, and launched ourselves backward over the side of the boat.

There's something about the shock of first hitting the water that never becomes routine. It's the feeling that your equipment, so heavy on land, has become effortlessly light. The sudden submersion, the bubbles rising from the regulator, the commitment to enter a whole other world for a while.

We made the "OK" sign to one another and let the air out of our vests, sinking down into blue space. Everything was beautiful down below. The choppiness of the surface subsided into a deep, wet calm. We swam side by side, Aaron and I. Schools of fish swam this way and that, reversing direction en masse. The reef was alive all around us. There was nothing to break the silence but the bubbling sound of my own breath. Everything was beautiful. Everything.

I looked over at Aaron, made the "OK" sign again, and got one in return. He gestured to go deeper down. With every exhalation I sank a little further, till we hovered over a patch of sandy bottom. I got the usual feelings of diving—being far beneath normal existence, somehow free of gravity, totally in my body yet really nowhere at all. I looked at my depth gauge: 90 feet.

He gestured me to sit on the bottom. I couldn't see a reason not to, so I knelt on the sea floor, stirring up a little sandstorm. He came over and knelt in front of me so close that our knees were touching. He laid a hand on my shoulder, and we stared at one another through our masks. I could feel my dick getting hard inside my wet suit.

Then Aaron grabbed my air hose. I took a big gulp of air. He tugged at the mouthpiece. I let him. I let him pull it out of my mouth. I held my breath.

I could die right now, I thought. *It would take so little. Just allowing my mouth to open, letting the ocean rush in.*

Why was I doing this, trusting him, letting myself believe he'd give the regulator back to me and let me suck in life again?

Letting go. Right here, right now, my last moment. The end.

My lungs began to ache for air.

Relief. The salty water, salty as my blood, bringing an end, a darkness, maybe peace.

I thought of the moment when he'd put his hands around my neck and squeezed. The girl with the big tits was right. Aaron was bad news.

His face would be the last thing I'd see. He would watch me shoot upward into blue shafts of sunlight, only to thrash, relax, and come to floating rest.

I looked upward. The surface was so far above. It might as well have been as far as the stars.

I should do it, I thought. *It would be so easy.*

My body was rebelling. I needed air. Fuck this shit, fuck Aaron and the places he took me and my hard dick and Kate and my life. Fuck it all. I needed air.

I could die right now.

I grabbed for his hand. He let go of the regulator, which floated upward out of reach. Through the glass of our faceplates, our eyes conveyed some primal, elemental message. Older than civilization: animal trust and betrayal. I made the "Out of Air" sign, fingers slashing across my windpipe. I was going to die. He would never let me breathe.

It would be so easy.

He blinked once and reached down for his spare mouthpiece, the "octopus." Gently, he held the back of my head with one hand and guided the octopus toward my mouth with the other. I opened my lips, he placed it between my teeth, and I clamped down greedily, breathing again.

He gestured to rise. I could have grabbed at my regulator hose, replaced my own mouthpiece. Instead, I remained breathing through his spare, the two of us sharing the same air as he put his arm around me and, locked in a wet embrace, we rose slowly toward the surface. When it came time for our decompression stop, he put both arms around me and hugged. Then he reached for his mouthpiece and his octopus, gently pulled the regulators from both our mouths, and kissed me, parting my lips with his tongue just enough for a trickle of salt water to rush in.

He replaced his mouthpiece, I got my own regulator back in my mouth, and we rose toward the surface, toward life.

I needed to go for a walk. I'd come to Utila to escape. To escape my life, but my life had followed me, hitched a ride with me on that Russian plane. If I'd come to Utila to simplify my existence, I'd come to the wrong place. Somewhere out in the middle of the sea, I was walking down the same small street again and again, wanting there to be somewhere to get lost.

I figured I'd finally hike out to Pumpkin Hill. I never got there. The Scandinavian girl was coming up the street, a bag of groceries in one hand. She placed herself in my path.

"The supply boat has come in, and the grocery store has now more food again. Look." She held the grocery bag toward me.

Jesus, I thought, *is this woman everywhere?* And then I realized it wasn't just her; since I got to Utila I'd been seeing the same faces again and again. Only Aaron was hard to find, always disappearing.

"So what," the girl asked, "have you learned?"

What a fucking weird question. Or maybe she'd been reading my mind.

"Huh?" I asked.

"About Aaron. Have you found out?"

"Found out what?" I didn't want to talk about it. I didn't want to think about it, about Aaron, about me. I wanted to relax, let the currents carry me, watch my thoughts swim off like a school of bright, mindless fish.

"How do you think someone gets that way?" she asked, an odd look in her very blue eyes.

Fuck you, I wanted to say.

Instead I said, "Excuse me. I've got to go." And I turned around and headed back to the hotel before she could catch up. Maybe Aaron would be there.

When he fucked me that afternoon he didn't use a condom.

"I'm okay," he said.

"Trust me," he said.

I did.

It didn't feel quite like I expected. A little pain at first, which was to be expected, and then just a funny, full feeling. Once he got going, though, once I relaxed, once he was all the way in, it all changed to pleasure. Sweat was glistening on his chest, dripping off the hairs of his belly.

I wanted him to choke me again, but I didn't dare ask him. I lost my hard-on from all the new sensations, but that didn't matter much. His pleasure was all that counted. I wanted to be nothing. When he shot off inside me, I hoped I could have been anyone. Even the girl from Scandinavia.

"Stay inside me," I gasped. "Please stay inside me." And I jacked off, getting hard fast, feeling an intense longing, a need to spew salty cum everywhere. It didn't take long for me to shoot. Jism arced all the way up to my face.

We showered. There wasn't much to say. I went off to find us a snack. In the heat of the late afternoon Utila's main street was nearly empty. Walking felt strange; I could still feel him in my ass. It was as if my body was carrying some barely concealed secret, something about being looser, more open. I was glad there were so few people out; discovery would be less likely.

When I returned to the room, every trace of Aaron was gone. No note, nothing. I felt resigned, then curious. I ran from the hotel, heading for the airstrip. As I got there, the last plane of the day was warming up on the runway, pointed toward the mainland. As the plane taxied down the field, I thought I saw Aaron's face at a window, looking toward me, but I couldn't be sure. I stood there stupidly, until the sputtering roar of the plane faded away over the deep blue sea.

When I got back to the hotel there was a boy with a backpack at the front desk, kind of scrawny, but cute. His neck was thin.

"You look exhausted," I said to him.

"Know of any place to stay?" he asked. "Every hotel seems to be full up."

"There's a second bed in my room," I told him. "You'd be welcome to spend the night."

I looked down at his legs, fuzzy with brownish hair, then back up at his face. It would be so easy. "You'd be welcome to spend the night," I repeated.

I caught a trace of motion from the corner of my eye; the Scandinavian girl with big tits was standing there, staring straight at me.

"Hey," the boy said, "that'd be great." So easy.

"This way," I said, and we headed up the stairs.

guts

Even before he joined the gym, his body wasn't bad. Tall, lean, and 25, Rand looked sort of like a skaterboy, only more clean-cut, less hip. But whenever he saw those pictures in the fag magazines, pics of boys with perfect biceps and chiseled chests, he felt some-how...inadequate.

Working downtown as he did, Rand decided against the glossy gay gyms of the Castro district and joined the nearby Central YMCA instead. The Y was big, funky, and convenient; he figured he could squeeze in a quick workout during a long lunch. The place was filled with an amazing collection of folks: men and women, young and old, buff and not-so. But this being San Francisco, there were a lot of other gay guys, including, thank God, other guys like Rand—young, cute, lean, some of them downright skinny. So he didn't feel out of place, even when he stripped down in the locker room and surreptitiously compared himself to the demigods of the place, pumped-up men with bulging calves and washboard abs. *Someday,* he said to himself, *with enough work, I'll have a body like that*. He left unvoiced the rest of the thought: *And then someone will love me.*

Three times a week—well, sometimes maybe two—he'd force himself to change into shorts and a tank top and surrender to the gruesome mercies of the Nautilus machines. He stopped working out at lunchtime as soon as he realized he was getting back to his office starving, exhausted, and glum. Instead, he slotted in the gym between the end of the workday and dinner. In place of the elderly, saggy Russians who jammed the sauna every noontime, the 5:30 crowd had a high proportion of queer young professionals. The showers were packed with guys giving each other the eye, some discreetly, others brazenly soaping half-hard dicks for unconscionable periods of time.

And then there was the steam room, its misty precincts dripping with overheated lust. Mostly the cruising was semi-discreet, but every so often Rand was witness to an unapologetic blow job or even a jacked-off spurt of cum.

He began to recognize the regulars. The muscular black guy with the dazzling smile. The middle-aged queen with too much jewelry who never took his towel off, never took a shower, and never, ever worked out. The matched set of maybe-18-year-old maybe-brothers who slowly, deliciously showered their impeccable bodies and long uncut schlongs; they chattered in Croatian or Italian or something, oblivious, while the trolls just stared and stared. And then there were the ones Rand had crushes on, the boys with perfect V-shaped bodies and flawless faces, the ones he never quite worked up the courage to speak to.

But, he'd remind himself, *I'm not at the Y to get laid. I'm here to get hunky so I can get laid. Some other time. Elsewhere.*

"Hello."

Rand had been toweling himself off; the insistent attentions of a steam room troll had persuaded him to cut short his post-workout lounging. He turned, letting his towel drape over his crotch. A cute guy, cute enough, about his age, but...big. Not fat, exactly, but stocky. Really stocky.

"Hi, I'm Chris. I've seen you around." Chris was naked, not even a towel.

"Yeah, I've seen you around a lot too." A lie: The guy didn't look anything more than vaguely possibly familiar. Nice smile, though. Pretty green eyes, light brown hair that would probably be curly if it grew out. Trim moustache, a close-cropped beard that was hardly more than stubble.

"And you are?"

"Oh, sorry. Rand." His gaze slid down Chris's body. Too big for him. At least 200 pounds more. Broad shoulders. Fleshy chest matted with hair. Tits you could grab hold of, nipples you could suck. Down lower, a round belly where washboard abs should have been. At least a 37-inch waist, at a guess. Nope, too big for him. So why, Rand wondered, was his dick, getting...

"Thirty-eight–inch waist, six-inch dick. You like?" Rand looked up, meeting Chris's broad smile, then down again, down lower. An average-size dick, maybe, but plump, nestled between big, meaty thighs.

"Yeah," said Rand, "I like."

What struck Rand about Chris, once they'd been to bed, was... well, the phrase that kept coming to mind was "his generosity of flesh." In place of the tense hardness of the muscleboys, Chris offered a body you grab onto, sink into, surrender to. Surrender not to the power of muscle, though Chris was plenty strong, but to something else, something Rand couldn't quite name.

Meanwhile, back at the Y Rand's efforts were paying off. He'd often sneak a glance at himself in the full-wall mirror, semi-amazed at his swelling chest and shoulders, the bulge that arose when he'd flex a biceps. Watching his reflection using the overhead press machine, he was gratified to note that his torso looked damn near V-shaped at full extension.

"Hey there." It was Chris. Rand had three more reps to go. Two. One. He let the handles return to shoulder level.

"Chris! How's it goin'?" He still hadn't figured out how to play things at the gym. Though he'd fucked with Chris four times in the last month, and even gone out with him to see some overrated queer movie at the Lumière, he didn't want the guys at the Y to know the two of them were having, well, maybe not an affair, but a *something*. Because Rand didn't want to get a reputation as a cub-chaser, which would give the wrong idea to the buff boys who were, he had to face it, still his ultimate quarry.

"How's it going, Rand?" A quizzical smile.

"Fine. Listen, I've still got a lot of workout to do. If I talk with you now and lose concentration, I'll never be able to finish."

"Yeah, sure." The smile faded.

"See you down in the locker room."

"Uh-huh." Chris turned to go. Turned back. "Maybe we should talk sometime." And then he was gone.

Yeah, maybe they should talk. About why he, Rand, thought this good-looking, funny, attentive, yes, sexy man was somehow...

Might as well say it. Not good enough for him. Because Chris was big. God *damn* it. Big.

Rand had just finished stripping down when Chris walked over, naked too.

"Talk now, Rand?"

"Here?" A few lockers down, a guy was zipping up his fly. "Sure, Chris. Why not?"

"You mad at me?"

"Mad? No. It's just...I need time." Or something. Jesus!

"We both know what it is, right? If I looked like *them*..." Chris gestured with his head across the locker room toward the Italian-or-Croatian-or-whatever brothers, looking yummy in their little matching Speedos.

"I just...I just want to be, I don't know, pumped up. Buffed. Hunky." Rand could feel himself starting to blush.

"It's important to your, as we say in California, self-esteem, right?"

"Yeah, and you…"

"Don't fit in?"

"No, you do. I mean I think you're really great, but…I don't know what I'm saying." Rand's face was hot. He hoped no one could overhear. "Listen, we're both standing here naked. Don't you think that…"

"No, *you* listen. You can like me and sleep with me and that won't change what *you* look like. Not a damn bit. What you want to be and what you want to fuck don't have to be the same. I mean, look at heterosexuals. Look at Arnold Schwarzenegger and Maria Shriver."

"I'd rather not."

"Well," Chris grinned, "you get the point. You like yourself skinny? *I* like you skinny. Be skinny."

"*Skinny?*"

"Okay, lean, slim, whatever. There's this myth that all bears go for other bears. Some of us do. I don't. Big fucking deal. And, believe it or not, some gym-body guys might actually lust after *me*. You, for instance. I thought sex was supposed to be where you could want whoever the hell turned you on, with no apologies. But for fuck's sake, as Mom would say, be happy being who you are, whether that's a Tenderloin drag queen or the president."

"I want to be whichever one's sleazier."

"Honey, it's a toss-up," Chris said.

And they stood there naked in the YMCA and grinned at each other, just grinned. Then Chris grabbed Rand in his big, strong arms and held him to his belly and his chest and his dick. And as soon as their dicks touched, Rand felt himself getting hard. The rest of his body tensed, but then relaxed; he realized he didn't care who saw.

As the next few weeks went by, Rand underwent a shift in his tastes. The young lean boys started looking distinctly undernourished. The muscle guys seemed armored and contrived. It was the big men who started catching his eye. At first it was just the stocky guys, boys like Chris, the ones whom he used to maybe glance at, then ignore.

Not any more. Whenever he walked into the steam room, he'd survey the naked guys and pick a nice thick thigh to sit beside. A thigh he could inch toward with his own lean leg till contact was made and cocks got hard—stiffies in the mist. Sometimes, if they were the only two men in there, there was time for a grope. But while the big guy was playing with Rand's hard-on, Rand would move his hand upward from the man's dick to his belly and slide his palm over convex flesh slick with sweat, stroking and stroking until they heard the door inevitably open and they jerked their hands away.

Rand cut back on his weight training and spent more time on the aerobics machines. It was where the guys who were trying to lose weight hung out. It was where he could, while climbing to nowhere on a Stairmaster, gaze across the room at men whose bellies hung over their gym shorts. There they sat on the stationary bikes, their big, naked legs pumping away in circles, and some of them, when they noticed Rand's stare, stared back in a friendly way.

Then Rand moved on from the stocky to the really overweight. Before, he'd focused on big young guys with largish dicks. But now he cruised them all as they stripped down or lathered up, all the extra-large ones, young or older, hairy or smooth, well-hung or with little dicks that half-disappeared beneath their bellies. The frankly fat. Anyone but the truly obese or old men with big guts and spindly legs—he still had *some* standards. *Oh, my God! What's happened to me?* he thought. But his dick kept getting hard. And as Chris said to him one Sunday afternoon in bed, "Hard dicks don't lie."

Still, except for Chris, whom he continued to fuck once or twice a week, Rand never got together with any of the big guys outside the Y. Things never went beyond a grope in the steam, or maybe letting somebody give him head for a few seconds when nobody else was around.

Until one evening in the spring. He went into the sauna and sat on a lower bench. Facing him on the other side, but sitting on the upper bench so his crotch was at Rand's eye-level, was a guy who was, frankly, huge. Not sloppy-obese, but easily in the high two-hundreds.

"Hey," said the fat guy, "how you doing?"

"Fine," said Rand. "Never seen you here before."

"Just joined." He spread his legs a little wider. Rand stared at the man's dick, which was medium-size, uncut, and shorn of hair, like a baby's. The fat man smiled and played with his cock in the halfhearted way that guys in saunas do.

"Can I touch it?"

"My prick?" the big guy said.

"Your...your belly," Rand replied.

The big guy nodded, and Rand sprang to his feet. Watching sidelong through the glass door for approaching intruders, he laid both hands on the man's belly and stroked all that flesh, all that flesh. The guy leaned over, grabbed Rand's head, and pushed it down toward his crotch. *But I'm a top, damn it,* Rand thought, *and besides, this is risky as hell.* Nevertheless, he took the guy's hardening dick in his mouth and sucked furtively for all of five seconds until, of course, the sauna door creaked open. Rand jerked upward, hard-on jiggling in the hot, dry air.

It was the black guy with the great smile. "I'll just pretend I didn't see that," he said, and his smile grew brighter still.

"Bob!" said the fat guy, unruffled. "How ya doing?"

"Oh, fine, Vince. Just fine."

Rand uneasily left the sauna and went to take a pee, but Vince followed him to the urinal and smiled. "Want to come home with me, guy?" And Rand did.

Rand had begun to feel like some damn *ABC Afterschool Special* about the pitfalls of prejudice, "Size Doesn't Matter" or "The Bigger They Come." He'd become an equal-opportunity lecher.

The thing with Vince *had* been kind of weird. Rand had let Vince fuck him, only the third guy who ever had, and the sight and feeling of all that weight above him bearing down and into him really got Rand off. But afterward it turned out that Vince really wasn't happy with the way he looked, with all that weight.

"Yeah, *you* wanted me to fuck you, sure. But most guys...most guys look at me like I'm some kind of freak."

And Rand realized he sort of did too. He was attracted to Vince not despite of his size, not regardless of his size, but *because* of his size. To him, Vince was just a big belly with a man attached. As if this guy, who had certainly suffered because he was so fat, were one of those weird-looking goldfish the Japanese prize for their physical grotesqueness. Rand had, in a way, become what he'd never been before: a size queen.

And things with Chris had become kind of strange too.

"Jesus, Rand. I didn't mind being objectified because of my weight," Chris said one day. "After all, every guy wants to feel like a sex object, whatever the hell he might say out loud. But this obsession of yours—well, I feel like an aging wife whose husband goes chasing after younger and younger girls. Only you're chasing after fatter and fatter. And short of binge eating," he went into his best Bette Davis impersonation, "I don't know how to compete, my darling, I just don't." Chris was smiling, but clearly something serious was there. And what could Rand say? "I don't love you only for your fat?"

guts

One afternoon at the gym, Rand remembered the way things used to be. He noticed a slim Latino guy on the back extension machine. The guy was wearing spandex bicycle shorts, and every time he leaned back into resistance the outline of his basket was clearly visible through the stretchy black fabric.

Rand had just finished his biceps curls, but he decided to skip his triceps and stand beside the back extension machine as though he were waiting to work in. Each time the Latino leaned back, his crotch jutted upward and his lean torso flexed beneath his thin tank top. And each time he sat upward, his eyes met Rand's. After his final rep he removed his Walkman's headphones and smiled at Rand, a dazzling grin.

"You waiting to work in?"

"Yeah."

Rand adjusted the footpad and began to strap himself in. The Latino was still standing there. "Or are you waiting for something else?" he asked.

Miguel ("Call me Mike") had damn near zero-percent body fat, a nice uncut dick, and hardly any attitude for such a gorgeous guy. Three days after they met at the gym, they had dinner at a place on Upper Market Street, Mike leaving over half of his curried-tofu and sundried-tomato wrap. Then they went back to Mike's apartment, which was, like its owner, spare, tasteful, and carefully arranged.

The sex wasn't bad. Where Chris's belly had been soft and yielding, Mike's six-pack abs were hard as a rock, his pretty brown butt taut as a drum. Rand knew he wasn't on a par with him, but he guessed he must be in the same league. After all, he was in bed with him, right? So all those hours in the weight room, all those squats and curls and presses, hadn't been a total waste of time after all.

Each had assumed he was going to top the other, so they never did get around to fucking. But they sucked each other's dicks and came and wiped up. And while they were lying there, Miguel on his stomach, Rand softly stroking those perfectly developed lats, the firm Latino said, "I like you. Let's see each other again, huh? Sometime."

Rand had made it: He'd had sex with one of the hunkiest Y guys, and now they were talking about a second time. So Rand said what gay men often say in similar situations: "Yeah, sounds great. But I'm real, real busy with work for the next week or two. So why don't I call you?"

Mike's folded-up number went into Rand's wallet, then to his desk drawer, but Rand didn't use it. Instead, day after day, he found himself thinking about Chris, his yielding flesh, relaxed smile, the way his big old ass moved when he walked.

"Chris," he said, finally, over the phone, "you're more than just 'some bear cub' to me."

"I know I am, Rand. But you had to realize it as well."

Aww, thought Rand, *just like in the movies.* But within 90 minutes, they were together, naked, in Chris's king-size bed.

"I thought you were going to call me," Miguel said the next time that Rand saw him at the gym.

"Well, I...yeah, but I've sorta gotten involved with someone." *I must be crazy,* Rand thought. "So thanks anyway, but..."

And indeed, Rand and Chris had become an item. Rand introduced the big guy to his friends, who tended to use the words "cute" and "sweet" rather than "big" when they talked about him afterward.

And within six months Rand actually did it, moving out of his overpriced studio apartment and into Chris's overpriced one-bedroom instead. They'd decided early on it was going to be an open relationship, so when Chris wasn't around Rand would take other guys back to the king-size bed, some of them big men, others lean. But the intensity with which he sought out the heaviest of the heavyweights was a thing of the past. Skinny, fat, or in-between, buff or flabby, Rand either wanted to play with a guy or not. But most of all he wanted to crawl into bed each night and find Chris there and throw his arm around his boyfriend's reassuring bulk, the two of them sleeping spoons all through the night.

He even thought seriously about letting his gym membership lapse and just forgetting about ever pumping iron again. Just let his body do whatever it was going to do. But *Oh, fuck it!* he decided. And so he continued to work out at the Y, sweating and straining and grunting, and, as a matter of absolute fact, he can be found working out there still.

dooley'sdick

I thought I knew from guilt, until I met Dooley.

It was two days before the Nazis marched into Paris. I'd been to the World's Fair out in Queens. My parents had already been to Flushing Meadows the year before, and once was enough for them, so I'd gone by myself—rode the subway out there, spent a sweltering June day wandering around The World of Tomorrow, then took the D train back to the Bronx.

Making my way up 170th Street, I could still smell the heat of the sidewalks, even after sunset. Kids played stickball beneath a streetlight. Old guys with cigars gossiped in front of the candy store. And there was Dooley, sitting on the stoop of my apartment house, in a sweat-soaked undershirt. I would have stared, but I was afraid he'd yell at me. It had happened before with a guy on the Grand Concourse. "What're you starin' at?!" the man had yelled. So I walked into the building and took the elevator to the eighth floor. Mom had cooked a brisket. "How was the Aquacade?" she asked. But I was still thinking of the curly black hair on Dooley's chest.

Only I didn't find out his name was Dooley till a couple of weeks later, when I saw him in the lobby. He was just standing there. I tried not to pay attention, but he was looking my way. He smiled. "You live here, don't you?" he said. "I've seen you around." My knees turned to Jell-O.

"Yeah, eighth floor. You?"

"Third." He spoke with a foreign accent.

"You from another country?"

"Ireland."

"So you're not Jewish?" Nearly everybody in the neighborhood was Jewish.

"No, Catholic." I didn't know what to say. There'd been some Catholics at my high school, a few of them Irish. But they had mostly kept to themselves, the way kids like to do. And we'd called them "stupid micks."

Just at that moment, the elevator opened again.

"There y'are, Ma. I was beginnin' to wonder what'd happened to you."

"Oh, now none of us is as young as we used to be." The plump woman in the print dress spoke with music in her voice, a music worlds away from the nasal cadences of the Bronx. Fading red hair, rouged cheeks, a look of loving kindness: the sort of mother I wished I'd had, instead of the angular, spiky neurotic who'd given me life.

"Ma, I'd like you to meet..."

"I'm Sol."

The woman half-smiled and nodded.

Her son extended his hand to me. "And I'm Seamus Dooley. But everyone just calls me Dooley." His grip was firm and strong and lingered just a little too long.

Don't get me wrong. I wasn't sexually experienced back then. Whenever I was around attractive men, I just stared and stared, while my aching hard-on struggled against my underwear. But since I'd started commuting to Cooper Union my world had opened up a bit. I'd become a college student, an art student all the way down in Greenwich Village. I suddenly found myself on the outskirts of bohemia. Effeminate men in berets. Naked models in life-drawing class. Girls with long, straight hair who talked about

Marx and free love. But I, a good Jewish boy, made sure I was always home in time for dinner. The closest I'd gotten to decadence was an occasional between-classes beer at McSorley's.

I'd been pretty busy with summer courses. But on my way home or on weekends I'd sometimes run into Dooley. And I began to notice details. The curve of his butt beneath his light-weight summer trousers. The deep blue of his eyes. His broad, strong hands, well-chewed fingernails, the dense, dark hair on his forearms.

When I was back in high school there'd been fights between the Jews and the Irish. But now with the troubles in Europe it seemed everybody had more important things to worry about. So I felt at ease when I finally got to talking to Dooley about his past.

"My Pa was killed by the Black and Tans," he began, "right before I was born."

"Black and Tans?"

"British soldiers. It wasn't easy for my mother, raising three of us on her own. Finally, a cousin who'd settled in New Jersey helped us to make the voyage over. My two sisters are still in Derry, married. Here it's just my Ma and me—her a clerk at Macy's, me down at the docks when there's jobs."

"Well, this war fever should mean more work for you."

"Ma had intended to move to Brooklyn, to be near other Irish. We just ended up living in the Bronx by accident. It hasn't been easy here, y'know, with my accent and all, surrounded by your people. Hard to make friends." He laid a big, strong hand on my shoulder and kept it there. "No offense."

I felt my dick beginning to swell. My mother's warnings about the *goyim* vanished from my mind. "Well, we should do something sometime, then. Go to the movies."

"That'd be grand. There's a Bogart at Loew's Paradise."

"Saturday night?"

dooley'sdick

"I've a date with my girlfriend then." My heart sank, but his hand was still on my shoulder. "How about Friday night?"

"That's *Shabbos*. The Sabbath."

"Sorry, yeah, sure." He drew his hand away. "Next week, then?"

"Sure, next week." And we exchanged phone numbers. He left the lobby of the apartment house to go heaven-knows-where. To his girlfriend's, maybe. I took the elevator up, repeating his phone number over and over until I got a chance to write it down. And after dinner I went into the bathroom, locked the door as silently as I could, and jerked off, thinking of Dooley. I stripped him down in my mind, made him more and more naked, but by the time I'd gotten him down to his underpants I'd shot all over my hand, cum dripping down to the white six-sided floor tiles, a stew of impossible lusts.

The phone call, when it came, was a total surprise.

"For you, Sol," my father yelled over the radio. We were listening to Charlie McCarthy. "Sounds foreign."

I pulled the phone as far from my parents as I could.

"Sol, it's my Ma. She's in the hospital. I don't know...I don't know what to do. Could you come over, maybe, please?" The grief in Dooley's voice was a strange aphrodisiac.

"Sure. I'll try. I'll be right there. What's the apartment number again?" He told me, then hung up without waiting for "Goodbye."

"Irish, Sol?" my father asked, only the slightest reproof in his voice.

"Yeah, a friend from Cooper Union," I lied. "Wanted to know if I could join him for a soda."

"To go all the way to Cooper?"

"No, up here. Grand Concourse."

"You never mentioned an Irish boy," my mother said, switching off the radio.

Well, I don't have to tell you everything, I thought.

"Poor Mrs. Silver's heartbroken," she continued. "Her Sophie ran off with a *goyish* boy. Not just Christian, a Catholic. Irish. Or Italian. Such a shame."

"I'll be back in a while."

"Don't be out too late, Sol."

I'm a big boy, Mom. "I won't, Mom."

"And be careful."

"I will, Mom."

"I worry."

I took the elevator to the ground floor, then went to the other side of the lobby and ran up three flights of stairs. Making sure there was nobody around, I found Dooley's door and knocked. I wasn't sure just why I was sneaking around. Not yet.

Dooley had liquor on his breath. His eyes were red. He looked like he might cry again any minute. "C'mon in," he said, draping one arm around my shoulder, leading me from the foyer to the living room. I looked around. A mostly empty bottle of whiskey stood on a table with a lace tablecloth. Above it hung a crucifix. I'd never been in an apartment with a crucifix on the wall.

"What's up, Dooley?" I tried to sound concerned but nonchalant. He was breathing fumes in my face.

"Oh, Jesus, Sol. Ma's in the hospital. I've been such a lousy son. If I'd been...if I'd been a better son none of this would have happened." His arm tightened around my shoulder.

"How is she?"

"The doctors say she'll be all right. They made me go home, no more visiting hours in the ward. But seeing her lying there...I know she...she's suffering for my sins."

"Dooley, that's just damn silly." I knew right away it was the wrong thing to say.

"No, Sol. You don't know what a bad person I am...I...I...with my girlfriend."

He started to sob. I felt embarrassed, then somehow frightened. I glanced around the room. My eyes landed on the cheaply ornate cross. This man, this adult man maybe five years older than me, was crying like a kid. I forced myself to look at him. His scrunched-up, tortured face was more handsome than ever. I wanted to stroke his cheek. So I did. I felt myself getting hard.

"Have a drink, pal," Dooley said through his tears. I was reluctant to move—I didn't want him to let go of my shoulder. But he followed me, hanging on, as I walked to the table. The neck of the bottle was slippery in my tear-wet hand.

The whiskey burned like fire. Except for sugary-sweet Passover wine, the hardest stuff I'd ever drunk was those beers at McSorley's. Still, I held on to the bottle.

Dooley grabbed me harder and stuck his face right up to mine. "I'm so ashamed, Sol. I know that God is punishing me. Punishing me by making me watch my Ma suffer."

I didn't know what to say, so I stroked his face some more. Suddenly he threw himself against me, arms round my neck. I was scared he'd notice I was hard.

"You're so...sweet, Sol. Sweeter than my...girlfriend." Nobody had ever called me "sweet" before, except my mother. He kissed me on the cheek. I froze. And then he clutched me to him and hung on for dear life. I didn't know what to say. How could I?

I ran my hand through his thick black hair. "You'll be okay, Dooley." I raised the bottle to his full lips. He nursed at it like a baby. Then I took another deep swig, and the bottle was empty.

"Sol..." he began. And then he started to press into me. I knew he'd notice my hard-on now, my shameful secret. And then, to my utter terror and delight, he began to grind his hips into mine, crotch against crotch. "Oh, Jesus!" he moaned. "Oh, Jesus, I'm so sorry." And he slumped into my arms.

"C'mon, let's get you to bed." I knew that's what I was supposed to say, what they said in the movies. And, much as I might have wanted to, I couldn't take advantage of his grief. I kind of wrestled him down the hallway to a bedroom. I could see that it was his mother's room, but he was getting too unwieldy to haul around any more. Once he was sprawled on the chenille bedspread I backed away a bit, uncertain what to do next. Slowly, deliberately, he reached up and grabbed my wrist and pulled me down on top of him. Fully dressed, we wrestled around on his mother's bed. At one point I managed to slip my hand between his thighs. He was hard too, now, a considerable bulge at his crotch.

I wanted him naked, as naked as the models at art school, as naked as I wanted to be with him. I tore at his shirt, but he pushed my hands away. "Hey, lay off," he snarled. "Lay off...fairy!" And he wrapped his arms around my torso, legs around my waist, and squeezed the breath out of me, squeezed so hard I was sure that he wanted to break me in two. So hard I thought I'd faint. I was terrified, but, astonishingly, my dick still was stiff. And his was too. There was a stink of liquor and sweat and violence.

"Oh, God!" Dooley yelled, and his body arched and squeezed and went into spasms. And then he was still. I stared at the statue of the Virgin Mary on the bedside table, half-burned candles at her feet.

When I brought myself to look at Dooley, tears were rolling down his cheeks. I kissed him gently, the only time I ever kissed him on the lips, and pried myself loose. He lay immobile on his mother's bed, a stain spreading across the front of his pants.

I found the bathroom, stood over the toilet, took my stiff cock out of my trousers, and pulled at it till I shot off into the porcelain bowl. Then, woozy with dread and booze and relief, I sank to my knees and puked.

When I looked in on Dooley his eyes were closed. I guessed he'd passed out.

I let myself out of the apartment, making sure the hall was empty, and ran down the stairs, over to Bernstein's Candy Store, where I bought a pack of Sen-Sen. "You look like hell," said Bernstein, bemused. "But don't worry, I won't tell your parents. Just hope that the Sen-Sen covers up that breath."

My apartment was dark when I let myself in.

"Sol?" called my mother from her bedroom.

"Yeah, Ma."

"Have a nice time?"

"Yeah, Ma."

"Good night, son," called my father, with a tone that said *Thank God, now we can get some sleep.*

In a couple of days Dooley's mother was back home. And every so often I'd run into Dooley around the neighborhood, but we never talked about that night.

Every August my parents would go to Far Rockaway for two weeks at the beach. When I was a kid I used to love staying in a bungalow, listening to the ocean, feeling sand between my toes. But now I was grown up. I stayed behind for classes. Four or five times while my parents were gone Dooley showed up at my apartment door. Each time we'd talk for a while, him sprawled on the couch, legs spread. Then I'd kneel between his thighs as he unzipped his fly and pulled out his half-hard dick. I'd never been so close to a foreskin before. I'd seen a few in the showers at school, freakish-looking things. But now I was fascinated by it. I slid it silkily back and forth along his cock head. As Dooley sat there wordlessly, I'd rub my face in his yeasty crotch, the hair of his ball sac soft against my cheek. Then I'd get his longish dick between my lips, into my mouth, going down on him till my jaws ached and I started to gag. My mouth still full of him, I'd reach up and unbutton his shirt, rub my hands up the thick hair on his belly, his chest, past the little gold cross he wore around his neck, eventually to the damp tangles of his underarms. Touching his pits made me nearly come. Then I'd bring my fingers to my nose and smell him, his dark male otherness. I thought I'd surely shoot off inside my pants. I went to work on his cock, sucking inexpertly but enthusiastically until Dooley filled my mouth with cum, tangy Irish cum that he pumped out with a grunt.

I'd wipe him off with my handkerchief, the same handkerchief every time, and he'd zip up, say "Thanks, Sol" and walk out the door. Then I'd go sit on the toilet and jack off.

Only the final time, when my parents were due back the next day, did he stick around after he came. He looked sheepish. "I told you a lie, Sol," he said.

I knew it! He doesn't have a girlfriend!

"What I told you about my father?" he continued. "It's not true. The Brits didn't kill him. He was a member of the Blue Shirts. They're a bunch of Irish fascists. He went to Spain to fight for Franco during the civil war. That's how he died."

I could see why he hadn't wanted to tell me.

"That's okay," I said. "It was him, not you."

"And my Ma, Sol, she says that you people killed our Lord. Thinks you're all going to hell." That rose-cheeked woman.

"And you?"

"You know me better than that, Sol."

I couldn't help but ask: "And your girlfriend? Do you really have one?"

Dooley looked surprised. "Anna? Oh, yeah, she's for real."

My parents came back, my father peeling from sunburn. And, for one reason and another, I never touched Dooley's dick again.

We never even talked about what we'd done. But every so often I'd take that cum-encrusted handkerchief from under my bed, hold it to my face, and beat off, thinking of the curve of his flesh.

When autumn came Dooley's mother went into the hospital again. This time she never came back out. Dooley packed up and moved in with his cousins in Jersey. When he phoned to say good-bye his voice was flat and terse. I invited him out for a farewell beer. He refused.

"Sorry about your mother, Dooley."

"Thanks, Sol." His voice was softening. "Sol, I hope..." And he hung up the phone.

I didn't hear from him again until December, when a greeting card came for me in an envelope with no return address. "Merry Christmas," the card read. Inside, Dooley had written "Hope this is okay" above his signature.

The next year passed fairly quickly, filled with drawing lessons, war jitters, and rumors about the German Jews. Nate Roth, who taught painting at Cooper, invited me to his place on 8th Street so I could suck his cock. Two weeks after Pearl Harbor another Christmas card from Dooley came, this one with a return address somewhere in Chicago. There was a note enclosed. Dooley had gotten married, not to Anna but to someone named Siobhan. They were expecting their first kid. I mailed him back a Chanukah card, not bothering to change the words.

By the spring of '42 I was in uniform. I served in the South Pacific and lost a leg at Bataan. When I got back to the Bronx, I fought, in turn, with my parents and with depression. Eventually, my self-pity ran dry and I moved down to the Village, where I achieved a bit of fame as a cartoonist for *The New Yorker*. And every year, and only once a year, Dooley and I exchanged cards. "Merry Christmas" from him, "Happy Chanukah" from me. And always a note with a little news. He moved to Michigan, went to work for

Chrysler, retired. He married off four daughters, had more than a few grandkids.

Then, three years ago, I received an envelope addressed in an unfamiliar hand. The Christmas card read, "I'm sorry to tell you that my husband has passed on. Sincerely, Siobhan Dooley." And that was that.

It's funny how things happen. How the memories of youth remain so vivid, how varied the paths of our lives can be. And how, so many years later, I can recall, in perfect focus, the feel, the smell, the taste of Dooley's dick.

young,dumb,andfullofcum

Slade, Block, and Blue: They looked like they'd just stepped out of a porn video.

Slade had been a pole vaulter in high school—he had a pole vaulter's shoulders, arms you could bounce a nuclear warhead off of, an ass any man would be proud to call his own.

Block was not just handsome—he was exceptionally, heartbreakingly, mindfuckingly handsome.

And Blue...you might have expected Blue to have blue eyes, but you'd be wrong. His African-American genes had given him dark eyes, darker hair, and one of those huge dicks that, when attributed to black guys, is surely a symptom of racist stereotyping, but what the hell. Oh, and the Jewish part of his background had left him circumcised and carrying his father's surname, Bluestein.

And if none of them was a rocket scientist—not even close— still you would not have thrown them, separately or together, out of bed, not Slade, Block, or hunky Blue.

Blue was the one who had the most convincing fake ID, so he was the one who usually bought the beer. This being the day he got his pay from the auto parts store, he walked out of the Circle K with two six-packs of Rolling Rock, got into the banged-up Jeep Grand Cherokee with three American flag decals and the Jack-in-the-Box ball on the antenna, and the three of them, Block, Slade, and Blue, pulled onto the interstate.

"So where you want to go?" Slade was the one in college, on an athletic scholarship to State, and it was nearing the end of August.

Though everybody knew he would most likely not last out the next semester, he couldn't help but feel his free time was nearly gone.

"Down to Loon Lake?" Block said from the seat behind Slade. He was wearing a joke T-shirt that read "Stupid...and prowd of it." It was perilously close to the mark.

Blue laid a noncommittal hand on Slade's bare knee. "How's that sound to you?" The two of them had been palling around all summer, ever since Slade had come home from State. That left Block, great-looking Block, who had a crush on Blue himself, with somewhat hurt feelings and blue balls—though not, of course, with Blue's balls, which, needless to say, were meaty.

"Fine with me, dude," Slade said, guiding the Cherokee down the blacktop. "Helluva day for a swim." He was secretly hoping that Blue's hand would creep up under the leg of his shorts. Except for one drunken blow job in July, they'd never actually had sex or anything like it. Not that Slade cared all that much about Blue, not really. There was a football player at school, Wayne Kretschmer, who was much more Slade's type, the blond Visigoth model. His friendship with Wayne had developed its own little protocol. Slade would go over to Wayne's dorm room, where they'd get drunk and fire up a blunt. Wayne would yawn and stretch and say, "Boy, am I tired," and when he'd laid back and ostensibly passed out, Slade would unzip Wayne's fly, fish out the dude's already-hard stiffy, and suck away. It would never take long for the blond boy's thick pink cock to feed a load to Slade. Afterward, Slade would Kleenex off the halfback's deflating dick and blond bush, replace his cock, refasten his pants, and head out the door, as Wayne moaned, stretched, and rolled over onto his belly.

But that was Wayne, and that was at school. Since Slade had been home for the summer he'd hardly had much sex at all, just several furtive fucks with an eager-if-nerdy librarian and that one suck-off with Blue. Mostly he'd beaten his meat two, three, maybe five times a day, and though he'd had to jack off after each time he left Wayne's, that had been different. Somehow.

The lake was down a rutted, boulder-filled road that kept all but the hardiest tourists away. The Jeep's four-wheel drive and high clearance didn't keep it from bottoming out now and then, but fortunately for Slade the car was his dad's, not his, so unless they lost the transmission or oil pan or something, it was all right. Slade, Blue, and Block could see the lake through the perfectly green trees, and then they were there.

Block had already peeled off his T-shirt, exposing a lean, hairy chest and a tattoo of the Tasmanian Devil. He swung out of the SUV, a six-pack of beer in his hand. "Man," he said, "it's nice here."

"Yeah," Blue said, joining him at the shore of the lake. "Gimme a beer."

Block handed over a Rolling Rock, thinking how cool it would be to get Blue's big, dark dick in his ass. "Wanna fuck?" he asked.

"Huh?"

"Just joking."

"Ha."

"Ha ha."

Slade was with them now, wearing nothing but shorts and a pair of flip-flops. "What's so funny?"

"Nothing," Block said.

"Man, this is the life." Slade grabbed a beer, uncapped it, and took a long, cold gulp.

They were on their second round when Block asked, "Briefs or boxers?"

"Briefs."

"Me too," said Slade, lighting up a joint. "Why?"

"I thought we should have a wet Jockey shorts contest."

"Oh, man," Slade said, making a face.

"No, man," Blue said. "Sounds like it could be fun."

"Maybe. After another beer or two, I'll consider it." Slade drained his green bottle and reached for another.

The three not-very-bright young men sat side by side on the lakeshore rocks, dangling their toes in the cool blue water, drinking beer and talking about nothing important. Block casually draped his arm over Blue's shoulder, and thought again about getting fucked. They'd all polished off three beers apiece and were down to the roach when Slade spoke up. "Okay, now I'll do it."

"What?" Blue asked.

"The Jockey shorts contest."

"Oh, yeah, I forgot about that," said Blue.

But Block was already clambering to his feet. He unbuckled his shorts and stepped out of them, down now to his Nikes and a pair of well-filled white briefs. The other two followed suit, Blue stripping down to BVDs with a humongous bulge, Slade standing there in the woods in a surprisingly bright-red thong, showing less of a basket than the other two guys. Maybe some god had figured that it would be unfair for a fellow with such a great body and terrific butt to have a monster dick as well.

"Let's get 'em soaked, dudes," Block said.

"Wait." Slade reached into his underwear and rearranged his smallish cock. "Just want to look my best."

Seconds later the three young hunks were splashing around in the water, wetly horsing around. Slade grabbed Blue from behind, wrapping his thoroughly strong arms around slippery, dark flesh, pressing his cotton-clad crotch up against Blue's delectable ass. As soon as Block noticed that bit of action, he preemptively yelled out, "Okay, boys! Time to dance."

He splashed out of the lake, semitransparent white cotton clinging nicely to all the curves of his basket and butt. Blue and Slade followed him, still playing grab-ass. Their effortlessly male voices rang through the otherwise quiet woods. They were, in their way, Dionysian...if, after the orgy, Dionysus had ended up going to In and Out for a burger instead of getting torn apart.

Block walked back to the truck and shoved *Aerosmith's Greatest Hits* into the CD player. By the halfway mark of "Dream On," he'd clambered onto the hood of the Grand Cherokee and begun swaying butchly to the music, turning his back to the other two guys. His wet briefs clung to the curves of his lean, well-formed, pleasantly pornographic butt.

"Yeah," Slade said, "work it." He reached down and gave his damp basket a squeeze.

Block pulled down the stretchy waistband of his underpants, exposing the upper part of his furry ass, just a bit of his butt crack. He hoped that Blue was getting an eyeful. Blue, yeah Blue. He fucking wanted Blue bad. Just the thought of the dude slipping it to him, shoving his big dick up his ass, made his own cock hard. He spun around on the dented hood of the Jeep, shaking his hips, thrusting out his crotch. His big piece of meat strained against his wet Jockeys. Blue, disappointingly, was looking more than a little unimpressed.

Oh, well, Block figured. He was, at least, having a great time, getting off on showing off. His prodigiously large penis was half-hard, its sizable head peeking out of the waistband of his briefs whenever he gave his underwear a vigorous tug. By the time Steven Tyler was caterwauling about walking this way, Slade had clambered onto the imperiled hood of his father's Grand Cherokee and started dancing too, his gorgeously muscled, cliché-perfect butt cheeks flexing to either side of his damp, skimpy red thong. Blue was, Block noticed with a pang of dim jealousy, starting to show interest now. Block stomped down hard, leaving a noticeable dent in the hood of the Jeep.

"Hey, watch it!" Slade said.

"Just dancing. Sorry." Block smiled and rubbed his barely concealed woody against Slade's thigh. "Nothin' wrong with that, is there, bro?"

"Fuck, guess not." Slade turned his back toward Block, stuck out his near-naked ass, and rubbed up against Block's swollen crotch. Suddenly, where Blue was or was not looking seemed a lot less important to Block. A lot.

"Hey, why'd ya stop dancing?" Block asked. Slade had stopped moving and was standing stock-still, his ass jammed into Block's crotch.

"Dude," Slade said, "look over there."

Block followed Slade's gaze. A young man carrying an overloaded backpack was standing in the trees not more than 20 yards away, staring in their direction.

"Hey," Block called out. "C'mon over here."

"Shh, what're you doing?" Slade slurred.

But Block was drunker than Slade, and after showing off for Blue he was horny as fuck. He called out again. The backpacker hesitated for a minute, then readjusted his pack and headed over. At least, Slade thought, he hadn't tried one of those "Who me?" gestures.

If Blue, Slade, and Block were pretty much like porn stars, the sandy-haired backpacker boy was like the son in some sitcom—cute, slim, and a little geeky. Headful of long curly hair, nose a bit too large, lingering traces of acne, cute as hell. Under the weight of his pack, he shifted from leg to thin, furry leg.

Blue, just feet away from the boy, stared uneasily, as though standing around outside in wet underwear wasn't the best idea after all. Slade looked down from his perch on the SUV. Only Block made a move, jumping down from the hood, walking over to the boy, and extending his hand. "Name's Block, dude."

The slightly geeky boy shook hands, his face more downturned than necessary; behind his dark sunglasses he was no doubt staring at Block's obvious wood.

"Like it?" Block asked.

The boy looked up, startled.

"Want to suck it?" The boy's blush got Block's dick fully hard. Block pulled down the waistband of his still-damp BVDs, and his erect dick sprang forth, long foreskin just covering the base of his cock head. "You know you want it."

"I...uh...uh..."

"You *know* you want it." Which was most surely the case; the boy's swollen cock had tented out his shorts.

Blue spoke up, the first thing he'd said for a while. "Aww, go on and suck it."

That was, apparently, all the added persuasion the boy needed. He struggled to remove his backpack, then dropped to his knees. He looked up at Block and stuck out his tongue. Block grabbed his shaft with a tight overhand grip, milked out a drop of precum, and guided the dark-red head to the boy's mouth. The backpacker swirled his tongue around the blood-engorged flesh, a move that made Block squeeze his eyes shut with pleasure. He took his hand away, the slightly-nerdy boy's mouth moved down the length of his shaft, and Block let out a long sigh. Slade, meanwhile, had descended from the Jeep and was standing beside the two, his stiff prick sticking out of his overstretched thong.

"He a good cocksucker?" Slade asked.

"Yeah. Want a shot?"

Slade had already pulled down his thong and started stroking. The boy backed off Block's dick and was looking up, his gaze moving from Block's incredibly handsome face to Slade's incredibly buff body, then down to Slade's prick. Though Slade's dick was just mediumish, he had big low-hangers, and his well-filled ball sac jiggled up and down as he jacked his cock. The boy scooted over and stuck his face into Slade's crotch, aiming his tongue at the trampolining nuts. In a moment of adventurous vanity a couple of weeks before, Slade had shaved his cock and balls, so the tender flesh was a bit stubbly against the backpacker's mouth, but the boy didn't mind. He liked it in fact, and he reached up and held onto Slade's hand until it was still, then gulped one of the big nuts into his mouth. That sort of thing—though the backpacker had no way of knowing it in advance—drove Slade wild. But he knew it now, as Slade moaned, grabbed the back of the boy's head, and pushed the nerdy guy's face against his almost-smooth crotch.

Blue, meanwhile, had moved in right beside Block, and was squeezing his oversized basket through his underwear. With a sidelong glance, Block ventured a hand on Blue's butt. He was afraid that Blue might shy away, but Blue didn't do anything, just stroked his fat hard-on through his Jockeys. Block stepped out of his own underwear and got on his knees. Blue took his hand from his crotch, and Block's mouth was on his friend's big bulge in a shot, caressing the hot flesh through the thin fabric. Block was suddenly in heaven, being able to make Blue's cock feel good.

Slade had a sudden thought, just as his cock hit the back of the boy's throat. "How old are ya?" he asked. Not that the law was always foremost in his mind, but the kid did look on the young side. The backpacker took his mouth away and aimed his face upward. The boy's sunglasses reflected Slade's cock, twice.

"Just turned 18, Sir."

Slade had never been called "Sir" before, but it didn't seem silly, even though the boy was just a year younger than him. Instead, it seemed hot, and it went to Slade's head. Both of Slade's heads, in fact. He growled, "Then suck that cock, boy," as if he was, in fact, in some porn video. And the boy did suck it, with even more enthusiasm than before.

"Hey, Slade?" Blue said.

"Yeah?"

"What do you say we fuck that boy?" *No-o-o,* Block thought, *I want to keep your cock all to myself...at least for a while longer.*

"Yeah, bro. Let's fuck him."

Shit, thought Block. He hurriedly reached up and tugged down Blue's briefs, and his buddy's huge, hard dick was in his face at last. He opened his jaws wide, like some hungry beast on the Discovery Channel, and slid his lips over Blue's fairly enormous prong. Fuck, it really filled his mouth, and it really felt great in there.

But Slade, taking his "Sir" position seriously in a drunken kind of way, had already ordered the backpack boy to stand up and strip down. Block watched him as he pulled his shorts over his hiking boots and then tugged his T-shirt over his head. Compared to the three of them, the newcomer's body was thin and underdeveloped, with a patch of sandy hair midway between two pink, prominent nipples. The boy stood there in nothing but his boxers, hiking boots, and bulky socks, shivering slightly in the hot afternoon.

"Underwear, too."

"Yes, Sir."

The head of the boy's dick was already sticking out of the boxers' gapped fly. He maneuvered it back inside, pulled off the boxer shorts, and stood back up. His dick was on the thin side, very long, and jutted sharply upward.

"Who gets his ass?" Blue asked.

"Sir, I've never been fucked before." Blue and Slade ignored his nervous-sounding protest.

"You go first. I've got some rubbers in the Jeep," Slade said. "Be right back."

When Slade returned, Blue pulled out of Block's mouth, to the cocksucker's disappointment. It took a bit of doing, but Blue managed to get the rubber unrolled over his big cock.

Slade told the boy to bend over and suck his cock. The boy did it, his firm ass stuck invitingly out, a line of swirly hair running down the crack. Blue figured he'd have to loosen that thing up before he plunged inside. He knelt down and spread the boy's butt cheeks. The backpacker's ass smelled of musky sweat. Blue stuck out his tongue and licked at the hole. *Considering it's virgin butt,* Blue thought, *it's opening up pretty good for me.* He stuck his tongue deeper inside. Slade groaned as the boy's cocksucking accelerated.

Blue stood up, spit on his hand, lubed his dick up as well as he could, and positioned the head against the backpacker's asshole. He pushed. The hole pushed back. Blue increased the pressure, but the boy's ass was too tight; he wasn't getting in so easily. Frustration was written all over his horny face.

"Maybe you better fuck him first, Slade, and loosen him up for me."

"Sure thing. Wanna switch places?"

"Nah. Too hard to get these damn rubbers off and on. I'll just watch for a while. Hey, Block, want to fuck this guy's face?"

"Sure," Block said, though what he really wanted was Blue's cock in his mouth again.

"He seems kinda awkward in that position, though," Slade said. Then, in a voice of boozy command, "Get down on all fours, boy."

The men shifted around in a little game of musical dicks. The boy got on all fours, Block knelt at his head, and Slade got on his knees, between the boy's legs. "Hey," Slade said to Blue, "hand me one of those Trojans, willya, dude?"

While the boy nursed away on Block's hefty cock, Slade jammed his shaft against the guy's puckered hole, which opened up gratifyingly, letting Slade's dick inside with a little pop. Blue stood beside Block, stroking his hard cock, watching Slade's muscular body flex and gleam with sweat in the late afternoon sun as he plowed into the stranger's ass. Block turned his head. Blue's dick was right at face level. He leaned over and started licking the latex-clad head. He hated the taste of rubber, but he loved the feel of Blue's cock ramming down his throat, so he kept nibbling at the cock head till Blue obliged, shifting over and slipping his dick into Block's hungry maw.

Now they were all one long chain of lust—Slade's dick, the boy's ass, the boy's mouth, Block's cock, Block's mouth, Blue's hard-on. In a perfect world, the chain would have been circularly completed with Blue eating Slade's awesome butt, but probably not even the Cirque du Soleil could have managed that bit of acrobatics.

"Hey," Slade said, trying to take his Dominant's Responsibilities seriously, "maybe we should tie the guy to a tree or something."

"Did you come?" asked Blue, enjoying the feeling of Block's throat muscles massaging his hard flesh.

"Not yet, don't want to. Not yet."

"Cool," Blue said. "There's some rope over there, hanging from the guy's pack."

Aw, shit, Block thought, once again relinquishing control of Blue's cock.

The rope wasn't great for bondage—it was the slippery nylon kind—but with a bit of ordering around and manhandling, Block, Blue, and Slade soon had the backpacker's wrists tied to the limb of a nearby tree. Legs spread, facing the tree trunk, the boy's body was pleasingly stretched out, long and lean and ready for more fucking, a fucking that Blue was only too happy to provide. While Block and Slade held the naked guy steady, Blue slid his humongous cock into the boy's already primed ass.

"That's it, fucker. You take that dick," Slade said, his enthusiasm compensating for his lack of verbal originality. He peeled off his rubber and stood very close to Blue, watching his buddy's dick slamming into tender flesh again and again. No doubt about it: he *did* like being a nasty top. It sort of surprised him, but then, a lot of things in life did.

Block was still hungry. If he couldn't chow down on Blue's dick, he'd take the next best thing. He got between the tree and the boy and dropped to his knees. He looked up at the backpacker's face. The boy should have been suffering. He'd been, after all, stripped naked and tied up by strangers and was being plowed by an enormous cock. But it didn't look like he was in distress. In fact, his cock was hard. His cock was *really* hard. And suckable. So Block sucked it, or rather, it fucked his face, snaking so far in it damn near bruised his tonsils, pounding into his mouth every time Blue rammed the boy's ass.

It didn't take long at all before the backpacker's dick shot off, spurt after spurt of jizz down Block's voracious throat. When the dick was finally deflating, Block let it slide from his mouth and wiped his face with his muscular forearm. Slade was standing right bedside him, stroking hard meat.

"Suck me too."

It felt weird to be bossed around by Slade, who'd been his pal since childhood. Still, Slade was a college boy and Block was hungry. He gratefully wrapped his mouth around Slade's dick. Slade was close to shooting off, just like the backpacker boy had been. Within a minute or three, Slade yelled out something unintelligible and his cum flowed copiously over Block's warm, talented tongue.

Blue was still fucking away at the boy's slim butt.

"You almost done, Blue?" Slade asked. "It's getting late. A mosquito just bit me on the ass."

"Man," Blue grunted, "this is so fucking awkward, fucking him this way. I don't think I'll be able to come, dude."

"Okay, then. Let's go," Block said. He was getting bitten by bugs too. So much for Eden.

Blue pulled his dick out, peeled off the tightly stretched rubber, and wiped off his dick with the boy's boxer shorts.

It was kind of tough to untie the kid; the knots were a tangled mess.

"There's a knife hanging from my pack," the victim offered helpfully.

After Slade had sliced through the restraints, Block muttered, "Sorry about the rope."

"It's okay," the boy said, rubbing his wrist.

Block, Slade, and Blue pulled their clothes on, and, for good measure, Slade gathered up the boy's clothing, too, and carried it to the Jeep. It wasn't till they were pulling away that Slade threw the backpacker's shorts and shirt out the window. Block looked back. The boy, still wearing nothing but boots and shades, was standing there watching them go. At the very last moment, Block thought he saw him wave.

"Dudes, that was fucking great," Slade said.

"Yeah," Blue said. He sounded a little less sure.

"Hey, you didn't get off, didja?" Block asked over his shoulder, knowing full well Blue hadn't. "I'll take care of that. Let me take care of that."

Blue saw no reason not to. "Sure," he said.

Block climbed over the seat, contorted himself to a position kneeling between Blue's legs, undid Blue's fly, and fished out his mouthwatering penis.

"Mmm," Blue said helpfully as Block hungrily sucked his cock.

"Yeah," Slade continued, obstinately proud of himself, "We sure showed that dude. Sure used him. Fuck yeah, really showed him who was boss. Fuckin' A."

"Unh," said Blue, hips thrusting upward as he shot his load into Block's thoroughly delighted mouth.

The backpack boy, whose name was Leif, watched the SUV drive off, then recovered his clothes, pulled on his shorts, sprayed himself with Off!, and set up his campsite. After he made dinner— freeze-dried chicken Tetrazzini—he crawled into his tent and lit a candle lantern. He pulled a book out of his pack, a book with a cover picture of a boy wearing only a jockstrap and boots, crotch thrust toward the camera, and began to read a short story in which leather-clad men did perfectly awful, totally exciting things to one another. He got halfway through, then closed the book and began to think of what had just happened to him. The three guys hadn't been bad—they were hot-looking if a little on the stupidly drunk side, and if they hadn't done *everything* Leif would have wanted, it had still been a good scene. Sure, he would have like to be slapped around a little bit; he'd always wondered what that would feel like. Still, a hot scene. Leif's dick was hard again. He stripped, got into the sleeping bag, and jacked off into a thick hiking sock. Then he rolled over and, smiling blissfully, drifted off to sleep.

AQBJatJB

We were heading down the hill, Jeff, Preston, and me, down from Preston's place on 21st Street. It was one of those unseasonably warm February days. There'd been a break in the winter rains, and the marquee of the Castro Theater hovered beneath an impossibly blue San Francisco sky.

"So *rude*," Preston was saying. "He's the kind of queen who'd eat asparagus before heading out to the Cauldron for a night of water sports." Preston's famously acidic tongue was sharpened by alcohol, and he'd already had his own private cocktail hour before we'd arrived at his flat.

"So where do you think?" very blond Jeff asked. "Moby Dick? The Nothing Special?"

"*Ma mère*," Preston said, "all these bars are so-o-o tired."

"Then why," I asked, "in the holy fuck did you suggest we go out for a drink?"

"Point taken," he replied. "Moby Dick?"

"Speaking of which," ostentatiously all-American Jeff said, "get a look at that hunk." A well-built man in his early 30s was headed up the hill toward us, muscles bulging under his partly unbuttoned flannel shirt, basket bulging in his 501s.

Preston purred, "He's sanded that crotch, for sure. And maybe stuffed it. No white boy has a..."

The dark-haired man approached and shot me one of those "let's fuck" looks that I'm usually too lost in low self-esteem to notice. This time, though, I noticed, and our eyes locked. He proceeded up the hill, hesitating just slightly as he passed, while the three of us were being carried downhill by gravity. But a split-second later, when my head swiveled to the rear, he was looking back at me too, a semi-nasty half-smile on his face.

"Go for it," Jeff murmured.

"Guys," I said, "I'll see you later."

And I trudged back up the Castro hill, encouraged by Mr. Hunk's frequent backward glances. He was climbing the hill at a pretty good clip, though, and I hadn't had time to catch up with him when he turned, ascended the stairs of a Victorian, let himself in, and closed the door.

Well, *that* was a letdown. Cocktease? Someone who just loved the art of flirtation for its own sake? Whatever. I looked back. Preston and Jeff had already leveled off at 18th Street. I hesitated. What the hell.

I went up to his house, climbed the stairs, and rang the bell.

A few seconds later the door opened. It was him.

"C'mon in," he said. "But my roommate will be coming home from work soon. We don't have much time. Coke?" I wondered if that was an offer of drugs till I saw the can in his hand.

"Sure."

"Kitchen's this way."

He opened the refrigerator and pulled out a soda, standing silent as I popped the top and took a swig. He was undeniably beautiful, but he apparently didn't believe much in small talk.

I told him my name.

"We don't have much time," he reiterated, and his hand went to his crotch. I put my Coke on the counter. He undid the buttons of his jeans—no underwear—and pulled out his dick. It might have been cunningly packaged when it had been inside his pants, but it was still, even not-quite-hard, impressively thick and mouth-wateringly pretty. I walked the few steps between us and took its warmth in my hand.

"Go on," he said. "Suck it."

Well, he was a little bossy, but I was certainly in no mood to argue. I dropped to my knees and filled my mouth with his flesh. He leaned back against the refrigerator, sipping on his Coke, while I sucked on the now-stiff cock that jutted from his denims. I reached up and unbuttoned the waist button. His Levi's descended to mid-thigh. I stroked his fuzzy ass and hard thighs. My own dick, meanwhile, strained inside my pants.

I could hear the front door open.

"Roommate. You can keep on sucking."

Which I did. There was the sound of footsteps in the hallway, into the kitchen. I glanced up on one of my outstrokes. Roommate was standing there, handsome and well-groomed, in a business suit. Hardly anyone in the Castro seemed to actually have a full-time job, and precious few of *them* wore suits to work, so this was something of a novelty.

"Mind if I get some juice?" the roommate asked.

"Back off, cocksucker," commanded the owner of the cock I was sucking. I did, long enough for my host to turn around, open the fridge, and hand a bottle of apple juice to his roommate.

"C'mon," he then said. "Finish me off."

I took his big dick in my mouth again. It was just as well he wanted to come; I'm not the best cocksucker in the world, and though I was trying hard, my jaws were beginning to ache. I tried deep-throating the thing, but the angle was wrong and it made me gag a little. So I used both my hand and my mouth on his hard-on, accelerating the pace until I could feel it swelling up for the final blast-off. Then I took it as far in my mouth as I could, reached around him to play with his asshole with my wet fingers, and used my tongue on his cock head until he shot a big, sweet-and-sour load down my throat.

I looked up. He was still sipping on his Coke, and his roommate, standing by the sink, had poured himself a glass of cider. I awkwardly got off my knees, which had begun to ache from the hard floor.

Neither of the men said a word. I finally came up with "Thanks," grabbed the rest of my Coke, and showed myself out. My unsatisfied dick was leaking into my jeans, the bright day was fading into evening, and as I walked down the hill to 18th Street, I bounced a little, feeling absolutely great.

A few days later Jeff and I were sitting around Orphan Andy's, eating pancakes and talking. It was Sunday and the sidewalk outside the restaurant window was packed with guys in jeans and flannel shirts, some of them locals on their way to buy shower curtains at Cliff's, others out-of-towners making a pilgrimage to the liberated zone of Castro Street. It was as if they'd gone through Checkpoint Charlie at some sexual Berlin Wall. *You are now leaving the Hetero Sector.*

"So I stopped in for a QBJ at JB," Jeff was saying. This was our private shorthand. Jeff had gone for a Quick Blow Job at Jaguar Books, the dirty bookstore housed in a Victorian building in the heart of the Castro. "I was looking through the magazines..."

"Yeah, you're like the breeders who read Playboy for the articles."

"Shut up. I was looking through the magazines, when you know who came in?"

"I have no idea." And I guessed the name of a man who owned a Union Square art gallery where Jeff had worked for a while. The man was ostensibly straight, very visibly married, but he had, like so many straight guys, wondered about what he was missing, so he'd persuaded Jeff to take him on a little tour of the lower depths. Within weeks he was a habitué of the backrooms at the raunchiest bars—Folsom Prison and the Boot Camp—where stand-up sex came fast and furious and nobody could have cared less who he was or whose lithographs he sold.

"Nope," Jeff said. "I'd be more likely to run into him at the Slot these days."

"*Fisting? He's into fisting?*"

"Only as a top. Guess again."

"Ronald Reagan?"

"Eewww." Reagan was following up his ghastly stint as the governor of California with a right-wing run for the Presidency, but even if a bad actor *could* be elected chief executive and things got scary, it seemed wildly improbable that the scene on Castro Street would be shut down. We'd all come too far in the decade since Stonewall to be forced back in the closet; the gay movement, whatever disasters lay ahead, was an unstoppable force, or so I wanted to believe.

"Um, hey?"

"Yeah?" I said.

"You're daydreaming. Guess again." Jeff mopped up what was left of his maple syrup with one last bite of pancake and took a gulp of coffee.

"Twenty questions? Male or female?"

"Scott O'Hara," he said.

"The porn star?" Porn actors were a dime a dozen around the Castro, but O'Hara was near-legendary for the size of his cock, which was truly remarkable, and for his talent at sucking himself off, which was pretty damn amazing.

"So?" I'd seen O'Hara around myself.

"So I followed him upstairs and put the moves on him."

"And?"

"And his dick really is fucking huge. Where other guys' cocks stop, his just keeps on going. But, get this: He's a bottom."

"What a waste."

"Not really. But surprising, like a misallocation of natural resources." Jeff had an Ivy League education.

"So Scott O'Hara did you?"

"Yep. One of the best cocksuckers I've ever had."

"Jeffrey, my lad, you're making me think you're nothing but a starfucker."

"So sue me." He finished his coffee.

The days had returned to a depressing, gray rain. Suicide weather. I'd been out late dancing at the Trocadero, hadn't gotten laid, and was sitting naked by the window, mildly hung over, so horny it gave me a slightly sick feeling, thinking about going to Mexico, Hawaii, Jaguar Books. In my current financial state only one of the options was viable. A QBJ at JB it was, then.

I pulled on a pair of jeans and a sweatshirt, grabbed a rain jacket, and headed out the door; the Jaguar was just a 10-minute walk away.

"Yoo-hoo!"

I looked across Upper Market Street. It was Camellia, who'd been in the Cockettes, then in the Angels of Light, and who was, in any case, one of the most flamboyant genderfuck drag queens in the universe. He was also—I knew firsthand—semi-viciously mind-blowing in bed. The bite marks had lasted a week. That had been a long time ago, though, and now Camellia and I were just air-kiss friends. He ran across the street, dodging traffic.

"Hello, hot stuff," Camellia said, breathy as Marilyn Monroe on acid. His usual flounces and ruffles looked more than a bit bedraggled from the rain. Somehow, now that I was all shorthaired, mustachioed, and butch, it was a little weird to be talking to him in sight of the boys at the Café Flore. I was about to escape when he asked, "Did you hear about Preston?"

"What about him?"

"He's been sick, really sick. He was in the hospital, but he's back home now."

"God, that's too bad." Preston could be a real bitch, but he could also be hellishly amusing, as long as he wasn't dishing *you.* "I'll give him a call."

"Yeah, cutie, you do that."

"Well, listen, I've gotta get moving before the rain starts pissing down again."

"Okay, then, see you." And Camellia blew me a kiss and flounced off.

I was in luck. My friend Kon was working the desk at Jaguar Books, which meant I could get into the backroom for free. I said hi to him, not thinking to relay the news about Preston, then walked past the displays of dildos and dirty magazines, through the turnstile, and up the stairs.

There were dirty bookstores where you could fuck around in the video booths if you kept plunking in quarters, and there were backroom bars that hosted stand-up sex till last call, but Jaguar's backroom was a low-cost, all-hours orgy room, like the baths, only without the steam room and Jacuzzi. It was perfect. In the Castro? Got an itch? Presto, here was the place to scratch it.

It took my eyes a minute to adjust to the sudden darkness. There were maybe eight or 10 other guys there, leaning against the wall, on their knees, or lying on one of the vinyl-covered bunk beds.

I edged over to the action. Immediately, one guy got grabby and stuck his hand in my crotch. I shoved him away, turned off by his lack of finesse, his belly, and the booze on his breath, but my dick got hard nonetheless.

I looked around. There were several guys there who, if not exactly my type, were damn sure close enough for a rainy Thursday afternoon. And one of them, the Castro being a small world (in a non-Disneyland sense), was the man from a couple of weeks back, the man in the kitchen with a Coke and a roommate. I sidled over to where he stood in the erotic gloom, his big cock hanging from his open fly. I looked him straight in the eye. He looked away.

"Hey," I whispered. "The kitchen, remember?"

He turned and walked away. Given the size of the orgy room, that wasn't too far, but it *was* away. What a fucking queen. Oh, well, maybe he didn't remember who I was? No. Fucking attitude queen.

I went over to one of the upper bunks, where a hairy guy, naked from the waist down except for a pair of work boots, lay stroking his pole. I extended a hand toward his crotch, then hesitated. He grabbed my wrist and guided my hand to his cock, really hard and hot to the touch. I pulled at it a couple of times then bent over and took him in my mouth. As my lips rode up and down his thinnish stiffy, I felt someone behind me pressing his hard-on into my butt. I took mouth off dick long enough to straighten up and see who it was: an ambitiously cute guy who, with his close-cut dark hair and well-trimmed moustache, looked a lot like...well, like me. I went back to fellatio.

The man behind me reached around, unbuckled my belt, and unbuttoned my 501s, pulling them down almost to my knees. I wasn't nearly in the mood to get fucked, so when he spread my cheeks I began to get a bit uncomfortable. But when I felt his warm wet tongue slurping away at my hole, I relaxed and pushed my ass out for better access.

The guy on the bed shoved a bottle of poppers under my nose. I closed off one nostril and breathed deep.

Boing! said the usual comforting, enveloping, overwhelming rush in which time and space cease to exist and only sex is real. I was flying into a long, dark red tunnel, and at the end of the tunnel was dick, the dick I was sucking, the dick that was in my mouth. Dick. Dick. Diiicck.

And when my head cleared, someone, a guy I couldn't see, was in the lower bunk too, pulling at my cock with his slippery hand, then taking it down his thoroughly talented throat.

We'd formed a circuit of flesh, the four of us—tongue in my ass, cock in my mouth, mouth on my cock. I gestured for the poppers, never taking my mouth off the thin, hard shaft, then handed the little bottle down to whoever was sucking me off. That guy grabbed it, handed it back after a second, and his sucking became even more skillful, even more intense. Just when he'd gobbled every inch of me down, had latched on to my cock head with the muscles in his throat, I took another hit of poppers and handed them back to the guy on the top bunk. And somehow, somewhere in that sudden onrush of dislocated timelessness, a tongue was pushing deep into my pulsing hole; I was swallowing cum, I was pumping out cum, we were men connected, deeply connected, by lust, and everything, one long, long orgasm, was all right.

It took me a minute to recover. By the time I stuck my dick back in my pants whoever had sucked me off was gone. On to the next dick, no doubt. The guy on the upper bunk, the one I'd sucked, reached over and tousled my hair, and I squeezed his shoulder in return. I turned around, and a handsome man with a moustache stroked my face and kissed me. I could taste my ass on his mouth.

"Thanks," he whispered when the kiss was done. I smiled.

On my way out of the orgy room, I spotted the attitude queen from the kitchen leaning against one wall, untouched, still stroking his lonely cock. I remembered a line from *Alice In Wonderland*.

Will you, won't you, will you, won't you, won't you join the dance?

And then I was back out on 18th Street, heading toward home. The rain had stopped, and the sky was a clear, cold blue. Reagan would never be elected president. Preston would get better. That weird growth on my foot, whatever it was, would go away.

And I would stop off at Orphan Andy's and have a cup of coffee and a piece of blueberry pie.

thefootwhoreofbabylon

Brandon "Biff" Large was an expert in niche marketing, if he did say so himself.

He'd decided, when the economy went south and his finances got persuasively bleak, to become a hustler. But not just any kind of hustler, because there was a small obstacle to his having sex with hundreds of well-heeled men: Biff Large was as het as Hefner. Money was, of course, money, and he didn't expect anything like love to change hands. That wasn't the problem. It was just that (and he'd thought about it long and hard) he wasn't like those "gay for pay" porn stars who could get it up for any man with a paycheck attached. Biff was afraid that, Viagra or no, if he were a conventional hustler, the kind whose dick gets sucked and who fucks willing ass, he'd be in constant danger of falling down on the job. There was always the prospect of screwing rich women instead, but he was concerned that his girlfriend, Dru, would object.

And then, in a single stroke of merchandising genius, he came upon the solution: he'd be a specialty hustler, a dominant footwhore. Large had heard that there were plenty of gay men who, for one reason or another, worshipped feet. He'd heard that the richer and more powerful the man, the more eager he was—perhaps for compensatory reasons—to abase himself before another man. And Babylon, N.Y., certainly had its share of wealthy, powerful men. Bingo!

He put an ad in the pages of the *Babylon Gazette*. It read, fairly discreetly, "Men with an interest in feet are encouraged to contact Lance" and closed with a phone number. It was no surprise at all when the phone started ringing the next day.

His very first john was a well-known businessman, a lifelong bachelor who immediately dropped to his knees and started stroking Biff's shiny black boots. "Get up," Biff said, in a tone he hoped sounded commanding. When the man rose, a spot of wetness was already seeping through the front of his khakis. *This is going to be easy,* Biff thought. It was the easiest hundred bucks he'd ever made. The fact that his dick never got hard didn't matter, not to Biff, and not to his john, Mr. Ronson, who was to become a steady patron of Biff's size 11s.

Within a week Biff was a busy guy. He soon learned that not all foot johns were alike; even in the small town of Babylon, there was plenty of variety. There were the suckers and there were the lickers, those who preferred his feet spotlessly clean and those who craved them reeking to high heaven. There was the hotel tycoon who liked to be toe-fucked, naked on all fours, while listening to Wagner. There was the handsome guy who enjoyed having his dick stepped on while his boyfriend watched. And there was the corpulent man with the digital camera who wanted nothing more than to take pictures and jack off; within days, Biff's bare feet were all over the World Wide Web.

Yep, it was a funny world, all right, and Biff was going to profit from it. He rapidly learned his trade, built a loyal clientele, and doubled his fees. The pay hike lost him a bargain-hunting pervert or two, but he more than made up the difference in increased tax-free income. And Biff liked being expensive.

"Honey," he said to Dru, "I think the hard times are over."

"It was about time you got some work," she said.

Bitch, he thought, but wisely kept silent. He'd take it out on his johns the next day.

The next day, as it happened, was the day he met Arnie

Runcible. Arnie was different from most of his clients. For one thing, he was as young as himself, no more than 30. And for another, Runcible wasn't rich. He was, he'd for some reason confessed, a teacher at Babylon Elementary, and he wore a Timex, not a Rolex, though the time it told was no doubt pretty much as accurate as that told by a much more expensive watch.

The session with Arnie started out uneventfully enough. Biff watched with disinterest and, if anything, pity as the young man stripped down to his swollen white briefs (BVDs, not Calvins) and began to stroke Large's boots, pull them off, nuzzle and sniff Biff's ripe gym socks. Moaning softly, Runcible groped the toes beneath the socks, then slowly, gratefully, pulled the thick white cotton away, revealing Biff's naked, well-formed feet.

"Oh, my God," Arnie Runcible said, "my God." Lying on his stomach, dry-humping the floor, he stroked the bare flesh, kissed the toes, licked at the instep. Biff leaned against a desk and lifted one foot. In a shot, Runcible was underneath, licking the sole, chewing at Biff's calloused heel. Arnie squirmed, his hefty hard-on evident beneath his briefs. Biff looked away, gazing around Runcible's underfurnished room. He realized he should have asked for the money up front.

"Sir?" said Arnie, looking up at the hustler through largely vacant blue eyes. "May I please touch your cock?"

"No." None of Biff's clients thus far had even seen his dick, much less played with it. Fuck, he was straight and, money or no money, he was going to keep it that way. No ifs, ands, or...

"Then would you touch mine?" The teacher had tugged down his underwear, and the shaft that sprung forth was enormous, the biggest Biff had ever seen, even in porn. To gay guys, it would have been an object of awestruck desire. To him it was just abnormally fleshy.

"No."

"Please? Please, please, please?" He grabbed Biff's foot, tried to drag it toward his hard-on. This was getting serious.

Inspiration struck. "I said no, you fucking sick faggot son-of-a-cunting-bitch."

And at that, Arnie Runcible's enormous penis shot off big spurts of cum, again and again and again. Biff quickly backed away, but one wad hit him anyway, square on his left foot. It was creepy.

"Get a towel and fucking wipe that up," Biff growled. "Cocksucker." Runcible meekly, submissively did so, posthaste.

While Biff was pulling on his boots, Runcible, still naked, went over to the desk, opened a drawer, and pulled out a worn-looking wallet. "Two hundred, right?"

Biff Large never thought of himself as having a heart, much less a heart of gold, but for some reason he said, "No, just a hundred."

"Thank you," Arnie said as he showed him to the door, his half-hard dick bobbing. "Thank you so much. Can I see you again?" He looked like he might cry.

"Sure, call me for an appointment," Biff said, wishing the guy had some clothes on.

On the way home Biff thought about his new profession. He wondered if he should he feel guilty about it. Biff Large had never felt guilty about much of anything, not since he was a small boy, and despite taking money from a pathetic case like Arnie he wasn't going to start now. After all, he gave good value for the money. Hell, he wasn't even claiming to be gay. He stuck his feet out, men paid plenty to play with them, and if he enjoyed anything about the situation, it was the thought of easy money. What was wrong with that? Nothing, Biff decided. Nothing at all.

Just a few days later, Arnie called again for an appointment. Biff had a vacancy, so despite the bargain rates he was giving the guy, he scheduled him in.

This time out Runcible was even more submissive than the first, trembling as he stroked and kissed Biff's naked feet, pushing up the cuffs of the hustler's pants to worship his hairy ankles. He could barely contain himself; his breath was coming in gulps. He reached down for his own enormous, dripping dick.

"Don't touch it," Biff said, but Runcible's hand kept going, starting to stroke the damp, swollen head.

"I said don't touch it, you fucking faggot!"

And the teacher's hand flew from his cock.

Pathetic. But profitable.

Suddenly, unexpectedly, Runcible curled into a fetal position, cuddled around Biff's feet, his dick at a respectful distance from the size 11s. "Sir, may I ask a question?" Owlish blue eyes.

One thing Large hadn't expected when he'd started hustling was how many of his clients would want to talk. It was a nuisance. But he figured it was part of his job description, like those ugly uniforms the kids at Burger Delite had to wear. "What do you want to know?"

"Do you enjoy this? Having men devote themselves to your feet?"

Biff was taken aback. As long as the cash kept rolling in, it was a question he wouldn't have thought to ask himself.

"What do you think?"

"I think," said Runcible hopefully, still curled up in a ball, "that it makes you happier than anything in the world."

"Yes, it does, faggot." It didn't, of course. But it was better than working at Burger Delite. And if the money was good, he'd be anything anybody wanted him to be. Within reason.

"Lance, sir?"

"What?"

"Can I tell you a little about myself?"

Large looked at his watch: 20 minutes to go. "It's your dime."

And the naked, scrunched-up man let it all spill out—his love of feet, his submissiveness, the tiresome details of his day-to-day life, his love of feet. Most of it Biff found tedious. Some he found pitiable or faintly disgusting. But Brandon Large had never before asked himself why the men who hired him needed what they needed, hadn't even wanted to know, and now he found himself on the way home from Runcible's house thinking about some of what the guy had said. Yep, kind of a nuisance.

The following week, as winter turned to spring, Biff had a new client. A really young client, as it turned out—he'd even demanded the kid's ID to make sure he was legal. He was Middle Eastern, and his family was, from the look of things, rich as holy fuck. The house was like a goddamn museum. The kid was gawky and anxious.

"You're parents aren't due back, are they?"

"They're in Abu Dhabi." Well, wherever that was, it was no doubt far enough away.

The kid didn't want anything special, just to get down on all fours on a very expensive carpet, his smooth, brown ass in the air, and to cozy up to a pair of big, strong feet. At the end, the boy, still tentative, lay on his back, head between Biff's arches, and jacked his hard-on till he shot, copiously, all over his own lean, young belly.

The kid rose, wiped himself with Kleenex, reached into the drawer of a costly piece of furniture, and handed over 250 crisp new bucks. Nice tip. "Hey, stay here while I clean up, okay?"

Left to his own devices, Large looked around the living room, all oriental fabrics and big-ticket knickknacks. One marble table held a collection of dozens of decorative little boxes, wood, porcelain, metal. He pocketed an ornate little silver one. A nice present for Dru, and he bet it would never be missed.

"Hey," the Arab boy said when he emerged, dressed in linen pants and a tan silk shirt, "want to go to dinner?"

"Don't you think it's a little risky to be seen together around here? Babylon's not that big a town."

"I meant go to the city to eat."

"Manhattan?"

"Sure," said the boy, pulling a sport jacket from the closet. "Here, put this on." It fit like a glove. A very costly glove.

"Listen, I don't even know you."

"Dinner? My treat."

"I have to go pee first."

Once in the bathroom Biff checked out the jacket: Armani. Nice. He stuck the little silver box into his jacket pocket, and on his way out of the house managed to slip it back onto the table.

"Your car or mine?" the Arab boy asked. His was a white Mercedes convertible. Of course.

"Yours," Biff said.

The maitre d' at the Manhattan restaurant recognized the boy. Hell, even the valet parker knew the boy. But they didn't have a reservation, and there was a wait of about 15 minutes for a table. Biff was feeling restless. "Want to go for a walk in the meantime?" he asked.

While they were strolling around the Upper East Side, Biff noticed a man leaning against a wall. He was a handsome, tough-looking man wearing black, knee-high, lace-up boots. *The competition,* Biff thought. The Arab boy noticed him too, but, being well-bred, quickly returned his attention to Biff. "Our table must be ready by now," he said, and they headed back to Au Pied.

The menu, with its lists of obscure ingredients, was only semi-comprehensible to Biff, and the portions were smaller than they had any right to be at those prices, but dinner was, finally, not bad at all.

The kid had spent the whole time nervously chattering about himself, so Biff finally asked point-blank, "Don't you want to know anything about me?" It wasn't that he wanted to confess to his tricks who he actually was; it's just that he'd found out he enjoyed being the center of attention.

"Not really," the young man said.

Slightly chagrined, Biff stared down at his tiny, expensive dessert. "And you don't feel like I'm taking advantage of you?" he asked.

"Quite the opposite," the Arab boy said, with a slight smile. And that was that.

And when, on the way home, the white Mercedes passed, perhaps not by accident, the corner where they'd earlier seen the hustler, he was still standing there. Maybe business was slow that night.

Two weeks later Dru's birthday rolled around. Things between the two of them had been a little tense of late, so Biff decided to go all out, and thanks to queer men's money he could afford it. He bought tickets to a Saturday matinee of a Broadway musical that Dru had been aching to see. And he made reservations for dinner at Au Pied.

After the show, which was every bit as awful as Biff had feared, they drove uptown to eat. Biff purposely took a route that would pass the corner where he'd seen the man in boots, though he certainly knew there wasn't a chance in hell the man would be there again. Only he *was* there, wearing those big boots, leaning against the wall, crotch thrust slightly forward, face impassive behind mirrored shades, even though it was after dark.

Over a dinner even more expensive than Biff had remembered, he and Dru made small talk, but his attention wandered. He kept thinking of the man in boots. Big boots.

"Honey," he said, after he'd signed for the check, "happy birthday."

"Oh, Biff," Dru said. "Sometimes you really do delight me."

"Um, listen, Dru. There's something I have to do tonight in

the city. Would you mind driving yourself home? I can take a late train back."

Dru did, in fact, mind. But she figured he'd just dropped nearly half a grand on her, so she agreed to make her own way back to Babylon. After she'd pulled away, Biff walked, somewhat reluctantly but inevitably, back to the corner where the hustler had been. This time, though, he was gone. A young, skinny boy was working the opposite corner, but he wouldn't do at all. Biff was about to head for the subway when he heard a voice behind him.

"Anything I can help you with?"

"Huh?" Biff said, turning. It was the man in boots.

"I just thought you seemed lost or something. Looking for anything in particular?"

"Um...I'm looking for...well, I'm looking for a good time, to tell you the truth."

"Not a cop, are you?" Did hustlers really ask that? Biff never did, but suddenly he was thinking he should start.

"Christ, of course not."

"Follow me, then."

"How far?"

"A few blocks."

"And how much?"

"Hundred for an hour." A bargain. Especially compared to dinner at Au Pied.

Walking slightly behind the booted man, Biff felt his brain go into overdrive. If this had been some gay porn story, he would be on his way to discovering that, yes, he was really, beneath it all, queer as anything. The two of them would have explosive sex, Biff would leave Dru, and he'd start going to Broadway musicals all on his own. But it wasn't a porn story, and Brandon "Biff" Large was totally, irrevocably hetero, full stop. Why was he doing this, then? Partly it was just curiosity, wanting to see things from the other side. But Biff had read in some how-to book about S/M, that most good tops learned their skills by being bottoms first, and he had somehow skipped that part. So here was a way to learn how a real gay man did the top thing, maybe pick up a move or two that he could in turn use on his own clients. Job-related research. Yeah, that was it: research.

"We're here."

"Here" was a pretty classy apartment building, the kind that might have had a doorman, though this one didn't. The hustler's apartment, though, was in the basement, just a barren little room with a mattress on the floor.

"Have a favorite safeword?" the man in boots asked Biff.

"Never use one," Large replied.

"Your choice. Now get on your knees."

Biff had watched fags going at it often enough to have a damn good idea of what to do and how to do it. He dropped to the floor and laid his forehead on the man's black boot.

"Now lick it."

Biff did, feeling both queasy and excited, hoping he wouldn't catch anything. He could understand something of what his clients felt, why they paid big bucks to be at his feet.

"That's it, get it nice and shiny." Biff's tongue made the leather wet. "That's a good boy. Now take it off."

"Yes, sir," Biff said, because that's what he was supposed to say. The man's sock had a ripe, not displeasing smell. Biff had to admit it—this was kind of exciting.

"Now take off the sock." The hustler's foot was, like his own, big and well-formed. "Kiss my foot. Kiss it."

Biff's lips met flesh. In the interests of research.

"Toes, suck my toes." Large had never sucked anyone's toes, not even a woman's, not even Dru's. But he opened wide and sucked on the man's big toe. It wasn't bad. He opened wider, got most of the guy's five toes stuffed into his mouth.

"Mmmf," said Biff.

"And now suck *this*."

Biff looked up. The man had taken his cock out from his pants, and it hovered, mostly hard, above Biff Large's head.

"No."

"What was that?" the hustler growled.

"I said no." Even though he'd been kind of enjoying himself, Biff was straight, he was paying good money, and he knew where to draw the line.

"And I said kiss it, faggot." And the hustler sent one foot, the one still wearing the boot, into Biff's crotch. Not all that hard, just hard enough to hurt.

"Listen, I want to stop this. It's over." But the hustler didn't listen to him. With no safeword, his protests could well have been part of the scene. The boot was grinding into Biff's crotch now, and to his dismay his cock was getting stiff. Twisting away to avoid the pressure, he lost his balance, landing with his face against the hustler's bare foot. He felt the boot pressing down on his neck, jamming his cheek into foot flesh.

"Suck me, you fucking sick fag!" It was just the sort of thing Biff would have said to one of his own johns. Since he wasn't a sick fag it didn't make him feel bad. But, conversely, since he wasn't a sick fag, it didn't make him feel good either.

"No, listen, sorry..." The boot came off his neck, then arced into his flank. It knocked the breath out of him. And again. Jesus, what had he gotten himself into?

Biff had a sudden inspiration. "Safeword," he said. "Safeword, safeword, safeword."

And the hustler immediately stopped kicking him. "Hey," said the man. "Sorry, I figured you wanted to do a resistance scene. Listen, you okay?"

"Fine," said Biff. He pulled himself to his knees, at eye level with the man's cock. He averted his eyes. "I just, I guess I made a mistake. Bit off more than I could chew, kind of."

The hustler was stuffing his penis back in his pants.

"You see," explained Biff, "I'm straight."

"So fucking what?" said the hustler. "I am too."

There was nothing, really, to say after that. Brandon "Biff" Large paid up, left the hustler's apartment, took the train back to Babylon, fucked Dru fiercely, rolled over, and fell into a sound and dreamless sleep.

number14

The Soviet submarine slices silently through the waters of New York Harbor.

The Communist commander is peering through the periscope...at the Statue of Liberty! "We shall destroy," he sneers, "this symbol of America—and all she stands for." There's a very evil grin on his face.

Meanwhile...on Bedloe's Island, a high school field trip stands at the foot of the statue. Philip MacReady, just turned 18, lifts his Brownie to his eye.

"Will ever stand as a symbol of the American way..." the teacher is saying.

A device in Philip MacReady's ear emits a secret signal from his mentor. The students make their way toward the statue's entrance, but young MacReady hangs back from the group.

The Soviet sailor's face is contorted by hate. "Ready the missiles, comrades! We shall DESTROY HER!!"

"Captain! Look! On the underwater television-scope!"

An awesomely familiar shape is streaking at jet speed toward the Soviet sub.

"Suffering Stalin! It's SeaScout!!!"

Kevin looked at himself in the full-length mirror. Not bad, really. Mid-thirties, just a bit of a belly. His dick was on the small side, but some guys liked small dicks. His face wasn't bad, though his ears stuck out a bit and he was getting the beginnings of a double chin. He would never pass for a superhero, but he was okay.

Enough—he had to quit daydreaming. It was a big day: Some kid named Jeromy was bringing him a copy of *SeaScout Comics #14*. His collection would be complete.

SeaScout #14 had been published before Kevin McHugh was born. It had originally belonged to his much older brother, one of a big pile of comic books in the basement; Mike had left them behind when he went off to Vietnam and never came back. Sprawled on a shabby old sofa, Kevin had devoured every garishly colored page. There were the science-fiction comics, the ones where square-jawed scientists fought off bug-eyed monsters while their buxom girlfriends cowered in a corner. The deliciously gory horror comics dripping with guts. There were a few soldier comics too. And then there were the superheroes. Kevin had especially liked the superheroes: Captain America, Superman, the less popular ones like the Blue Beetle.

And SeaScout.

Mike had collected all the *SeaScout* comics, all the way back to *SeaScout #1,* which featured a cover drawing of SeaScout thrusting upward from the waves, silhouetted against the New York skyline, fist upraised, all supple strength and American courage. Atlantic foam gushed around his powerful body. Seawater coursed over his chiseled half-naked chest and muscular belly, swirled around his astonishing thighs. His form-fitting costume, aqua blue and sea green, accentuated every rippling curve. There was even the suggestion of an erect nipple. Only his crotch remained hidden, the merest suggestion of bulk.

THE BIRTH OF A SUPERHERO! the cover exclaimed. And in a dialogue balloon SeaScout shouted his soon-to-be-famous call to action: "Sail ON!"

"Sail ON!" commands SeaScout, and the ocean itself leaps to respond. Waves begin to churn, underwater currents rise to typhoon

strength. The Soviet sub is tossed about like a bathtub toy. Volcanoes sprout from the sea floor, belching lava with a ROARRR! And amazingly, the tights-clad hero hoists the entire Commie warship above his head, heaved skyward on a gigantic waterspout.

The bearded captain, looking suspiciously like Lenin, spits out, "Curse you, SeaScout! Fire the warheads!" Two missiles flare forth from the ship, only to spiral wildly and head off harmlessly into space. But...

"The force of the missiles has knocked me off balance!" says SeaScout to no one in particular. The sub begins to wobble, and SeaScout starts to plummet toward the ocean.

Of all the comic books in his brother's collection, the *SeaScouts* were Kevin's favorites. He'd loved the elemental strangeness of it all, how Rick Roman, a Navy research scientist whose atomic experiment had been sabotaged by the Reds and gone horribly wrong, could command the mighty ocean itself. And then there was the way he looked, his bulging-yet-streamlined muscles flexing beneath the ocean-colored costume.

When summer came and his family went to the public pool down the road, Kevin would imagine himself clad in clinging blue tights as he dove beneath the chlorinated surface, held his breath till his lungs were close to bursting, then pushed off from the turquoise-painted concrete of the pool bottom, shouting, as he soared into the muggy July sky, "Sail ON!"

"Can't...hold...on..." gasps SeaScout. And then—miraculously—the sub rights itself, lofted skyward again. It's Flip, SeaScout's teenage sidekick, holding up the vessel's stern, steadying the Red sub. He's shown up in the nick of time. And now it rings out from them both, their rallying cry: "Sail ON!"

Inside the lead sub, panicked sailors grab onto anything in a futile effort to save themselves, the commander frozen wide-eyed in fear.

And, at SeaScout's gesture, the ocean floor itself opens up, split by a huge, yawning fissure that sucks the lava, the submarine, everything but SeaScout and Flip, deep, deeper, down into the bowels of the Earth.

By the time Kevin left for college, the simple good-always-triumphs worldview of '50s comic books had been replaced in the public's fancy by the darker, more neurotic stories in the Marvel canon. Kevin would get stoned and read the latest about Spiderman's self-doubt and the mutant bonding of the X-Men. Something in him, though, still longed for the stories of SeaScout he'd left behind in the basement.

Kevin graduated from college just before his mother moved out of the house on Oakdale Road. Kevin's father had dumped her and remarried. And left on her own in the suburbs she was bored to distraction. Kevin had one last chance to rescue his childhood relics before she moved to a condo in Atlanta.

The SeaSub glides into its subterranean dock. Flip and SeaScout clamber out.

They get into the private high-speed elevator that shoots them upward to their penthouse, far above the city. "Another job well done, Flip." SeaScout lays a powerful hand on young Philip MacReady's shoulder. The elevator doors glide open and the two superheroes, arms around each other, walk down the marble-paneled hallway.

"It's time for bed, Philip." SeaScout turns, and, gazing out the window at the city lights far below, strips off the top of his costume. His back is broad and well-muscled. Flip can see the semitransparent reflection of the older man's brawny torso in the window, V-shaped, perfect.

He'd gone down to the basement first thing. The comics were still there. Most of them were now valuable collectors' items, but they still sat there in a couple of raggedy corrugated-cardboard cartons. All except *SeaScout #14*, the rarest of the bunch. That one had somehow been left lying on the floor, and at some point the water heater had sprung a leak. The comic, what was left of it, was a water-damaged mess—its pages were wrinkled, the front cover spotted with mold, the last few pages stuck to the floor. It was not only worthless, the end of the story was totally unreadable. Stranded midway in the badly damaged comic, Kevin had invented the climax of the tale, just made it up the way he wished it had been.

> *Flip walks over to SeaScout, now standing naked at the window.*
> *"Rick?" asks Flip, using SeaScout's given name. He lays his hand on the bare flesh of SeaScout's powerful shoulder.*
> *"Philip, don't."*
> *"But Rick...all this time together...I mean, how much longer can I stand this torture?"*
> *"Philip, you're stronger than this." SeaScout is still staring out the window, out at the night. "We both are."*
> *A tear falls from Flip's eye, leaving a salty trail on his cheek.*

The years passed, flipping over like illustrated pages. Kevin, now in a low-level high-tech job at Princeton, got married; nothing special, the kind of thing you do because that's what's expected of you. Then, somewhere along the line, he discovered he liked to have sex with men. The divorce had been friendly but final, and since then Kevin's romantic life had been basically nonexistent. He didn't think of himself as "bi," exactly, much less "gay," but when he got horny he would, from time to time, head out to a dirty bookstore, where some stranger in a grimy video booth would blow him. No muss, no fuss, no big deal. As his granny had said, in a slightly different context, "In the dark, all cats are black."

And there *were* those memories of SeaScout...

Suddenly there's a shattering of glass. Four men with gas masks over their faces—Soviet soldiers—burst through the broken picture window, propelled by rocket packs strapped to their backs.

Clouds of noxious gas swirl through the penthouse. Within moments, the men carry the unconscious forms of Flip and the naked SeaScout out through the broken window, out into the night.

For years he'd let his comic book collection, carefully repackaged to reflect its amazingly high value, remain untouched in storage. Then Kevin had had an astonishingly vivid dream about SeaScout. He, Kevin, had been Flip, and he and SeaScout had been swimming effortlessly, weightless in azure seas. They circled, touched, whirled like dolphins, rubbed against each other. It was magnificent.

Kevin awoke to a damp spot in his bed; he'd had his first wet dream since high school.

It was then he'd taken his *SeaScout* comics collection out of storage. It was complete except for #14, which had mildewed and rotted and finally been thrown away. He resolved, for old times' sake, to somehow get his hands on a copy of the rare missing issue: # 14.

Kevin placed ads on a couple of Internet newsgroups, but *SeaScout #14* wasn't the easiest comic to come by. Amidst the anti-comics frenzy of 1950s America, renowned Dr. So-and-so had warned Congress about "the harm that comics can do," waving a copy of *SeaScout #14* and railing against the cleverly coded perversion contained therein. The writer of *SeaScout,* a right-wing Republican, protested that he, in fact, hated sex perverts every bit as much as he hated Commies, but to no avail. Though *SeaScout #14* was already on the stands, the publisher recalled the copies that remained unsold and mulched them all, thereby courageously protecting America's youth from the unspeakable.

number14

Flip comes to. He's lying on his back, firmly tied down to a table in some dark dungeon. He turns his head and sees...

"Rick!" SeaScout is tied spread-eagle to a wall, arms and legs outstretched against cold concrete, a web of ropes binding him to hooks set into the stone. He's still naked, though a small scrap of cloth drapes modestly across his crotch.

Flip struggles against the ropes, but it's in vain. He's firmly trussed down, all right.

A green-painted metal door in a corner slides open and a long shaft of light shoots across the floor.

"And now, SeaScout," says a man silhouetted in the doorway, "you shall see what lies in store for those who seek to foil the will of the working class!"

Kevin had started fantasizing about SeaScout often. After a hard day at work he would fill the tub, light some candles, and slip into a hot bath, imagining that SeaScout was there with him. In his fantasy Kevin had taken Flip's place, he *was* Flip. He and SeaScout played beneath the waves, swimming weightless among endless reefs of coral and forests of seaweed, the simple colors of comic books transformed by the tides of desire. SeaScout's aqua-colored costume just barely concealed a hard-on of titanic proportions, and Kevin glided up to it, his hands grasping its underwater heft, working it free. It was, of course, magnificent, the killer whale of pricks, arching toward the eerie blue sunlight that filtered from the surface far above. Kevin took it into his mouth. It tasted of brine and legend, and it filled his mouth as no other cock ever could. Together he and SeaScout spiraled in a subaqueous dance of lust in timeless blue space, startling the fish, trailing bubbles in their wake. Meanwhile, back in the real world, Kevin's hand, lubed with soap, coaxed an orgasm out of his own hard cock. Salty white spurts arced upward and landed in the bathwater, for a moment leaving little trails like the stuff in Lava Lamps, only to disperse, fluid into fluid, and be no more.

SeaScout squirms against his restraints. The little piece of cloth flutters to the floor.

"You won't get away with this!" Flip's face is contorted with anger, drops of sweat popping from his forehead.

"Ah, but on the contrary, we surely will." The Russian is dressed in an elegantly tailored suit, and he fairly purrs. "Face it, little fishy, you've been hooked."

He'd contacted Jeromy through an online newsgroup for comic book collectors. "SeaScout #14, anyone?" Jeromy's posting had read. No price was mentioned, just the words "not greedy." Kevin had sent e-mail to the poster and was astonished when, a day later, a response appeared in his in-box offering to sell him *SeaScout #14* for a mere fraction of what had been demanded on the online auction sites. At $500, Jeromy was asking far, far below fair value. It made Kevin suspicious.

"Can we talk by phone?" his response had read. When Jeromy called—a 19-year-old kid, it turned out—his doubts were put to rest...almost. Jeromy even lived in Jersey too, not very far away.

"The comic book was my Dad's. He died last year, and I gave most of his collection to charity. That's what he would have wanted; he was a generous guy. But...well, I could use a little cash right now. I feel funny about selling any of his comics at all—he always said that money was the worst reason to collect comics."

"You gave away his collection?"

"Yeah, I did. But I knew this SeaScout thing was the most valuable comic he had."

"You gave away his collection."

"Comic books don't mean very much to me. Sorry."

number14

"Did you read #14?"

"Yeah," said Jeromy, "it wasn't bad."

The Russian walks over to SeaScout and takes the long cigarette holder from his mouth, bringing it close to SeaScout's naked chest. The Russian looks over at the tied-down teenager. "First we shall take care of you, little Flip, and then we'll deal with your...friend."

He touches the glowing cigarette to SeaScout's pec, and the super-hero's face contorts in pain. There's a smell of scorched flesh.

"You Commie bastards!" Flip shouts. He stares at his naked hero and gets a shock. Could it be that SeaScout finds this situation... exciting?!?

After the phone call, Kevin started having ideas, kind of crazy ideas. Ideas about, well, about this boy Jeromy becoming his very own sidekick.

Kevin tried to picture what it would be like. He'd lie back on the sofa in the dark, stroking his dick, imagining the two of them, Kevin and Jeromy, being buddies like SeaScout and Flip. Two superheroes floating side by side through the night. He'd never had a more intense fantasy. Nothing had ever made his cock harder, more sensitive to his touch, more ready to gush a load of cum.

SeaScout and Flip. Kevin and Jeromy. Gliding through an underwater world. Swimming around one another, their costumes soaked through, becoming translucent, transparent, vanishing alto-gether, the two of them circling around one another, naked beneath the sea, swimming closer and closer, stiff cocks like twin dolphins that finally rubbed up against each other, hard wet flesh against hard wet flesh.

And when he thought of that, Kevin would squeeze his dick just a bit harder, until the wave was inevitable, juices splashing across his naked chest. Once the spasms subsided he'd rub his hand over the dampness that covered his chest and bring it to his mouth. It tasted like seawater.

"And now we shall see how long you can survive underwater, my young enemy," the Red agent sneers. *"Guards, prepare the room!"*

Half a dozen Russian soldiers deploy themselves around the concrete cubicle. Metal shutters drop down over the walls. A drain in the center of the floor is sealed off. A light goes on in the middle of one wall; it's coming from a window into an adjoining cubicle.

"And now, SeaScout, prepare to watch your little guppy drown. There's not a thing you'll be able to do about it except shut your eyes, and even then..." he takes a puff of his cigarette *"...you'll be able to hear him scream."*

The doorbell rang. It was Jeromy; no one else would be coming to the door this late, nearly 11. Jeromy worked nights as a waiter at a seafood restaurant, of all places. And now, after his shift, he was bringing by, as arranged, a copy of *SeaScout #14* that, Kevin hoped, was the genuine article, the object of his desire.

As he walked toward the door Kevin's dick shot upward, instantly hard. He'd expected that might happen and so he'd put on an oversize T-shirt and tight briefs under baggy pants, but as he opened the door he still felt self-conscious.

Jeromy. Jeromy was a...surprise. He'd expected someone who seemed like a 19-year-old boy. And though Jeromy *was* a 19-year-old boy, he was a tall one, about 6 foot 5, with a surprisingly mature, solemn face topped by an unruly thatch of jet-black hair. He was a lot more imposing than any teenage sidekick had a right to be.

"Kevin?"

"That's me. C'mon in. Beer?"

"Please."

Jeromy opened the manila envelope he was carrying and pulled out a smaller envelope, a clear plastic one that held a near-mint copy of *SeaScout number 14.*

"So that's it."

"Yep. You want it?"

Kevin, unexpectedly, felt like crying. He carefully opened the envelope and pulled out the precious issue. It had the unmistakable smell of old comic book, as delicately flowery as fine Chardonnay.

"Yes. I want it." *And I want you,* Kevin thought.

The guards are uncovering four large spigots in the corners of the room.

"Once your protégé has become a shipwreck, I'll be back to take care of you, Comrade SeaScout," the Red sneers. "Oh, and one thing, little Flip. You can so easily escape the fate that awaits you...if you'll just agree to kill SeaScout yourself."

"Never, you Commie pig! Never!"

The Red turns toward the exit.

"Ah, well. Pity. Guards, make ready."

The guards file out the door, followed by the Communist agent. The door is shut and bolted. In a moment, Flip can see the Russki through the window, still puffing on his cigarette, his eyes evil slits.

There's the sound of valves being opened. From all four corners, water gushes into the sealed-off dungeon.

"Is a personal check okay?" Kevin had taken a close look at #14. If it *was* a forgery, it was the most convincing damn one imaginable.

"Of course."

Kevin pulled out his checkbook. "I've wanted this for so long. You've made me very happy, Jeromy."

For the first time that night the tall young man smiled. It was dazzling.

Kevin handed Jeromy the check and, without asking, fetched a couple more beers. He handed one to Jeromy and sat down beside him on the couch.

"So you're 19, huh?" Kevin was acutely aware of how much older than the boy he was, pudgier, and less attractive too.

"Yeah, and let me tell you, it's not easy."

"Being 19?"

"Yeah. Figuring it all out, who I am, what I want." He leaned back, stretching slightly, and his leg brushed up against Kevin's and stayed there.

Kevin's cock was so hard it hurt. If he was ever going to risk a move, make his dreams real, this was the time. Kevin took his left hand and placed it deliberately on Jeromy's right thigh.

The boy stopped drinking his beer. "Hey!"

"Oh, God, I'm so sorry. I'm so sorry. I'd understand if you just walked out of here and took the comic with you." Blood rushed to Kevin's face, and he felt slightly sick, then out of breath, as though he were drowning. But his hand stayed on Jeromy's thigh for a moment more, as though it were anchored there.

"Listen, it's not that I don't like you or anything. It's just that..."

"Jeromy, I just feel so awful about this." Like he was drowning.

The water is pouring into the room with astonishing force. Flip, tied down to the table, is surely doomed to drown.

He looks over at SeaScout, his mentor, his friend, his protector, bound naked to the wall. He can't read the expression on SeaScout's face, but the superhero's dick is, astonishingly, very hard, curving magnificently upward.

Flip can move his head just enough to see the water filling the room. It's a foot or two above the floor now and rising rapidly. The end is near...

And yet, looking at SeaScout's gorgeous body, impassive face, eager cock, Flip feels a stirring in his crotch too, and as the tide rises, so does the blood in his dick.

"Rick..." Flip begins.

"I know, Philip, I know..."

"Please, let me say it..."

"Philip, you don't have to say a word..."

"Rick, I love you."

And the water continues its inexorable climb.

Kevin had finished telling Jeromy the story of himself, his brother, and *SeaScout #14*. Though he left out the parts about wet dreams and masturbation. Some SeaScout he'd be. He didn't feel like a superhero. He felt pathetic, felt like breaking down in tears.

"Want to split another beer?" the tall, handsome boy asked.

"Sorry, that's all there was. I could maybe go out for some..."

Jeromy smiled again, a gentle smile. "Kevin?"

"Yeah?"

"Don't worry about it."

"But..."

"Kevin?"

"What?" He felt like he *was* going to break down and cry.

The boy was staring deep into his eyes, and Kevin's dick was hard, as hard as ice.

"It's just that you startled me, okay?" Jeromy smiled again, reached for Kevin's hand and guided it back to his thigh. "Which way's your bathroom?"

Life, Kevin suddenly realized, was full of surprises.

The water is rising quickly now, almost up to SeaScout's swelling crotch, nearly reaching Flip's helpless body.

The vicious Communist agent is watching through the window, a satisfied grin on his face, but SeaScout and Flip don't notice. They stare into one another's eyes, and not a word need be spoken.

A sadistic, cold voice comes from a loudspeaker: "Last chance, herring-boy. Kill SeaScout for me and I'll let you live."
No response.

Jeromy led Kevin by the hand down the hall to the bathroom.

"We could try filling the tub, but there's no way in hell both of us could fit in there" Kevin said.

"The shower, then?"

Jeromy reached over and turned the knobs, flipped a handle, and water started pouring from the showerhead. He stood very close to Kevin and started unbuttoning Kevin's shirt.

"Jeromy, you don't have to..."

"Shh," Jeromy gently said, and he kissed Kevin on the lips. He slipped the shirt from Kevin's torso, then reached down and unbuckled the older man's belt. When he unzipped Kevin's fly, his fingers brushed against Kevin's hard dick.

"I *want* to do this," Jeromy said, and once again Kevin felt close to tears.

And then Kevin was totally naked, and he stood in wonderment, watching as the tall, good-looking boy slowly removed his own clothing.

Jeromy's body was trim rather than muscular, even a little bit gangly, but Kevin thought he'd never seen anything so beautiful in his entire life. The boy removed his briefs, revealing a startlingly black bush nestled between snow-white thighs. His big, thick cock stood straight up above a generous set of balls. Kevin said a silent thank you to God.

They climbed clumsily into the tub, and then they were together beneath the shower, together, their flesh shiny-wet, stroking, kissing, holding each other's slippery bodies tight, cock against cock, water flowing down.

"Let me suck you off," Kevin said, silently adding *SeaScout*.

But Jeromy didn't say anything. He just awkwardly got on his knees and took the older man's hard-on in his mouth.

"Oh, my God," Kevin said. "Oh, my God."

He could barely breathe.

And then Jeromy reached over for the bar of soap, lathered his hands up, and, taking Kevin's stiff dick all the way into his mouth, reached up and slid his soap-slick fingers up to Kevin's ass. The tight hole resisted at first but soon let one, then two fingers in. If there were tears falling from Kevin's eyes, they were invisible beneath the shower's incessant flow. Kevin didn't want to come, he tried not to, but he couldn't stop himself, couldn't turn back the irresistible tide. His cock pulsed into Jeromy's mouth, and the boy gulped down every salty drop.

The freezing-cold water begins to cover SeaScout's muscular thighs. Flip shivers from the spray of the onrushing flood. SeaScout flinches as the frigid liquid reaches his balls. Flip feels the water seeping beneath his back. In a matter of seconds the rising tide engulfs the tied-down young man. A trail of bubbles escapes from his lips.

And then, just as Flip is about to breathe his last, just as SeaScout is about to watch his loyal partner die, just as SeaScout's dick is about to shoot tortured streams of cum into the flood, big red words appear across the scene: "IS THIS IT?? CAN THIS BE THE END OF SEASCOUT AND FLIP???"

After it was over, after Kevin's hand had jacked the cum from Jeromy's big dick, spurts of jizz joining the shower water spiraling down the drain, after the two men had dried off and dressed and kissed good night, promised to meet again and probably meant it, after the front door had closed and the boy was gone, Kevin found himself alone with his thoughts.

There was no way, really, to make sense of all that had happened.

He'd try tomorrow, he figured, after a good night's sleep filled with underwater dreams. He walked over to the table where *SeaScout #14* lay. He just stood there looking down at the long-sought prize for a while, remembering the touch of Jeromy's lips, Jeromy's wet body against his.

Then he shook his head slightly and picked up the comic book, carefully rewrapped in its plastic shell. Beneath it, lying on the tabletop, was the $500 check, slipped there by Jeromy. Where the recipient's name was written, Jeromy had crossed off his name and written "Flip." Kevin's own name had been replaced by "SeaScout." Across the top of the check, Jeromy had scrawled "Enjoy your comic book."

And in the lower left of the check, in the space left for comments, Jeromy, beautiful Jeromy, had written just two words: "Sail ON!"

Kevin picked up the check and looked at it a good long while. He walked over to the window and looked out at the night, at the city lights, each one representing a person's life. He thought about things until he got tired of thinking, then ripped the check into little pieces. SeaScout and Flip were, after all, dead.

He turned away from the window, threw the shreds of paper in the trash, picked up the plastic envelope, and pulled out *SeaScout #14*. He turned off the lights and headed for the bedroom; he figured he'd read himself to sleep.

mongrels

He was in a doorway on Broad Street, sorta scrunched up, backpack to one side and guitar at the other, hairy knees sticking out of cutoff jeans. Cute. Bo walked past him on the way to the liquor store, then later, heading back to the hotel with a 40 in his hand, saw him still sitting there, just staring into space. A few steps past him Bo stopped and turned around. The kid wasn't looking his way.

If Bo had listened to his head instead of his dick, he would have just continued the half block to home. But Bo never had been very smart that way.

"Hey," Bo said when he was standing right by him, looking down at his 20-ish face, his scraggly beard and tired eyes. "Hey."

"Yeah?" the young man said, looking up at last. "What do you want?" He certainly could have been friendlier.

"Want a drink?" Bo asked, gesturing with the brown paper sack containing the 40.

"Don't drink."

"Oh." This was going nowhere. Bo turned to leave.

"Can you get me high?" the kid called out from his doorway, loud enough for passersby to hear, as if anybody gave a fuck—somewhere down the street, some crackhead was no doubt shearing off the top of a motorcycle's spark plug so he could throw it through a car window and get to the CD player. Bo shambled back to him. It had been days since he'd come, and his cock was just pounding away in his pants. Already.

"You got some place to sleep tonight?" Bo asked. God, the kid was cute; what the fuck was he doing on the streets?

"Here."

"Want to come back to my room?" Bo asked, not even trying to sound casual. "I'll see what I can do."

"Sure. Whatthefuck." The young man was already standing up, unfolding his grimy body. Bo could smell him, could just imagine what his crotch smelled like. Jesus, he felt like coming right there on the fucking street.

Luckily, Bo's jacket covered his hard-on while they headed to the hotel. "I'm Beauregard," he said, "though maybe somebody'll call me Professor. That's because I used to teach college, though I wasn't a full professor. Junior college, really."

"Cool," the kid said, loping along beside him, pack slung over one shoulder, guitar under his other arm. He smiled. Even by the light of the street lamp Bo could see the kid had perfect white teeth; apparently he hadn't always lived on the sidewalks. "My name's Clint. Glad to meet you."

"Clint, huh?"

No reply, and then they were at the hotel. The fizzing neon in the window read "DuRoy Hotel," and below that a hand-painted sign advertised rooms by the week or month.

"Hey, Professor," Maurice said from behind his metal grill at one end of the lobby. "Who's your friend?" A sly smile split his fleshy face.

"His name's Clint. We're just going to go up and talk for a while."

"Professor, you know that ain't allowed. 'Specially not after dark."

Bo walked over, reached deep into his pocket, and slid a five-dollar bill under the grill. Maurice's chubby hand lay next to it but didn't pick it up. Bo found another few bucks and shoved them at him. Maurice grabbed the little wad of bills. "Have a nice night." His smile grew wider, shiny with spit.

The elevator stank even more than usual, like someone had cut an enormous fart in there, but it groaned and got up to the sixth floor okay.

"It's down this way," Bo said, hitching up his pants with the hand that wasn't hauling the malt liquor.

"Cool," Clint replied. "Thanks again."

"Sure thing." Bo unlocked the door; all around the keyhole there were scratches and pry marks.

Clint looked around what there was of the small room, the narrow bed.

"You can sleep on the floor," Bo said, hoping for an argument.

"Whatever." The young man tossed his backpack onto the room's only chair, then laid his guitar on the floor beside it.

"Make yourself at home."

Clint collapsed onto the bed, lying back, legs dangling over the side. "This is all right," he said.

"Sure it is," Bo said, staring straight at the crotch of the boy's jeans.

"So you said something about getting me high?" Clint kicked off his battered sneakers. He wasn't wearing socks and his feet really smelled.

"No, you're the one who said that."

"Oh, man..." Clint started to sit up, like he was thinking about splitting. Fuck, Bo really wanted to suck his cock.

"Okay, okay. What do you want? I know somebody in the hotel, he probably can get you crack, crystal, whatever. Just no smack, okay?" An OD'd boy in his room was the last thing Bo needed.

"Shit, none of that. It's fucking bad for you."

Bo knew that all too well. It was why he wasn't teaching any more, why he was living in a fucking welfare hotel and trying to get his life back together.

"What, just grass?"

"Yeah, man. 4:20. If you got it."

"Not here, but my friend has some, I'm sure of it. You want me to go get a joint?"

"That'd be sweet." The kid had lain back on the bed again, one of his hands casually reaching inside his baggy jeans.

"I'll go get it. Want to take a shower meanwhile?" Bo didn't like his guys too clean, but Clint, frankly, stank. The kid looked around the room, his eyes landing on the sink.

"Shower's down the hall," Bo said. "Here's a towel. I'll leave the door open so you can get back in."

"You sure that's okay?"

"I trust you," Bo said, though the truth of the matter was there wasn't jack shit to steal, not unless somebody craved an old hot plate.

"I'll get undressed here?"

"Sure," Bo said. "Get undressed."

" 'K."

"Where's your family from?" Bo asked as Clint tugged off his jacket and pulled his dirty long-sleeved T-shirt over his head. Bo got a nice, strong whiff.

"St. Louis."

"No, I mean originally. What country?"

"Oh," Clint kind of laughed. "I'm part Chinese." Which explained his exotic looks. "And there's some Portuguese in there somewhere, and German. English. My Dad always said we were mutts. He's dead now, my Dad."

Clint was naked from the waist up now, smooth and trim with just a little V of dark hair on his chest, midway between two small, dark nipples.

"Got a towel?" Bo handed it to him. Clint turned his back and undid his cut-off jeans. The young man wasn't wearing underwear; when he reached down for his crumpled pants, the pretty cheeks of his ass parted enough to give Bo a peek of a line of dark hair. Clint had a blue yin-yang symbol tattooed at the base of his spine, a spider web drawn on one elbow. Bo wanted him fiercely but didn't want to spook him, figuring there was time to make a move.

Clint wrapped the ragged white towel around himself and turned to face Bo. "Where's the shower?"

"Here, let me show you." Christ, Bo's dick was hard. He was sure the kid couldn't help but notice.

Luckily, Patrick was in his room down on the third floor, and when Bo told him what was up, he offered to bring a joint upstairs. He was a tough little fireplug of a man, mid 30s, black Irish with a face like a broken nose, and a luxurious tuft of hair at the collar of his shirt that made you think he was hairy as hell, only once he got his clothes off, he wasn't. He also had, Bo had heard, one of the most stupefyingly long dicks west of the Mississippi.

Bo returned to his room. Clint was in there, lying on his back, towel wrapped around his now-clean body, nearly naked in the broken-down bed. Bo couldn't tell whether the kid was trying to be seductive or not. Maybe even Clint himself had no idea.

"Clint, this is Patrick," Bo said. "It's his grass."

The boy in his bed looked up. "That's nice of you, Patrick," Clint smiled. "Real nice."

"The boy's nice, Professor," Patrick said. "Real nice." And he pulled a fat joint out of his pocket. When Bo had told Patrick about Clint, the Irishman said the boy had no doubt been turning tricks. Bo said he didn't think so. But really, he had no way of knowing,

Patrick handed the joint to the boy and pulled a lighter from his pocket, an unexpected moment of courtliness. Clint took a big drag and held it for a long minute before letting it out with a hacking cough. The towel shifted around, slipping off his thin thighs, nearly exposing his crotch. Tough little Patrick took a hit and handed the joint to Bo, who figured he might as well get stoned too. But when it was the kid's turn again, Patrick took the joint and placed the lit end into his mouth. He leaned over Clint, grabbed the homeless boy's head in his hands, and slid the other end of the joint into the kid's mouth, forcing a big steamroller blast of smoke into the boy's lungs. The sight of the two of them lip to lip made Bo weirdly jealous. It also made him horny as hell. He moved around the room, hoping for a glimpse of the boy's balls.

"Wow," said the kid, exhaling. "Good dope."

"I bought it from somebody where I work. A warehouse." Patrick inhaled and handed the dope to Bo. Standing between Clint's naked spread legs, still holding in the hit, Patrick laid both his calloused hands on the boy's bare shoulders and started kneading softly.

"Hey, fuck, watch it," Clint said.

"What?" Patrick asked, pugnacious in a wreath of smoke.

Just..." Clint hesitated. "Don't get the wrong idea. Just that I don't have sex with guys. No offense."

"Never?" asked Bo, surprised to hear himself speak up.

"Neither do I," said Patrick. "I only let guys suck me off sometimes. Don't you?"

"Well, yeah, but..."

Patrick shoved the boy back onto the unmade bed. The towel fell away; Clint's soft, cut dick lazed against a hairy thigh.

"So what are you doing here?" the muscular little Irishman asked, stoned.

"My mom has a new boyfriend. I'd been living with her, but he threw me out."

"I mean, what are you doing in this room? Huh, Clint?" Suddenly belligerent.

"I needed a place to sleep, is all." The boy didn't sound

alarmed at all, and he didn't reach down to re-cover himself.

"So you'll get sucked off and then you'll go to sleep. Not a bad deal, huh?" Patrick turned to Bo. "You want to, don't ya? You want to suck Clint's dick?"

Bo was silent; everything was swimming in surprise.

"Well, go ahead, Bo, do it." Patrick's voice was low, insistent. "He'll let you. Go ahead and suck his dick. Don't be a fucking pussy. You'll let Bo suck your cock, won't you, Clint?"

But the young man just lay there, stoned eyes half closed, the towel around his waist gapped wide, cock and balls and pubic hair lit by the room's single bare bulb.

Bo couldn't figure out what Patrick's game was, and maybe he didn't want to know. What he did want was Clint's prick, and he moved slowly toward it, afraid of what might happen, or might not.

Patrick stepped away from the naked boy. He grabbed Bo's 40, unscrewed the cap, dumped Bo's toothbrush out of a not-very-clean glass, and poured himself a drink, handing the open bottle to Bo. "Put this in your mouth," he said.

Bo took a long swig, then handed the bottle back.

"Now go on," Patrick said, "let me see you suck him off. I gave you the fucking grass, didn't I? Suck him. Jesus Christ Alfuckingmighty, suck his damn dick."

Bo was standing beside the mattress, looking down at the naked boy. Clint's eyes were wide open now, a direct stare. Not a challenge, not an invitation. Just watching.

Bo let his dark hand brush up against the boy's knee. Clint didn't flinch. Bo slid his fingertips partway up the boy's leg. The naked dick began to stir. Maybe a surprise, maybe not. Bo dragged his fingertips toward the boy's balls.

Clint began to hum something pretty. His eyes were closed, his dick was jerking upward, almost totally hard. Bo hesitated, thinking. Back when he was a teacher, married, he hadn't been able to deal with any of this. Then he'd gotten involved with a student, a guy who'd introduced him to meth, and though the affair hadn't gotten him in trouble, the speed had fucked him up good. His wife left him just about the time everything began to fall apart, and now here he was, living in some cheap-shit hotel, being commanded by an Irish maniac to suck homeless cock. Bo's hand moved up the boy's thigh. It wasn't bad to be commanded to do something he *wanted* to do more than anything else in the whole fucking world. He slid to his knees and laid his head against Clint's leg.

"Go *on!*" said Patrick. Bo looked up. The muscular little Irishman had a glass of malt liquor in one hand; his other hand occupied itself with a prominent lump in the crotch of his pants.

Bo reached up. When his hand found the young man's dick, the heat of it, the slightly moist stiffness, Bo felt like he wanted, in a stoned sort of way, to cry. Maybe from happiness, maybe from something else. His hand squeezed and released, squeezed and released.

Clint had stopped humming. He was thrusting his hips ever so slightly against the resistance of Bo's hand.

Bo looked up at the boy's hard dick, less than a foot away, then maneuvered his face toward Clint's crotch. He took a deep breath, stuck out his tongue, and began to lap at the young man's tight, hairy balls, still gripping the warm, hard shaft.

"Now we're fucking getting somewhere," Patrick said. Bo wasn't sure whether he wanted Patrick to leave or was glad he was around. Whichever. He'd waited long enough. His mouth moved from the balls to the underside of the shaft, lapped its way up the swollen flesh to the large slit at the head.

"Go ahead, dude. Suck it," murmured Clint, then, when Bo's eager mouth had wrapped itself around the tasty, swollen head, "God, it feels really good." Bo's hands moved up from the wiry pubic hair, over slightly curved belly, up to the boy's nipples, where they traced lazy, stoned circles as he moved his lips down over the shaft. He felt a hand on the back of his head, shoving him downward till the whole of the young man's cock filled his mouth. The hand was Patrick's.

This whole thing with Patrick was a surprise and a puzzle; the guy always seemed to talk about nothing else but cunt. Better not to think too much about it. Better to concentrate on the hard-on that filled his throat. That was what really mattered, the only thing that mattered. Clint was thrusting his cock now, fucking Bo's face, and when Patrick's hand pushed down again it made Bo gag. He struggled to the surface for a second, pulling his mouth partway off the dick, drooling on the boy's crotch, then hungrily gulped the flesh down again. It was amazing, Bo thought, just how great sucking cock could be. Better than speed, better than teaching junior college, better than any-fucking-thing.

Bo felt an insistent pressure on his ass—Patrick had started dry-humping him. Then, as he slid his tongue over Clint's dick, he felt hands unbuckling his pants, pulling them partway down, the heat of a hard dick rubbing up and down his crack. It made him a little nervous. Patrick wasn't going to fuck him without a condom. Patrick wasn't going to fuck him at all. He took his mouth off the boy and twisted around to have a look. The Irishman was standing there, his long, hard cock jutting from his fly.

"Want to suck mine?" Patrick asked.

"Go on, Bo, do it for a while," Clint said. Then to Patrick: "He sure sucks good. Better than any girl I've ever had, better than damn near anyone."

Bo had never found Patrick attractive. Now he looked at the angry-red Irish cock, foreskin still half hiding the head. It was a lot longer than the kid's, not all that tremendous maybe, not compared to its reputation, but pretty damn big anyway. Sure, why not? He got down on his knees and opened his mouth. But instead of fucking Bo's face, Patrick relit what was left of the joint and held it to Bo's lips. Not that Bo needed it, but he inhaled another lungful of smoke, then held it in while he tried to swallow Patrick's cock. The Irishman's crotch was pretty ripe, but that somehow just made things even better. Bo was hoping the kid was watching, having a good time, maybe jacking off, but not, Bo prayed, coming yet, not till he would be able to swallow his jizz.

"See, man," Clint slurred from somewhere, "what'd I tell you? As good as any damn girl. Better."

"Shit, yeah," said Patrick, then to Bo: "Keep it up, just like that."

Clint got up from the bed and stood right next to Patrick, his hard dick just inches from Bo's face. For two straight guys, Bo thought, they sure were enjoying this a lot.

"Now suck the kid's cock again," Patrick commanded. "I want to watch you deep-throating his prick."

Bo was rushing from his last hit of grass; he moved from one cock to the other, hobbled by his half-mast pants, damn near lost his balance and toppled backward. He threw one arm around Clint's naked thigh, one around Patrick's clothed leg, and set to work on the boy's cock.

"Yeah," said Patrick, "I should fuck your ass. I should fuck your ass." The idea scared Bo, but excited him too. He managed to relax enough to take the head of Clint's cock down his throat. He was just a cocksucking machine now, and these guys could do whatever the fuck they wanted. He might not be good for much, Bo saw through the clarity of the marijuana haze, but he sure as hell was going to be good at this.

Patrick had peeled off his T-shirt and unbuttoned his pants; now he removed Bo's arm from his legs and, kicking off his shoes, stepped out of his wrinkled chinos.

"Okay, cocksucker. On your back on the bed so I can fuck you." Bo backed off Clint's dick and looked up at Patrick, naked now except for a pair of dirty white socks. Bo gasped in surprise—beneath his shapeless clothes, the little Irish guy was damn near wonderful: sharply defined chest, big round nipples that were twins of perfection, a blue tattoo on each pec. And not the artsy MTV crap inked on Clint's body—Patrick had a picture of a heart on one tit, on the other a weeping Jesus with a crown of thorns. And across his lower belly, right above his hefty dick, in jailhouse script: "BORN TO RAISE HELL."

"There's rubbers and lube in the drawer over there," Bo said, pulling off his pants. He thought Patrick might object to using protection, but the Irishman walked over, dick pointing straight ahead of him, pulled out a foil packet that Bo had gotten for free from the clap clinic, and ripped it open. It took a few seconds to maneuver the tight latex over the heft of his swollen shaft. He lubed up and walked the few steps back to Bo. "Legs in the air," he ordered, "and suck the kid's cock some more."

It took a bit of doing, but Bo managed to twist his head to one side and start sucking Clint's still-hard dick. Patrick, standing at the foot of the bed, shoved some lube up Bo's asshole, grabbed Bo's ankles, and pulled Bo's legs over his shoulders. Bo could feel the wet head of Patrick's dick pressing up against his tight hole. Born to raise hell. Bo sucked harder. He tried to relax his asshole, really tried to relax, but he didn't get fucked often. It had been months really, nearly a year, and Patrick was damn big.

"Let me in," Patrick commanded, but Bo didn't. It hurt. It hurt.

Just then Clint did something that astonished Bo. He pulled his dick from Bo's mouth, bent over, and placed his lips on Bo's dick head. The feeling of the boy's mouth around him, hot and wet, got Bo really close to coming, really quick. Meanwhile, Patrick mercifully had given up trying to stuff his hard-on into Bo's ass.

"Oh, fuck, I'm gonna nut," Bo gasped out. Clint's mouth was off him like a shot, but the kid's hand took its place and with a few strokes it brought Bo's dick to a mind fuck of a climax, big gobs of cum shooting all over Bo's own chest, one wad barely missing his eye

"Hey, now you want to suck on mine, kid?" the Irishman said.

"No, man, don't think so," Clint said. Bo was surprised to feel glad about that.

Still standing between Bo's raised legs, with Bo and Clint watching, Patrick reached down to his lubed-up cock and jacked fiercely at it for a long minute or two, every muscle in his tight little body clenched hard, until his uncut dick pumped the transparent tip of the rubber full of cloudy sperm. Then he walked around the bed, stood next to Clint, pulled off the rubber, and said to Bo, "Open up." Bo did as he was told, and Patrick poured the cum into his mouth.

Which still left Clint, the original object of Bo's desire, the scruffy stand-in for all those junior college kids Bo had wanted when he was still living with Annie.

"Okay, Bo, back to sucking Clint's cock."

Bo reached for the base of the boy's dick, but before he could get his mouth on it again, the kid let out a weird groan and shot his young load onto Bo's face, the cum dripping down over nose and mouth. Bo stuck out his tongue and licked his lips clean.

"All right," said Patrick. "All right all right all right."

"I just wanted to see what it felt like," said Clint to no one in particular, "to suck dick."

And what *did* it feel like, Bo wanted to ask but didn't.

Patrick was already at the wall sink, washing off his cock.

After Patrick had gotten dressed and left, leaving what remained of the joint on the bedside table, Bo and Clint got even more stoned.

"You still want to spend the night here?"

"Sure, okay, thanks," said the young man. "Why not?"

"Share the bed?"

"Okay."

Once they were naked, lying side by side in the narrow, sagging bed, Bo wanted to stroke the boy's body, touch his cock, maybe even kiss his mouth, but despite everything that had happened, it felt like it would be awkward to even try. It wasn't until Clint threw his arm around him that Bo let himself sink into a deep, stoned sleep.

When he woke up the next morning, Bo looked around the room. Bare, streaked walls, suitcase in the corner, pile of clothes on the chair, stacks of used books on the floor. Morning flooded in through the ripped shade.

The boy was gone. Of course.

saintvalentinewasamartyr,youknow

"I want to kill you and fuck you and eat you," I said, and I meant it, sort of, because it was true, sort of, and he looked up at me with that smile of his and I put my hands around his throat and squeezed and he closed his eyes, opening his mouth, his beautiful mouth, for a kiss, which I gave him, my tongue going as far down his throat as it could, my knee pressing into his crotch, where his dick stood stiff as a soldier, and when he sighed I squeezed his thin throat harder, stopping the kiss so I could watch his face, which got pink but not alarmingly red, so I squeezed still a bit harder and then backed off, and that's when he threw his arms around me, pulling himself up against me, his nakedness against mine, his chest against mine, two heartbeats, his ear near my mouth, my mouth that whispered, "Kill you and fuck you and eat you...in that order," which made him give a little shiver of pleasure, hearing what nobody had ever said to him before in his short life, and when he replied that he figured being dead would mean he wouldn't enjoy the fucking very much, it was with a tone of bemusement and peace, not irony or fear, so I answered back in the same tone, quiet, confident, the tone of a man, I hoped, very much in control, "Maybe not, but *I'll* enjoy it," and hauled off and slapped him across the chest, a slap that landed with a resounding *whap*, a dick-hardening noise that made me want to do it again, so I did, I slapped him again, and then a third time and a fourth, each time a little harder, at each blow his face expressing, not astonishment, since neither of us was the least bit surprised, but expressing a genuine pain, that look of pain that made my heart race like a truck driver on bennies heading home, like a dog smelling his own piss on a tree, like a man who'd finally spotted what he was after, and I would have dry-humped his crotch, his hard-on, which was always glossier than mine, more insistent, but he was already straining that shiny purplish hard thing against my belly, leaving generous trails of precum on my flesh, and I slapped him a few more times, on one naked place, then another, till I saw it in his face, that look that says, "You're reaching my limits, you son of a bitch," a look that I'd gotten used to seeing on his improbably lovely face, an expression that sent affection up my spine, so I stroked his cheek, softly, softly, with one hand, while my other hand squeezed his little nipple hard, really hard, and that face I was stroking just beamed, a child on its birthday, just beamed, what a happy kid he was, which made me want to make him even happier, go even deeper, so I grabbed hold of his pec, a handful of flesh that I twisted, my grip refusing all compromise, his face reflecting something like love, something wordlessly real, or at least something that *seemed* real, and that made me want to kiss him again, made me want to sink my teeth into him, into the meat of his chest, his viral flesh, into his heart, like some Hannibal Lecter of desire, and I remembered when we first met, he and I, on Easter Sunday, late the night before really, at some tired sex club, when he looked at me and figured out that, of all the guys there, I was the one, the only one who could take him all the way down, as deep as he needed to go, though he really had no idea then, neither of us did, how long and how low that would be, and we left the club, with its masses of gayboys fucking blindly as those fish that live in caves and, never seeing the light, having no need for the eyes that they'll never in any case have, and we went off together past good people headed for midnight mass, we headed off toward some hunger that would terrify those good, pious folks, would terrify most people, sometimes even terrifies me, and now I looked at him, into his eyes, and punched his chest, not hard enough to crack a rib, not nearly, but hard enough to make him wince, probably hard enough to leave the bruises he craved, and he just nodded, and I said, "Yes?" and he said what he always says at times like that, two words, "Church bells," just that because no more was needed, and I punched him right in his gut, not hard enough to bust something, and when he turned his happy-kid face upward, I kissed him again, mouths locked together like some apocalypse, the two of us drinking each other's spit for a long, long time, me still flailing away at him half-ineffectually, until at last I grabbed his head in both hands and pushed it down, further down over my body till his lips reached my cock and I said, "Eat *this*, motherfucker," as he, not really needing encouragement, gulped me down, and while he sucked me, my straining hardness, down his throat, I asked him, "So what if you knew that my cock was the last thing you'd ever taste in this world?" and as I said that, I slid my hands around his throat again, which made him moan and suck even harder, his face starting to turn red again, red as meat, as blood, a valentine, a simile for God knows what, the cape before the bull of life, whatever, and his dick, when I let up on his neck and reached downward, was slug-slippery with his juices, and I gave it a hard yank, like I was going to tear it from his body, something I would never really do, I don't think, but it made him suck all the more hungrily, muscles in the back of his throat working my dick head, so I had no choice but to hit him again, slapping his pale shoulders with a satisfying sound of flesh against flesh, which is, after all, what life on earth is all about, flesh against flesh against flesh against flesh, church bells indeed, and I wondered if I actually *could* kill him, kill anyone, and really there was no answer to that, hypothetical oblivion, except to grab him by his wrists and drag him to the floor, and he had that look then, that look he gets when he's so far gone, so far into himself, that there's fuck-all he

can say, not that he's ever very verbally adroit, but he has compensatory virtues, as I'm sure you know by now, he really does, so I
have him pinned by his breakable wrists, which if they snapped
would make a sound like church bells, I guess, and he's in this fucking absolute-zero state where nothing but lust is in motion, the
fucking silence of the fucking Lamb of God, and I *did*, at that
moment, a big chunk of me *wanted* to kill him and fuck him and
eat him, in that order, the procession of desire, the urge to own, to
destroy, to incorporate, and to be destroyed in turn, as though
Shiva ruled the world and not some watery naked blond on a cross,
which is when he broke the silence and asked, "Fuck me?" two
words like "church bells" is two words, and I said, "Fuck you," and
I reached over to the lube and got my hand as slippery as his cock,
which, though smaller than mine, was also almost always even
harder, purple as bad prose and twice as overreaching, and then
two of my fingers were inside him, three, four working around his
yielding guts like I was kneading bread dough, and his ass, which
is amazing, opened up for me like heaven is supposed to open up
at the End of Days, and after twisting and prodding for a while, I
slid my hand out, and his hole, remarkable fuck hole that it is,
stayed all the way open so I could see into him, actually into him,
and I thought, *Red, that's what red really is,* and I wanted, with all
my soul, to fuck that bread dough, and if I did put on a condom,
it was to save myself, not him, and if I did slap his face when I slid
my cock inside him, it was because he wanted it, and if I did pump
my desire into that soft red meat, it was because that was what was
meant to happen, which was easy to tell because, though some
guys' dicks don't stay hard when you fuck them, his did, riding
tight against his damp belly, and if I didn't kill him before I fucked
him, it's because most gods that people worship are merciful gods,
and I was a merciful god, too, and if I wouldn't eat him that night,
it was no guarantee I never would, and what most people don't

know is that there are supposedly not one but two Saint Valentines, good Christians I guess who got martyred in Rome, two people, like me and him are two people, though they might, we're told, have just been one single martyr after all, and I wished at that moment, as I sometimes do wish but not all that often, that I could just have *stupid* sex, like almost everybody else, mindless and untouched by the knowledge of God or hell or whatever, smug and happy as salvation by faith, but hey, you play the hand you're dealt, and I guess I hit him across the face hard enough to split his lip, because now there was a new shade of red, and then I pumped and pumped and pumped while he grimaced, till I came, hard, gasping, like a fish out of holy water, and when I looked down he'd come too, wet on his belly, and when I kissed him I tasted his blood and figured I'd probably get away with it, though there are some things you can't get away with, but he wasn't one of them, and then we wiped up and went to bed, to dreams, to be devoured, him in the dark, in my arms, like two dead saints.

boysintrouble

Fuckin' Eisenhower.

Fuckin' McCarthy.

Fuckin' House fuckin' Un-American fuckin' Activities fuckin' Committee.

Fuckfuckfuck.

Otis had been raised not to use profanity, so his outburst felt both naughty and cathartic. "Fuck!" he yelled once more for good measure, pounding the wall. His fist hurt. He slouched to the sideboard and fixed himself a martini.

Phil wouldn't be home for hours. "Working late at the office," he'd said, "don't wait up." Which left Otis with anger, anxiety, and nothing much to do.

The juniper tang of gin hit his throat like a wonder drug. He switched on the television. Milton Berle in drag, his horribly lipsticked mouth working overtime. Uncle Miltie.

Otis should have known better. Lawrenceville, Princeton, a job in a prestigious Foggy Bottom law firm. And then, at 25, he went and fell in love with Phil. Smart, smart-mouth Phil, a Jewish lawyer from the working-class streets of New York, a guy with a big dick and an eye on the main chance.

Uncle Miltie made him want to scream. He switched off the TV, downed what remained of his drink, and tried to read *The Washington Post.* When he got to the story about Howard Rosenmann's refusal to name names to the committee, he laid the paper down, paced restlessly, stripped down to his Brooks Brothers boxer shorts, mixed himself another martini, and went upstairs and climbed into bed.

He was roused from sleep by Phil slipping between the percale sheets, pressing his hairy, naked body against his own. Otis didn't let on that he was awake till he felt Phil's hand trailing down toward his crotch.

"Unh, please don't. I just jacked off. To get to sleep."

"Hi, Otis."

"Get your hands off me."

Phil drew away. "That's a bit harsh, don't you think?"

"No." Otis felt like he wanted to scream, like he was going to scream. "Telling me you are moving out, *that* was harsh. It was shit." Just saying "shit" still gave him a bit of an illicit thrill.

"Honey, you know how things are here. Every day, some poor queen over at State loses his job. I'm not going to give up everything I worked for..."

Say it, Otis thought. *Say "I'm not going to give up everything I worked for just to stay with you."*

Phil put his hand on Otis's shoulder. "You know I didn't mean it that way. We can still see each other. But even with two bedrooms in this place, people are starting to talk."

"Have you *heard* them?"

"I know they—"

"*Have you heard them, damn it?*"

"Honey, I'm not as fortunate as you've been. If I lose this job..."

"Oh, fuck you and your self-pity."

But somewhere in his fury, Otis knew that Phil was right. Years back Phil had lived in a cold water walk-up, working nights to put himself through NYU law school; meanwhile, Otis had been sipping sherry and playing bridge with his queer college chums in a frat house on Nassau Street.

Phil was tugging at Otis' boxers, stroking his ass. "Can't we at least make this a night to remember?"

"Like on the Titanic?" Otis snapped.

"Otis, please don't. I'm sorry if I caused you any pain." There was a hurt quality to Phil's voice, a quaver that meant defeat, and knowing he'd won got Otis's dick hard. He reached back, grabbed Phil's wrist, and twisted his arm away. "Tonight, my little Jewboy, *I* fuck *you*," he hissed.

Phil had been on the wrestling team at NYU and could easily overpower his boyfriend, but he didn't even fight back. Legs in the air, he let Otis into his ass with nothing but a little spit for lubrication. Otis tore into him with the fury of moral certitude, class superiority, and general lust.

"Hey, Otis, not so rough, huh?"

"Move...out...on...me...will...you?" He spat in Phil's face.

Phil looked as though he were going to cry; his cock shrank limply on his belly. But Otis pounded away until, watching his partner grinding his teeth in discomfort and fury, he couldn't stop himself from shooting off in Phil's ass.

"I love you, Otis," Phil said weakly. "I do."

"Go to sleep," Otis said, and got up to wash his dick off.

When Otis awoke the next morning Phil was gone. Not in bed, not in the kitchen drinking black coffee, not in the downstairs bedroom that was "his" for the sake of appearances.

After he finished his cornflakes, Otis dragged two big valises out of the hall closet, threw them onto Phil's bed, and began packing all of Phil's clothes. Anyone else, given the situation, might have thrown the clothing in all willy-nilly, but Otis packed it neatly, keeping things precisely folded, and when he was done he slid Phil's suits into several garment bags.

Afterward, when he was done, he went into the bathroom and

jacked off. It was odd what Otis found arousing. After wiping up he started to shave, pondering his mirror image. He could certainly see how other men thought him attractive, but at 28 he already felt sometimes so terribly, terribly old. He razored off the lather, baring freshly smooth skin.

The second Saturday of every month was Otis's day to see his father. He took a taxi to the French restaurant in Georgetown where they always met, and though he was punctual, his father was already there, studying the menu through half-glasses pushed down to the tip of his nose.

"Good afternoon, son."

"Good, afternoon, Father." This was all about custom, not love.

The waiter, an obvious middle-aged queen, kept staring, looking hungrier for Otis than Otis felt for his meal.

Over vichyssoise and *boeuf bourguignon,* father and son tiptoed through the usual minefields.

"I must say," his father said, not for the first time, "that as little as I approve of McCarthy and his vulgar minions, it's about time that someone rid this town of its fairies and Reds." There was a time he would have felt free to say "Jews" too.

"Yes, Father."

"Your roommate works for McCarthy, doesn't he? What's his name?"

"Phil, Father. Not for McCarthy, really, but..." Did his father know? Suspect? Should he tell him Phil was moving out? If he did tell him, would an odd moment of misplaced emotion give the game away?

But his father had already lost interest and was pontificating on the stock market instead.

When the waiter brought the check he rubbed his crotch, briefly but blatantly, against Otis's shoulder.

"Oh, excuse me, monsieur," said the troll, all mock sincerity.

But it had given Otis an instant erection inside his neatly pressed Saturday chinos. It was odd, he pondered, not for the first time that day, what he found arousing.

Otis had left his father puffing on a big Havana. He was relieved that the meal had gone no worse than he'd expected, but he wasn't quite ready to go home and face the Phil situation. Instead, he took a cab to the Tidal Basin. He'd always liked the Jefferson Memorial, the Roman-style rotunda with its vaguely pagan overtones. Today, with April's cherry blossoms all around, it was especially lovely. Knots of tourists wandered through, dreary families with bucktoothed kids aiming Kodak Brownies at Jefferson's oversized statue. Off to one side a young man was seated on a little folding stool, working away at a sketchpad. Otis looked away, then back again; the boy was cute.

Otis thought of Phil, perhaps sitting and crying amid his packed valises, perhaps already gone. Why couldn't life be simpler? Why couldn't Phil have been born rich? And why did they have to care so much for each other?

Otis took a step toward the sketching young man, who noticed the motion, looked up, and smiled. And held the smile just a beat longer than necessary.

"Afternoon," said the boy, who was as dark as Phil, but even more exotic-looking, with high Slavic cheekbones and quizzical, slanted brown eyes.

Otis smiled and walked toward him. "Drawing Jefferson?"

"Something like that."

Otis looked at the sketchbook. If it *was* Jefferson, it was unlike any Jefferson he'd ever seen.

"Like it?"

"Uh, it's...*interesting*."

The boy laughed out loud. "You don't get it. Not familiar with Picasso, Braque, that kind of thing?"

"Picasso, yeah. Noses where eyes should be, that kind of thing."

"The cubists taught us a new way to see. And this is Jefferson as I see him, disintegrating under the burden of what's going on today."

"The war?"

"No, the conformity, the stupid, bourgeois blandness of this capitalist country. And the quashing of dissent."

"HUAC."

"Yeah, the House Un-American Assholes Committee. But sorry, I should get off my soapbox and shut up. For all I know, you could be..."

"The enemy?"

"No, not 'enemy.' " The boy smiled, his thickish lips revealing large white teeth. Pretty. Very pretty. "I should just shut up."

"No, I'm interested in what you have to say. Really."

"Then maybe you should come back to my place and I'll show you some other drawings I've done. I don't live all that far from here."

And there it was, as easy as that.

"So are you a Communist?" Otis was sipping cheap Chianti from a cheap glass, sitting in a cheap apartment that pretty well defined the word "bohemian." Dark window shades were drawn against the day.

"No, I'm not a Red, and even if I were, I wouldn't say so in times like these." The boy, whose name was David, smiled. "I'm an anarchist."

"Ah, like Kropotkin."

"Bingo. You win the 64-dollar question."

"I had a good education," Otis said.

"Ivy League, no doubt."

"No doubt."

"Don't take it so hard. I went to Swarthmore till junior year. By then I'd had enough, just left." The boy rose and laid a firm hand on Otis's shoulder. "More wine?" he asked, but Otis guessed that he was asking something else. Otis's hand closed onto David's. The boy squeezed harder.

"You're handsome," David said.

"And you're very direct."

"Anything wrong with that?" David's hand moved down over Otis's chest, dragging Otis's hand along for the ride. "People like us shouldn't beat around the bush. Unless we have to. Which it seems like we always do. Have to."

People like us.

"Fairies?"

"I'm not a 'fairy,' Otis, and neither are you. I hate that word." David glanced toward the mattress lying in the corner. "You know what I want, and you want it too, yeah?"

David took his hand away. Otis stood up and started to unbutton his shirt.

"You'll see, we'll have a good time," David said. He walked to the record player in the corner, switched it on. Otis expected the record to be some awful jazz thing, but it was Bellini. *Norma.* Then the boy flicked open a Zippo and lit half a dozen candles stuck into old wax-covered Chianti bottles. "You like Callas?" David asked as he snapped off the light switch.

"Yeah. Sure." Otis felt as if he were someone else. He unbuckled his belt and let his trousers drop to his ankles. His Brooks Brothers boxers were already tented out.

"Hey," said David, "you look good in your underwear."

Within a minute, they were naked, rolling around on the mattress. Otis had never been on a mattress on the floor before, unless you counted summer camp. And he'd never had sex with an uncircumcised man before, either. David's ample foreskin half-covered his cock head, even though his thick penis was bulkily erect. When

Otis reached down to slide it back and forth, the surplus flesh seemed somehow generous, secret, and exciting.

David made it very clear that he wanted Otis to fuck him. Otis took excited notice—Phil never, ever let on that he wanted to be fucked, and Otis had almost never fucked him. The artist lay on his back and raised his legs, exposing a pink hole nestled in an abundant forest of dark fur.

"You want to, don't you?" David asked. Otis nodded.

As Otis entered David, he stroked the coarse black hair on David's ankles. Despite his youth, David seemed pretty expert at this sort of thing; his hot, wet ass gripped Otis's elegantly curved cock enthusiastically. Otis looked down at the boy's beautiful face then impulsively bent over and kissed those thick lips. Within a couple of minutes, they'd both come.

"You grit your teeth when you climax, know that?" David asked.

Otis looked around at the candlelit apartment, the collaged pictures taped to the wall. The body of Betty Grable with the head of Mamie Eisenhower. Karl Marx hanging from a cross. And some of David's drawings, all convoluted shapes and unclear emotions. Otis wanted to get out of there.

"I'll give you my phone number, though I know that you won't use it," David smiled wryly. "Too much to lose, right? You got a boyfriend?" He changed the record. This time it *was* jazz, a saxophone.

"Had," Otis said. "*Had* a boyfriend." It felt odd to say it out loud, to confirm to a stranger what was already true.

"And I won't even ask for *your* number. Hell, 'Otis' probably isn't even your real name."

"Who would make that up?" But Otis cursed himself for not being quick enough to have given the boy a phony name.

"I like you, Ivy League," said David, as Otis headed out the door. "Call me."

Otis hurried down the stairs. It was a pretty crummy neighborhood. He prayed for a taxi and, miraculously, one came. On the way back to his apartment, Otis watched the twilit world. Normalcy. Little girls playing hopscotch, well-dressed families going out to dinner, men and women and children who fit in. Unquestioning, obtuse, happy. Otis felt the stirrings of self-disgust. But, curiously, he also felt something else when he thought back on ramming his cock into a stranger's ass, something like elation. *I've got a secret,* Otis thought to himself, and smiled.

When he paid the cabby, he realized that he still had David's phone number crumpled in his hand. He tossed it into a wastebasket in front of his house, then thought better of it and fished around to recover it, a well-dressed, handsome young man rummaging around in the garbage, for once not caring how he looked.

"Philip?"

No answer. Phil's bags were gone. There was a note on the bedside table. *I've taken a room at the Tarleton. I'll be in touch soon. Love, P.*

Otis smoothed out David's phone number and carefully laid it down next to Phil's note, just inches from the phone. He stared at the telephone, the two pieces of paper, till his eyes began to blur. He went back downstairs to the living room, fixed himself a drink, and switched on the TV. Ed Murrow was talking about the Congressional hearings; yet another poor bastard had been caught in the gears of the witch hunt.

Who knows, maybe Phil was right. Maybe what they'd had together would never have lasted, *couldn't* last in the middle of this shit storm. And that was nobody's fault, not really. Otis downed the rest of his martini.

Because, if the truth be told, if it came down to it, Otis wasn't so sure of his loyalty to Phil. If their positions had been reversed, what would he have done? He stared blankly at the dancing cigarette packs on the TV screen. "So smooth, so mild," they sang.

Actually, Otis knew. He knew the answer. If it had come down to a choice between Philip or a life of comfort and ease, he'd have done what he always did. Taken the easy way out.

"Philip?" he called out, knowing there'd be no answer, but enjoying the sound of pathos in his voice. "Phil?"

He stood up unsteadily, not bothering to turn off the television, and returned to the master bedroom, sat on the bed that had been "theirs," and now was only his. Scarcely thinking about what he was doing or why, he picked up David's phone number, lifted the receiver, dialed the number, intending to say...what? Fortunately, there was no answer. He hung up and just sat there in the gathering gloom, staring at the two pieces of paper for a long, long while.

thelastgayvampirestory

"I think what you've done is very good, so far."

Tod knew what that meant: It was Carrington's gentle way of saying the paper needed work.

The professor looked over his gold-rimmed spectacles and smiled. "What you've done with *Buffy the Vampire Slayer* is quite clever, but you might give a little more thought to what you've said about Anne Rice."

"You mean," Tod said, "about how a heterosexual woman basically *defined* the gay vampire back in the late 20th century?"

"Right," Carrington said. "You do bring up the issue, and what you say here makes sense, but you might tie it in more closely to the era's public discourse around queers, HIV, and contagion."

I did do *that,* Tod thought. He looked down at his paper, perched amid the benevolent disorder of his professor's desk. Maybe he hadn't done it quite as well as he'd thought.

Carrington's class, *The Rise and Fall of Queer Culture,* was a popular elective, dealing as it did with the era before prebirth genetic testing and elective orientation-associated abortion made queer people a thing of the past. There were, reputedly, a few non-heterosexuals still left, but they would have to be in their 80s or 90s at least, and if they indeed existed, they were keeping quiet about it. For a long time it had only been through the interest of academics like Professor Carrington that queers' impact on the popular and political culture of the times had remained a topic of any discussion at all. But recently a new wave of interest in dissident cultures had arisen, and now Carrington's class was always overen-rolled. Queers had even seized the popular imagination: The tabloid press had lately retailed sensationalized rumors that a few old supposedly surviving queers had been joined by bands of new, younger, clandestine homos. Like vampires, they walked among mankind, yet were never truly *of* mankind.

"Tod?"

"Yes, sir?"

"Distracted?"

"Sorry, professor. What were you saying?"

"Just that what you have here is very promising, and I'm sure that by the end of the term you'll come up with something truly excellent."

"Thank you, sir." Tod gathered his paper from the desk and stood to leave.

"Oh, Tod?"

"Yes?"

"If you ever want to get together to discuss your paper, go for a cup of coffee or something, feel free to let me know."

There had been rumors about Carrington, but that was par for the course for anyone in his field. He was unmarried, which didn't help matters, and never was seen with a girlfriend. But Carrington—tall, slightly stooped, sandy-haired, an eternally quizzical expression in his pale eyes—did not, in his early 40s, look anything like the queers that Tod had seen in the photos in his history texts. And he most certainly did not look like a vampire, not even the most unlikely ones in *Buffy.*

"Okay, sir. Thanks." He turned and headed out the office door.

"How did it go in there?" Tod and Kyrill were heading across the campus. Kyrill had been Tod's freshman roommate; they were still best buds.

"Not bad. But I think maybe I should have chosen a different topic."

"Yeah, something that Carrington's not so involved in, huh?" The professor's interest in the cultural implications of vampire narratives, both queer and het, was well known. Kyrill, for his part, was doing a paper on *The Twilight of the Golds,* a so-so late 20th-century play that had foretold the genetic elimination of queers. Boring but safe.

"Kyrill, do you ever get the feeling that Carrington is, oh, I don't know...coming on to you?

"Nope," Kyrill said decisively. "Not a bit."

That was that, then. If Carrington were somehow queer, he most certainly would have chosen Kyrill, with his perfect cheekbones, broad shoulders, and dazzling smile, over Tod, who would always be, he told himself, a bit shlumpy by comparison. Tod was the one who mooned over the girls; Kyrill was the one who got them into bed.

"Guess my imagination was working overtime."

"Yep. Everybody knows there are no fags anymore," Kyrill smiled, dazzlingly as usual. "Hey, want to party later?"

"Nope," Tod said, "I've gotta work on this damn paper. Maybe Saturday?"

"Sure," said Kyrill. "You have fun with your gay vampires tonight."

"The idea of homosexuality as contagion was an old one but given new motive force by the rise of the HIV epidemic," Tod typed out. "Around the time of the 1980s, when AIDS first was recognized as a transmissible medical condition, the queer vampire story saw an exponential rise in popularity. Ever since Stoker's *Dracula,* vampirism had been conflated with outlaw sexualities, and LeFanu's *Carmilla* had an explicitly lesbian text. But now gay male sexuality took the place of unbridled female lust as the predatory conduit of death-in-life."

Tod took another swig of coffee. He was *so* tired of reworking this damn thing.

"It was a strophe that might well be read as homophobic, particularly when purveyed by such hetero authors as Anne Rice, creator of the Lestat mythos. But that would hardly account for the continuing popularity of queer vampire literature among gay and lesbian readers of the era, who..."

Who *what*?

"Who..."

Oh, fuck it. He shut down the computer and, coffee or no coffee, crawled into bed.

That night, not for the first time, Tod jacked off to thoughts of Carrington. It's not that Tod was at all queer; he liked girls as much as the next guy, maybe more. It's just that—as an experiment—he had tried, back at the beginning of the semester, to eroticize another man, purely as a matter of research, to see what it might be like. Focusing on someone like Kyrill would have been both too easy and too hard. Easy because his friend was so conventionally attractive, difficult because Tod's experiment might have repercussions in the real world, somehow soiling their friendship.

It all had begun simply enough. He'd actually seen Carrington near-naked at the university pool, so Tod would get into bed, turn off the lights, and imagine Carrington's poolside body, not really muscular but in good shape, imagine running his hand down the little forest of dark blond chest hair, maybe touching one of the professor's prominent dark nipples as his hand trailed down toward Carrington's well-filled bathing suit, peeling down the tight fabric till Carrington's cock spilled forth, then touching it, hesitantly at first, touching the man's penis, thumb nestled in wiry pubic hair, fingers gripped around the warm, swelling shaft, pinkish flesh sliding back and forth over darker cock head. The image was far from repulsive, but at the beginning it was hardly stimulating either—

Tod had had to masturbate to get himself at all excited. Soon enough, though, in a matter of days, just beginning the fantasy got Tod's dick at least half-hard. It was then Tod began to elaborate on the scenario: Carrington would return his attention, stripping the clothes from Tod's trembling body, stroking Tod's chest, his thighs, grabbing hold of Tod's hardening prick, jacking him off as he was jacked off in turn. It wasn't long before Tod imagined Carrington's mouth on him, the imaginary blow job keeping time with Tod's spit-wet hand stroking himself. Sucking Carrington came next, imagining opening wide, taking the head of another man's cock between his lips, feeling it sliding against his tongue, filling his mouth. It was surprisingly easy to eroticize all this. Not that Tod could be queer; genetic screening had taken care of that. And not that homosexuality was a learned behavior; that sort of superstitious nonsense had disappeared at about the same time as fundamentalist Christianity. It just was, well, easy to masturbate while thinking of sucking on Carrington's swollen cock.

At about that time Tod had settled on the theme for his paper, and his late-night imaginings quickly followed suit. So now, as he lay in his narrow bed, one hand stroking his hairy chest, the other caressing his hard, curved dick, Tod's imaginings took a decidedly vampiric turn. He never imagined being the vampire, the undead victimizer. He was always the ravished, Carrington's prey. The professor would sneak into Tod's room as he was jacking off, swoop down on the boy, pin him to the bed beneath his ageless body, force Tod's hands from his crotch, press his engorged cock against the student's helpless body, bring his face close to Tod's, closer, close as a kiss, then part his lips, bare his fangs, and, as Tod's naked form arched upward, place his teeth on the boy's throat, slight pressure at first, two little points of pain, then, effortlessly slide his fangs into virginal flesh, blood welling upward, Carrington sucking, sucking, supping on the boy's precious lifeblood...which is usually when Tod's cock throbbed and shot sticky-hot cum all over his hand, dripping down onto his furry belly, dribbling onto the sheets, and that was that, at least for the night. Night: the time when vampires roamed the Earth, even if they were only vampires of the mind.

Tod was hard at work on his still-untitled paper, revising what he'd written. "*Buffy's* Weltanschauung was an extraordinarily ambiguous one, calling into question the very nature of 'normality.' The title character's circle of close friends included a werewolf, a vengeance demon, two male vampires of dubious morality, and a witch who came out as a lesbian. Far from equating heteronorma-tivity with 'good,' the program—"

There was a knock on the door. Kyrill.

"Hey, guy. I thought we were going out tonight."

"Jeez, sorry. I just got really into revising this paper, and..."

"Carrington's vampire thing again?"

Tod looked sheepish.

"Tod, you have a crush on the guy or something?"

"What the fuck do you mean?"

"Take it easy, Tod. I was just kidding."

"Can I ask you something?"

"Ask away."

"Why did you take Carrington's class, Kyrill? You seem to be what they used to call 'homophobic,' dude."

"Jeez, lighten up, will you? It's just an easy credit, yeah? In bio I wrote a paper on slime mold. That doesn't mean I love pond scum. I mean, you're doing a paper on gay vampires, but you don't want some guy to bite your neck and drink your blood."

Just hearing Kyrill say that sent a strange feeling to the base of Tod's belly.

"Sorry, Kyrill, I'm just preoccupied is all."

"You're spending a *lot* of time on that paper."

"I want it to be good, okay?"

"No problem. Sure I can't persuade you to drop the intellectual pursuits for a while?" Truth be told, Kyrill's every-night partying was taking its toll on his grades.

"Rain check?"

"Sure thing." Kyrill headed for the door. "G'night."

As soon as Kyrill was safely out of sight, Tod pulled down the shades, turned off the lights, and slid his pants halfway down his thighs. His cock was already getting hard.

For a moment the image of Kyrill lingered in his mind, but that soon was displaced. Being attracted to Kyrill, handsome, sexy Kyrill, would have meant that Tod was actually queer, an obvious impossibility. So the image of naked Kyrill—an accurate one from the days when they'd roomed together, when Tod had even, on occasion, seen Kyrill fucking one or another of his girlfriends—vanished. In its place came Carrington, the older man grasping at Tod, savagely tearing at his clothes. Tod's hand quickly brought him to the brink of orgasm, then backed off just the tiniest bit, keeping him on the edge. Carrington's oversized canine teeth gouged the tender flesh of Tod's neck; his lips suctioned the boy's warm blood. Tod threw his head back, his entire body ruled by the sensations in just a half-dozen inches of his flesh. The loss of hemoglobin was making Tod light-headed as Carrington, teeth still inserted, reached down and grabbed his student's hard cock. Swoon—Tod felt like he might swoon. When he could control himself no longer, when his penis finally shot its load, one errant wad of sperm nearly hit him in the eye.

The rest of the revisions could wait till the morning.

"And in the same way that the myth of the vampire had

changed, the creature having its factual roots in the historical figures of Vlad the Impaler and the Countess Bathory, but accrued
attributes—sensitivity to sunlight, fear of crucifixes—as the
archetype evolved, so 'the Queer' gained a plethora of signifiers
with time."

No, that was bullshit. The vampire was made up, folklore and
authored fiction, while homosexuals had actually existed. And the
word *plethora* was all wrong. Start again.

"Unlike the evolution of the myth of the vampire, which
accrued attributes—"

The phone buzzed.

"Tod?"

"Yes?"

"Carrington here. Did you forget we had an appointment to
discuss your paper?"

Oh, shit. "Oh...Sorry, sir."

"Well, I'm ready to leave my office." He didn't sound angry.
"How about we meet at my house?"

This was certainly not an untoward suggestion for a teacher to
make to a student; at-home conferences happened all the time. But
Tod's overactive mind sprang into action, giving the simple invitation all sorts of libidinal overtones. He tried to keep his voice level
while he imagined being ravished and sucked dry by his undead
professor.

The arrangements were made. "I'll see you at eight tonight,
then, Tod."

"Yes, sir." Tod hung up. He had an insistent erection.

"I like what you've done with the paper, Tod," Carrington said,
putting aside the last page.

Well, that was a relief.

"But I'd like to see you tackle the persistence of the myth of the queer vampire—the way that, long after the genre seemed played out, even after homosexuals had ceased to exist, gay vampire stories continued to be written, bought, and read."

Tod took the bait. "As though the archetypal figure of the predatory gay man spreading contagion served some vital function in human consciousness?"

"Sure, the possibility that heterosexuals in some way *need* the external threat of the queer vampire, even though there are no vampires. And no queers, for that matter."

"Interesting." Actually, Tod had thought of that before, but for the sake of politeness, he acted as though the notion were brand new.

"You sound a bit dubious. You don't buy that hooey about a new generation of queers rising from the—as it were—homo grave, do you?" Carrington's pale blue eyes gave Tod a coldly piercing look.

Tod stared back, seeing himself half-reflected in the older man's glasses, and felt his dick start to swell. He imagined Carrington naked beneath his clothes, pictured taking his foreskin between his lips, could almost feel the chilly bite of Carrington's fangs, the gush of his own hot arterial blood. Never taking his eyes from Carrington's, Tod surreptitiously rubbed his palm against the hard curve of his cock.

"Tod? You *don't* believe that queers still exist, do you?" The pale stare became even more intense.

It was true, then! Carrington *was* a...a...

"Tod?"

The young man had risen to his feet, the front of his pants tented out by his importuning cock.

"Professor Carrington, I..." He took a step toward his teacher, who leaned back slightly in his chair, spreading his legs. An invitation?

Yes!

"Take me. Please take me, sir." Tod flew to Carrington, dropped to his knees before him and tilted his head to expose his veined and vulnerable throat. His eyes shut, he waited. Nothing, no movement from Carrington.

"Tod, I..."

Tod opened his eyes. Carrington's mild face was wreathed in an inscrutable smile. The boy half-rose and pounced. He threw his body upon Carrington's, his hard-on awkwardly hitting the man's thigh as he, barely able to breathe, bit into his teacher's neck.

"Tod!" Carrington's surprisingly strong hands pushed Tod away. The boy toppled backward, sprawling on the floor, hard-on still swollen beneath his jeans. He didn't breathe at all.

"Tod, I'm really sorry. I hope I didn't make you think...that I was...well, make you think anything, really. I hope I didn't in any way lead you on."

Tod finally exhaled, a surprisingly rackety sound. His face flushed with embarrassment. "Sir, I'm so very, very..."

"Don't worry about it."

"...sorry." He felt like crying.

"Relax, son. What happened here will never go further than this room, okay? I swear to you."

That was reassuring, but it didn't really go to what upset Tod most. He scrambled to his feet, his cock deflating at last. "Can I go now, sir?"

"Of course. We'll talk later." He held out Tod's paper.

Tod took it from him and wordlessly walked toward the door. Turning back, he looked around the room: a clutter of Chinese antiques, piles of books and journals, a sandy-haired, middle-aged man still sprawled in a chair, a thoroughly unreadable expression on his bespectacled face.

Tod went home, barely able to focus his eyes, profoundly embarrassed, deeply disappointed. As soon as he shut the door, he dropped the manuscript on his desk and walked over to the full-length mirror in the corner. This time he didn't bother to turn off the lights. He kicked off his shoes, unbuckled his belt, stepped out of his jeans and underwear, and stood before his own image, wearing only a red sweater, white socks, and a hard-on that pointed toward the ceiling. Slowly, watching his own every move, he cupped his balls in one hand and stroked his cock with the other, thinking of Carrington, of Carrington's teeth, Carrington's deadly, lost embrace, watching his hand sliding up and down, his hairy legs tensing. He kept himself on the brink as long as he could, pulling at his balls till he was on the edge of pain, and then, with a sigh, he shot off, jism coursing down the silvery mirror. If he'd been a vampire, the legend went, he'd never have been able to watch himself do that. Would he even have been able to see his cum?

Fuck the paper, he thought, after he'd wiped up. He picked up the phone and called Kyrill. A short while later, Kyrill picked him up and, as he usually liked to do, drove out of the college town to the bars in the nearest city.

Tod wasn't much of a drinker. Two vodka Collins and he was pretty much flying, bold enough to approach one of the approachable women hanging out at the bar, but not horny enough to want to risk it. Instead, he nursed a third drink while Kyrill, Kyrill with the dazzling smile and shoulders, trotted out his pick-up routine and, as usual, scored.

"Vicki, this is my somewhat inebriated friend Tod. Tod, Vicki."

Vicki, who was pretty but wore entirely too much makeup, already had her hand slipped partway down the back of Kyrill's pants.

Tod looked up. "Pleased to meet you."

"Vicki and I want to leave now, okay?" *So we can go fuck* went unspoken.

On the drive back, Tod huddled woozily in the back seat, hoping that Vicki's hand working on Kyrill's dick wouldn't cause them to end up in a ditch.

"You okay, buddy?" Kyrill asked over his shoulder. "You seem really distracted tonight."

Tod could never, of course, tell his friend one damn thing about what had happened with Carrington, what he had hoped would happen, what he had done. "Fine, fine," he said, the last word either of them spoke till Kyrill dropped off Tod and said good night.

Tod turned on every light in the house and staggered to his sofa. He stared at the manuscript on his desk. "The Persistence of the Queer Vampire Archetype in Popular 21st Century Discourse," that was the title he'd finally come up with, a thicket of academese. In the morning, he figured, he'd scratch that out and call it something else. "The Last Gay Vampire Story," maybe. He imagined Carrington standing naked before him, nodding in agreement, licking the blood from his lips.

He thought he would just close his eyes for a moment. As he drifted off to a sleep that would last till a fuzzy-tongued midmorning, what Tod didn't know, what he had no way of knowing, was what Kyrill was up to.

Kyrill had driven Vicki, not back to his house, but to a secluded spot in the countryside. He'd parked the car and the two of them began to make out in earnest. Vicki had Kyrill's hard, dripping cock in her hand when he bent over, placed his teeth on her throat, and bit down hard, hard enough to break skin. She cried out sharply and shivered as he began to suck the blood from her veins. When he'd had his fill, he opened the car door and dragged Vicki's limp body onto the grass. He tore open her clothes and reached down to her cunt. She was, as she'd told him, on her period. He brought his bloody fingers to his lips and licked them clean, a taste of salty metal, then lowered himself down onto her unmoving form and fucked her until he came.

After he was finished, Vicki's eyes fluttered open. "Mmm, that felt good," she said with a suddenly pointy-toothed smile.

fist:aloveletter

I'm going through some old photos on my laptop when I come across a folder titled "Brian," dated over three years ago. Mouse click and there he is. I'd totally forgotten.

But I recognize him from the first shot. Of course. He was memorable, perfectly handsome in a bland-but-gorgeous way, longish spiky hair, charming smile. The smile's just a potentiality in the first photo, though. His face, in near-profile, fills the right side of the frame, slightly blurry—no doubt from the movement of my hand—and his mouth is wide open, just beginning to encompass the shiny-wet head of my dick, a sliver of his tongue reaching out for the underside of my shaft. He's apparently quite content to be sucking me off. I wasn't anticipating seeing him this afternoon. It's been a long, hot day and the sight of him sucking my cock a few years ago gets me unexpectedly, piercingly horny.

Next photo: Brian in my bed, lying naked on his back, eyes closed, hands behind his head, my leather collar around his throat. The collar dates the picture; I haven't had it for years, ever since it was stolen at a sex party. I'm standing at his feet, looking down at him. I'd forgotten quite how handsome he was; there's even a charming little cleft in his chin. Nice patches of dark brown hair under his arms, erect pink nipples, a slight thickening around his waist. His body's a bit fleshy—I can recall that even now—and you can see that he's chunky even though he's lying down. He's got a tan line, and the head of his erect cock lies above it, on golden flesh rather than white. From this angle you can't tell if he's cut or uncut, and I've forgotten. There are a couple of lovely veins running up the underside of his shaft, though.

Next picture: I've moved around to the head of the bed, shot his beautiful face full-on, his eyes still closed, lips slightly parted, a fallen angel in a black leather collar, maybe lost in dreams. (What he might be dreaming of is unknown, unknowable.) Just a bit of his underarm is visible; I'd love to remember what it smelled like.

Next: I've backed away from him. It's nearly a full-body shot. He's wearing my leather wrist restraints now, though it's unclear whether they've been tied down to the bed. I'm guessing they were. Light floods through the window behind him, catching the arc of his long, curved dick lying against his belly. I wish I could bend down into the frame, lick the inside of his naked thigh, my cheek nuzzling up against his balls. I wonder whatever became of him. We played a few times then lost touch. I don't even remember his e-mail address. God, what a beauty.

Next image: I'd forgotten this, too. Once again, I've photographed him from the foot of the bed. His face is at the top of the frame, head turned to one side, eyes still closed. One shackled hand is behind his head. I must not have tied him down after all. His legs are raised, bent all the way back, and his right haunch, looking pale in the afternoon light, fills the lower right third of the frame. There's a little roll of flesh visible between his chest and his belly, then just a hint of his cock, then his ball sac, a pale and inviting pink. Follow his perineum and there's his asshole, nearly the same pink as his balls, stretched way out over my gloved hand. I can tell just how far in I'd gotten my hand: up to the last knuckles. I can imagine what has happened so far, though it's more a reconstruction than actual memory. I've pulled on the regrettably necessary white latex glove and lubed it up well. (You can see the sheen, even on the screen of my laptop.) Brian has pulled his legs up, exposing his hole, and I reach down and smear it with lube. I massage it gently, feel it relax, then slide in a finger. Two. Even through the latex, I can feel the warmth of his insides. I slowly pull the two fingers out, then slide back in, my pinky and thumb linked as my three middle fingers enter his fleshy white ass. Brian moans softly. I look up. He seems happy, at peace, eyes still closed. I rotate my three fingers, pump them in and out. He's ready for the next step. I pull away my hand, scrunch all four fingers together, put them back up against his hole, push in. He opens up in welcome. More gentle rotations, till I can get the tip of my thumb in too. That's the point at which I reached over and took, a bit unsteadily, the picture—before he opened up enough to let me get my knuckles inside him. The knuckles are the trick. If you can get them past the resistant ring of muscle, a man can almost always take your full hand, at least up to the wrist. So seemingly impossible. Was I able to get my whole hand in him, to be in that precarious place where I'd be surrounded by the soft, tender membranes inside Brian? I don't remember.

My cock is hard.

Next picture.

Amazing, totally amazing. It's a tight shot. At the bottom, the inverted-heart shape of his ass cheeks is just visible against my blue sheets. At the top, the base of his balls. The rest of the screen is filled with his butt. I've taken out my hand; it's there, still scrunched up and shining, on the right-hand side of the frame. And in the middle, dead center, Brian's asshole is wide open. Wide open, a deep black upside-down teardrop shape, dilated—what?—an inch, two inches? Probably two. It's beautiful, an angelic guy's open hole. Celestial, even. I find myself wishing I'd had some way to shine a light up in there when I took the picture. To see up (continuing the metaphor) past the gates of heaven, into the deep-red promised land. The provisional paradise of Brian's guts. How the hell could I ever have lost touch with this guy? Christ, what an idiot I can be.

I've unzipped my pants now, and I'm jacking off. I hope that no one walks in on me.

One more picture left in the folder. I'm almost reluctant to open it, but I do, fingertip moving on the touch pad, then a click.

Another close-up, even nearer than before. His hole hasn't closed up yet; it's still a deliciously dark void, a bull's-eye of lust in the middle of expanses of pale ass flesh. His hole has perhaps shrunken down just a bit, but you can see it even better now—the folds and pleats of the swollen, dark pink opening are clearly visible. The light has caught a trail of lube oozing from his ass. And I swear you can see a little way inside him, the camera's flash catching the secret places just right. Brian. That's his real name. In my stories, if they're true, I always change guys' names. That hardly seems necessary here. There are plenty of men named Brian out there, more than a few of them no doubt like to be fisted, and Brian, if you should by some chance run across this story, I want you to know for certain that the sight of your wide-open body has made me shoot my load this beautiful, late-summer day.

stonedin10languages

Everyone should fall in love in Barcelona, at least once. Even if it's with a guy who's due to fly out the next morning—funny what the over-the-counter availability of stimulants in Spain will do to one's emotional equilibrium.

Spring had gone by. It was the summer of 1972. His postcollegiate hitchhike through Europe, virtually a requirement for guys his age, was what the Germans, who seem to have a word for everything, call *wanderschaft*. Week after week had oscillated between tedium and excitement. He'd stand by the side of some motorway in Belgium, France, or Greece, a highway that pulsed with hundreds of cars sweeping past, uncaring, imperious. He was so small in the strange landscape, the horizon far off, unreachable. He would think *Enough. I wish this damn trip was over.* Then came the moment of hope fulfilled, a car slowing down, him getting in, "Where are you going?" negotiated in one of a number of languages that he spoke haltingly if at all.

He'd spent a rainy week sleeping in a wreck of a house in Amsterdam, in the company of half-a-dozen acolytes of a boy guru who'd always seemed, to him at least, to be full of shit. He'd been whisked through Yugoslavia by a rich French Marxist author in a brand-new Citroën, who'd taken pity on him and bought him lunch at a tony seaside café. He'd stowed away on a train through the Alps, just barely escaping getting caught. And he'd fallen in love in Barcelona.

Greg was a redheaded American who wore a baggy undershirt

that let Simon glimpse nipple, coppery chest hair, freckled flesh. They'd met outside something by Gaudi. It was 10 in the morning, and Simon was already stoned.

"Hi," said Simon.

"Hi," said Greg.

Simon's very neglected cock started to do a little flamenco, or whatever kind of dance they did in Barcelona.

They talked for a while, then went for a stroll down the Ramblas. Greg was studiously noncommittal about his sexuality; no mention of a girlfriend but no sign he liked boys either. Still, when Simon somehow managed to rub Greg's shoulder—on just what pretext?—Greg had sighed and shut his eyes. Right there in the Catalan sun, Simon's "back rub" went as far as slipping his hands beneath the undershirt, stroking Greg's furry chest, touching his maybe-erect nipples as casually as he could under the circumstances. That's when Greg mentioned that he was due to fly back to the States the following morning and had to go finish a few last-minute errands. His voice gave nothing away.

"Okay," Simon said.

"Good to have met you," Greg said. His eyes were really, really beautiful.

"Okay."

Simon gave Greg a suitably manly goodbye hug, patting him furtively on his butt, then dropped another upper and went off to a big department store with a listening station in their record department, where he could listen to Led Zeppelin through headphones and grind his teeth. He felt a bit like crying. Maybe it was the road-weariness, too much time sticking out his thumb beside roads in the middle of nowhere. Maybe it was the speed he'd taken, which had a name that sounded like "Boost-aids." Maybe he'd really fallen in love with the shaggy, cute, peripatetic Greg. And maybe his moodiness reflected how lonely he was, full of unfulfilled longing. He'd left college still struggling his way out of the closet, and the grand adventure of life on the road was no substitute, it turned out, for another warm male body up against his own. In any case, he listened to "Stairway to Heaven" one last time, stole some bread and cheese from the deli department, and decided to head south. Way south. South to Morocco. Camels and hash cookies. The Marrakech Express and all that. Okay, it wasn't Kathmandu, but at least he wouldn't have to overland through Afghanistan with a case of hepatitis to get there.

He knew the border police would want him to cut off his long hair. Morocco had a strict "no hippies allowed" policy, which is why he had his passport photo taken wearing a short-hair wig, why he'd packed the unconvincing polyester shag in his duffel bag and hauled it all over Europe, from Amsterdam to Athens and then back west to Spain. It had hibernated in that overstuffed khaki duffel for months as he'd hitched thousands of miles, smoked dozens of joints, and tripped on acid in Salvador Dali's hometown.

He'd been riding through France with Eric and Gary, two butchish American guys, in a VW van, getting increasingly nervous as they neared the border of Franco's Spain, and so, right before they reached the customs station, just to be safe he'd downed the last three ancient hits of orange sunshine LSD he'd brought from the States. The acid was stronger than expected, the line at the border moved as slow as paella, and by the time the van sailed through, uninspected, into España, he'd been well and truly flying.

They'd driven to the village of Cadaques, his ego on the verge of total dissolution. He perhaps saw melting watches. He surely saw God. Maybe God even saw him. At one point, a gorgeous behind-the-eyelids mandala had morphed into a giant asshole that—though he'd only rarely fucked anyone—sucked him in until he was kundalini itself, making his way up the spine of some huge cosmic boyfriend, then shattering into a thousand wet, squirming dicks, a plethora of penises, all of which, in some way or stoned other, made Simon think he'd overheard the ticking of eternity. It was only after he'd come substantially down that he realized he was, in fact, piercingly horny. Even so, he never could entirely disabuse himself of the notion that he'd glimpsed the face of cosmic truth that night.

Somehow he found himself outdoors in Spain, where the widows in black on their way to midnight mass looked rather...odd. But the dawn...ah, the dawn was glorious.

He'd just barely gotten back down on Earth when the jocks in the van had taken off again, with him huddled in the back mumbling about Jesus. Eric and Gary were good, red-blooded, straight American boys and in a hurry to get to the Costa del Sol, where desirable chicks paraded around without their bathing suit tops. That would mean stopping in Granada only long enough to refuel the VW; the Alhambra, after all, was less of an architectural wonder than big tits. So when the VW reached Barcelona, he dropped some pesetas-for-petrol into Gary's hand and bid the boys a fond farewell.

But then came Greg, Led Zeppelin, and the decision to head to Marrakech. Swallowing his pride and good judgment, he sought out the hostel where Gary and Eric were spending a couple of days getting drunk—even the Costa del Sol could wait, it seemed, for the sake of cheap red wine—and arranged to head south with them, the Alhambra be damned. Oh, well.

He said a final goodbye to the VW in Torremolinos. It didn't take him long to hitch to Algeciras, a less-than-lovely port city where he could catch the ferry to North Africa. Actually, Algeciras was pretty much a pit, and he caught the first boat out, sharing the deck with dozens of other hippie hitchers tucked up in smelly sleeping bags.

In the morning he disembarked in Ceuta, the Spanish post-colonial outpost dangling from the northern tip of Africa. The border wasn't far from the uneventful town. Too cheap to take a cab, he made his way down the shabby streets, wearing a semireputable sweater he'd shoplifted in France. Ducking into a side street, he dug into his duffel bag and pulled out the short-haired wig. The poor little critter had been through a lot, and showed it. He smoothed its polyester locks and pulled it on, taking care to hide his real hair beneath. As he hauled his duffel beneath the late morning sun, the wig made him sweat, then started to itch. By the time he reached the road to the border he was almost ready to tear the short hair off, fling it to the dusty ground, and head back to Europe. Almost.

On the way to the customs station he passed a pair of cute long-haired boys coming the other way. He imagined them naked.

"How was Morocco?" he asked them.

"Dunno," said one of the boys.

"Didn't make it, huh?" With hair like that, it was no wonder.

"Nah," smiled the other, showing stained, but even, teeth. "We've been trying for a week, off and on. It's bloody impossible. We're heading back to Spain, we are." They didn't look particularly discouraged.

"Back to Spain?" he asked. "Rather than just cut your hair?"

"I've been trying to talk him into that," the other one said. He was the cuter of the two, with hair that reached the small of his back. "But he's not going to do it."

And you're going back to Europe with him rather than going on alone? he wanted to ask. And the most impossible question to ask of all: *Are you guys boyfriends?*

"Cheerio," the one with stained teeth said. "Good luck to you." And off they went, knapsacks slung over shoulders, trailing their intact hair and unwashed smell behind them.

He straggled up to the border. There was a line of people waiting to get into Morocco, many of them identifiably hippies. The queue moved fairly rapidly; Western women, whether nicely groomed or clad in disheveled skirts made from Indian bedspreads, got into Morocco. Young men, though, were turned back if their hair was even a bit shaggy, no longer than the Beatles' had been back in 1964.

He was next. A bored-looking old Moroccan behind a worn counter peered briefly at his passport.

"How much money?"

He pulled out a sheaf of traveler's checks. He still had a goodly portion of the dollars he'd started out with months before. Sleeping in fields and filling up on bread were great ways to save cash.

The tired Moroccan clerk looked up. His rheumy eyes widened slightly. He said something, angrily. "Peruke?" "Peluka?" Simon couldn't understand.

The clerk pointed at his own head. "Weeg," he hissed. "No. Go away."

Maybe he could make a break for it. He looked across the border. Men armed with rifles. Forget it.

He spent that night crashed out in a hopelessly cheap hotel; sleeping outdoors anywhere in Ceuta seemed both impractical and unwise. The whitewashed walls of his room were spattered with blackish spots of dried blood—bedbugs. To save money he decided to find a roommate for the night. As fate would have it, the first guy to come along wanting to share a room was a beautiful blond surfer from Southern California. His name was Randy, and, no, he didn't mind sleeping in the same bed.

He and Randy shared a hash-laced cigarette, and then they stripped for sleep. The surfer's body was trimly muscular, with just a sprinkling of honey-colored hair. Wearing only white briefs, the blond boy turned out the room's single lightbulb, pulled the thin blanket over himself, and fell asleep.

Simon watched Randy sleeping so close to him, so very close, though he might as well have been a continent away. Whatever he might imagine happening wasn't worth the risks—rejection, humiliation, possible violence. Forget it.

But as he lay there, stoned and nearly sobbing with desire, he felt as if something alien were taking control. He reached a hand toward the sleeping blond. Slowly, cautiously, he moved his hungry fingers toward male flesh. He could feel Randy's heat as it radiated from a body much more perfect than his could ever be. Just an inch farther. And then his fingertips brushed naked, miraculous flesh. Did Randy's breathing alter, even ever so slightly? No. No. His hand slid itself, with excruciating caution, onto the boy's muscular belly. The soft rise and fall of breath, the heat and smoothness. Just a little farther. The waist of his briefs. Over the elastic, the cotton, down just a bit. Down. Down to his dick.

It was hard. Randy's cock was hard beneath Simon's palm. He had to remind himself to breathe. Nothing—not even the ruins at Delphi—was as beautiful as this, the hot curve of hard, illicit flesh pulsing through a thin layer of cloth. *Don't wake up,* he thought. *Please, don't wake up.* He moved his hand upward to the surfer's belly, slipped his fingers beneath the elastic band. Hard-on. Slightly sticky, hot, the pubic hair silkier than his own. Simon's cock had never been harder. His fingers pressed cautiously against Randy's dick, which jerked away and then swelled up even more. He could have—had he been more shameless or more brave— jacked off the stranger's cock. He imagined what it would feel like, the spurting of the surfer's jism into his hand.

And then Randy stirred, made moaning noises, and rolled away to lie on his side, leaving barely enough time for Simon to extract his hand.

That was it. That moment of near-discovery left him defeated.

He slipped from the bed, knelt in a corner, and quickly beat off, spurts of cum falling inaudibly on the floor.

The next day he put on his wig, tried again, and got into Morocco. The same old man was on duty, and it was highly improbable that he'd forgotten about the phony hair. Still, the clerk waved him through into Morocco, stamping his passport with a faint smile. (Later someone told him it had been an Islamic holiday, that's why he had gotten through. Maybe, but he found it improbable that Moslems celebrated Let a Hippie Over the Border Day.)

Simon saw the German boy soon after crossing the border. He hadn't even started to hitch to Tangier. He was just wandering around, really, walking down a seaside road, elated, inhaling a place stranger than anywhere he'd ever been.

There was a battered old panel truck parked near the road, perhaps 10 yards away, on a rocky shoreline next to the gray-green sea. Beside it lay a young man sunning himself on the rocks. He walked over to see the sunbather better; it was, after all, a public road, and the man was displaying himself in plain sight.

The man was in his mid 20s, with a near-naked tanned body and a handsome face wreathed in medium-long hair; once a guy made it into Morocco he was free to grow his hair as long as he wanted, unmolested by authority. Simon remembered he was still wearing that miserable short-haired wig and snatched it off his head, stuffing it in his pocket before the sunbathing man could see.

He looked down at the young man. His body was even nicer up close; the only thing that covered his nakedness was a green towel loosely draped across his midsection. The sunbather looked up and half-smiled. He had bright blue eyes, luxuriant dark lashes.

"Hello," he said.

"Hi."

"Did you just get here?" He had a German accent.

"Yeah. Just now." Simon's scalp still itched.

"I see." He shifted his body a little, and the towel shifted too, revealing most of his lower belly, a line of hair leading to his hidden cock. "My name is Josef."

"Hi. I'm Simon." He put down his duffel and squatted just a foot or two from almost-naked Josef. He'd never seen anything so beautiful. Not Delphi, not the surfer in Ceuta. He hoped the German boy hadn't noticed his dick stiffening beneath his shorts.

"Simon," the German repeated, and half-smiled again.

What next? Simon absently picked up a stick lying on the rocky shore. He started drawing circles on the ground. The German boy closed his eyes, put his hands behind his head, and stretched. The towel slipped even more, revealing the upper reaches of his tangle of pubic hair. Surely Josef was aware of what he was doing, how seductive he was being. Surely. Surely. Simon moved the stick till the tip brushed the German's shoulder.

"Mmm," the boy purred faintly.

Emboldened, Simon trailed the end of the stick over the boy's collarbone, tracing lines of desire over bare flesh. The young man arched his back slightly. Simon moved the stick to his chest, pressing down slightly, drawing little circles that zeroed in on a stiff, brownish nipple. He looked down at the towel; the boy was getting hard, no mistake.

So far what he'd been doing had been semi-innocent enough, nothing to conceal from the sparse traffic that passed on the road above. But though the road, as it said in *Lord of the Rings,* goes ever on, he'd reached a horny little crossroads. He decided to go for the road less taken, drew the stick slowly but inexorably down Josef's torso, over his belly to the towel, and pushed the covering aside. The boy's perfect uncut dick was fully hard. Simon looked into Josef's pretty face, and Josef smiled in an absent, noncommittal way.

There was a noise; an old Dodge rattled by on the road. Josef reached down, replaced the towel over his crotch, then stood up and climbed into the panel truck's open door. "Come on," he said. Standing, his body revealed a slight pudginess, a heaviness around the thighs.

Simon followed, hauling his duffel bag after him. Josef shut the door. The truck had been fixed up as a living space. A mattress lay on the floor, a little table held a jumble of groceries, and some clothes lay in the corner. The van smelled of grease, incense, and grimy laundry.

Josef picked up a half-smoked cigarette, lit it, took a drag, and handed it to Simon, who inhaled a mixture of harsh tobacco and potent hash. Josef sighed, threw the green towel aside, and lay down on the mattress, legs splayed, head thrown back. His cock was still hard. It was, clearly, an intentional temptation, and Simon eagerly succumbed.

Simon hadn't sucked much cock, and he hoped he was doing it right. He tried to imagine what would feel good to him and did that. Apparently it worked. Josef thrust upward into his mouth. He was glad the boy's dick wasn't too big, smaller than his own, in fact. Easier to handle.

"Moment," Josef said, pushing Simon's head away. He sat up, lit a candle on the bedside table, and grabbed a small wooden box from the floor. He lifted the lid and pulled out a spoon, a ball of cotton, a hypodermic syringe, and a little clear bag of brownish powder.

The hash had been good, better than good, and Simon sat in a daze as the beautiful German cooked up an injection of heroin. Somewhere along the line, probably while Josef was tying off his arm, causing his well-used veins to roadmap up, Simon pulled his own hard dick from his shorts and started stroking himself. He'd never seen anyone shoot up before.

The boy drew the drug up from the bent spoon, slid the point into the flesh of his arm, let his blood mix with the smack, then slid the plunger home. He put the works aside, undid his belt from his arm, sighed heavily, and fell backward onto the mattress. His legs were spread wide, his almost-soft cock lolling against one thigh.

Simon didn't know what he should do. He knew what he wanted to do, though, and he did it, bending over the semiconscious boy, taking Josef's dick into his mouth again, tongue playing with foreskin as he stroked his own stiff cock.

There was still a lot Simon didn't know. He had no way of foreseeing the time he'd spend at a hashish farm in the Atlas Mountains, where he'd get explosive diarrhea from tainted food drenched in olive oil. He didn't know how many nights he'd spend in Marrakech, staring at the ceilings of dollar-a-night hotels while he rode rush after rush from the hash-laced cookies they sold in the bazaar. His future was—as with all futures, no matter how wise we think we are—a big, stupid question mark. All he knew for now was that through an apparent wink of benevolent fate he'd made it into Morocco long hair intact, that he'd met a gorgeous German heroin addict, and that he was crouched in a stuffy, dim van, a drugged dick in his mouth. For a moment, but it was just a moment really, he wanted to go home. And then he sucked harder.

theboywhoreadbataille

Because he was actually French, he stood out in the class. That, and because he was gorgeous.

The class was Transgressive French Literature, otherwise known as Kink Lit 101. It was a popular one at my grad school. We got to read all the really twisted stuff: De Sade, Genet, Bataille. And Philippe was always on top of the class, not having to struggle to translate things; after all, it's not so easy to find the translation of "cocksucking motherfucking fag" in your *Larousse Dictionnaire Bilingue.*

I was attracted to him—I'm guessing everybody in the class was, both male and female—but he never gave a clue as to where his interests lay. His sexual interests, anyway. It was quite clear that as a reader he loved the thoroughly filthy works of Georges Bataille.

"God," he said one night, when a few of us—me, him, Ben, and Mary Anne—were polishing off a pizza at Vito's, "I could just read *The Story of the Eye* over and over again."

"Really?" I said. I was more inclined toward Genet, who didn't seem to always be straining to shock.

"*Oui.* Ah, Bataille. The scene with the piss and the wardrobe? *Magnifique.* And especially the one where Simone breaks raw eggs with her ass."

Well, I was glad he wasn't fixated on the part about Sir Edmond at the bullfight, or the one with Marcelle's eyeball in Simone's vagina. Eeewww!

"I'd love," he continued, "to try that out."

"Yeah?" I was excited, but cagey. I looked at his pretty, smooth face, which nearly always wore a quizzical, almost distant expression, eyes lively but remote behind his glasses, his countenance crowned by a shock of dark brown hair.

"Oh, God!" said Mary Anne. "Not me! That's gross."

"But you're taking a class on transgressive literature," said Ben. "Lighten up."

"Just because I read *Macbeth*," Mary Anne said, "that doesn't mean I want to kill a king."

Good retort, but my mind was elsewhere, wondering how Philippe, body obviously well knit even when he was fully clothed, would look naked, sitting in a bathtub full of raw eggs. I finished the last gulp of my pesto pizza and followed the procession to the cash register, a picture of his slick-wet butt throbbing in my mind.

Once outside the pizzeria I managed to get rid of Ben and Mary Anne without arousing suspicion. Philippe and I were by ourselves, walking back toward his place. The four of us had polished off a couple of pitchers of beer, so I'll blame what I said next on that.

"You really meant that? About the eggs?"

Philippe didn't look at me, just somewhere off in the distance, and he seemed a bit nervous when he nodded. "Very much, yes," he said, though he sounded more uncertain than that. "Why?"

"Because..." And then I hesitated, drunkenly tongue-tied.

Philippe helped me out. "Would you like to try something like that? With me?"

Well, I couldn't say I'd ever considered it before. In fact, I wasn't too committed to it even then. Kink had never been my thing, not even in my masturbation fantasies, which generally centered on smooth-bodied guys bending over to show me their butt holes. But if this was my big chance to see Philippe with his clothes off, maybe even touch him...

I nodded.

And soon we were gathering groceries at an all-night supermarket, my hard-on visible, I guess, to anyone who'd take the trouble to look. What the hell, transgressive is transgressive, right?

It wasn't a long walk back to Philippe's, but it seemed endless. He lived on the third floor, but I swear there were nine flights of stairs. Once we were inside his small, cluttered living room, we set our bags on the thrift-store coffee table. Awkward silence. Without a word, he stripped down to his undershirt and jeans. Then, never looking me straight in the eye, he slowly peeled down his Levi's.

I'd never seen anything so ostentatiously perfect as Philippe standing there in just his undershirt. Slightly stocky, broad-shouldered, he didn't look like the kind of guy who'd want to discuss Derrida. His soft dick had a long, luxurious foreskin. His thighs were creamy white, muscular, perfectly shaped, amazing.

And then he turned around.

I've seen plenty of asses in my young life, but Philippe's was the best, by far the best, a Greek god's ass, a Michelangelo-statue ass, the ass of the heavenly host. Philippe sauntered over to the bags on the table and pulled out the plastic shower curtains he'd bought. He tore open the package and, with the nonchalant attitude of someone decorating the high school gym for a prom, he laid the curtains on the floor, keeping his back toward me. I figured that he *must* have been aware of the effect his astonishing, creamy ass had on those lucky enough to behold it. He bent over to spread out the plastic, his pure white butt cheeks parting just enough to let me glance a thin line of dark hair around the hole. I almost came in my pants.

When the floor was covered in clear vinyl, he strolled over to the table again, his butt cheeks shifting with every step, and unloaded the grocery bags: two cartons of 18 extra-large eggs, a bottle of chocolate syrup, tins of vanilla pudding, spray cans of whipped cream.

"Are you ready?" he asked, turning to face me, his eyes quizzical behind his owlish glasses.

Turn around so I can see your ass again, I wanted to reply. Instead, I said, "Yes."

"And you want to do this? Really?"

I unbuttoned my fly and pulled out my hard cock. "See?" I said. "Now get down on all fours, okay?"

"Sorry," he said, pulling his undershirt over his head, revealing a flurry of armpit hair, nearly knocking his glasses off, "I guess I'm a bit nervous."

"Well, it's my first time too. On the floor, okay?" I really wanted to be a badass, kinky motherfucker, but as I stood there, watching Philippe getting on his knees, then all fours, stood there with my big, stupid hard-on jutting from my pants, I just felt tentative. If Bataille or De Sade or Genet had been watching, they would have thought: Pathetic! Or *Pathetique!*

"Well?" Philippe's voice was giving nothing away.

"Can I, um, touch you first?"

"Of course."

So I got down on my knees, just behind him, next to the pure European beauty of his ass, and extended a shy hand. The flesh of his butt flinched a bit at my touch, then relaxed as I stroked the cheek, running my hand over its classical curves, gently trailing two fingers down the crack, down from the tailbone till I felt the soft warmth of his hole. With my other hand I reached between his lean thighs, brushing his pendulous ball sac, then aimed upward till I grabbed onto his dick. It was getting gratifyingly stiff, but the generous foreskin still covered the head; I slid it back and forth over the moist head flesh as my other hand massaged his hole.

"*Les oeufs...*" Philippe said. The eggs. He was sounding impatient. All I wanted to do was fuck him, and he was thinking about groceries. Damn this kink stuff.

I reluctantly got up, walked over to the table, and opened an egg carton. The egg was slightly cool in my hand. I cracked it on the edge of the table.

"Ready?" I asked, like something momentous was going to happen.

He looked up at me, straight at me through his glasses, and sort of smiled. "*Oui.*"

I stood above him and pulled apart the shell, letting the raw egg drop onto the smooth, white flesh of his ass. I wanted it to drip right down the crack, but my aim was a bit off.

Philippe was muttering something. In French.

"Pardon?" I said.

"I was just reciting Bataille," Philippe said, and when he started in again I realized he was doing just that, apparently having memorized the bit leading up to Marcelle's suicide. The guy was amazingly weird. But his ass was amazingly fantastic. I got another egg, cracked it, and, holding it close to his flesh, hit the target, the yolk oozed right down his ass crack. I spit in my hand and worked my throbbing dick for a minute while I watched raw egg slithering down his thighs, down to the plastic-covered floor.

"Oh, fuck," I said. And meant it.

Then I went back to the table and picked up the open egg carton—16 left. Standing above him, I dropped the eggs one by one onto Philippe, onto his shoulders, the small of his back, but especially onto his wonderful, wonderful ass.

By the time I'd gone through most of the carton, the place filthy and Philippe was thoroughly covered with viscous whites and bright streaks of yolk. I was about to suggest that we'd made enough mess, when he reached back with both hands and pulled his ass cheeks wide apart. His deep pink asshole gleamed beneath a raw egg glaze: boypussy tartare. Sometimes it's a matter of hygiene-be-damned. I dropped to my knees right between his kneeling legs, stuck my face into his sloppy-wet ass, and started lapping at his high-cholesterol hole. He paused in his recitation of Bataille long enough to say "Fuck, yeah" and backed up against my tongue. I reared back, reached for an egg, and smashed it into his open hole. I was, my oozing cock and I agreed, beginning to really enjoy this.

The chocolate syrup was next. I stood over Philippe for a moment, looking down at his egg-slick ass, all its beauty slippery and wet. Then I opened the nozzle of the syrup bottle, inverted it, and let just a drizzle of dark brown syrup fall onto his wet, white skin. If this was the final exam for Transgressive Lit class, I had a feeling I was passing with flying colors.

I squeezed the bottle and a stream of sweet syrup hit his hole, drenching egg whites, yolks, bits of shell. It was beautiful, that hole, those food-covered butt cheeks. As gorgeous as his ass had been when it was clean and white, it was even sexier all sullied, filthy with food. I wanted to fuck it. And I *was* going to fuck his ass. I was glad I'd slipped a package of Trojans into the grocery basket.

The syrup bottle sputtered to emptiness. I dropped it onto the dirty floor, then picked up the whipped cream container and shook hard. With a flourish, I topped the egg-and-chocolate slop with swirls of whipped cream, shooting a big white rosette right on Philippe's asshole. He took his hands away and his cheeks came together, squeezing out a big glob of chocolate cream. I ran my fingers up the crack of his messy ass, getting a handful of the brownish goop, bringing it to my lips. Sweet.

I went to fetch a rubber. I was tearing the packet open with my teeth, my slippery fingers straining to get a grip on the foil, when Philippe asked, "What are you doing?" I glanced his way. He was looking up at me through those glasses of his, expression vague as ever.

It was a stupid question.

"What does it look like? I'm putting on a rubber," I replied.

"No." Just that, sounding the same in French or English. No. While I hesitated, wondering if all the work I'd done still wouldn't get me into his butt, Philippe rose to his knees. He grabbed his dick with his filthy hand, quickly jacking his foreskin back and forth over his swollen, shiny cock head.

At last his face changed expression. Looking somewhere in the room, but not at me, never at me, he scrunched his face up in a stereotype of preorgasmic lust. "Oh yeah oh yeah oh yeah," he chanted. His glasses were sliding down his sweaty nose.

If I'd been smart, I guess I would have gotten behind him and at least stuck my fingers up his ass. Maybe even my dick. But I wasn't smart. I was polite. I just stood there gaping as Philippe shot a big load of sperm, gush after gush, onto the swamp of eggs, chocolate, and cream.

"That's it," Philippe said, recovering quickly. "You can wash up in the kitchen sink. I'm going to go shower."

I didn't know what to say. "Fuck you, asshole" came to mind, but when I thought about how gorgeous his asshole actually looked...

By the time I'd rinsed my hands and stuffed my poor hard-on back into my pants, the shower was already running. I went into the bathroom to say goodbye. There behind a clear plastic curtain, the French boy was washing his butt. His back turned toward me, he spread his cheeks, soaping up, lathering, drawing small wet circles on his hole. My dick stretched to full hardness again.

"Philippe?"

He turned. Amazingly, he still had his glasses on. He didn't say a word. I'd been dismissed, my part in his little literary experiment apparently at an end; he'd had his transgressive fun.

When I left Philippe's, the door locked itself behind me with a click.

vaporetto

Fifteen years had not been particularly kind to Venice, nor to his memories of Venice. Nor to him.

The Hotel des Bains, for example. Tadzio remembered it from his childhood as a grand and silent place. But these days, breakfasts echoed to the sort of nouveau riches American tourists who bellowed "Good morning" and clapped one another on the back. And the hotel, for its part, responded with signs of incipient decline. The carpets were tattered, the cherrywood paneling no longer polished to an impossible sheen. The once-perfect service was now too often negligent or peremptory. But then, he thought, perhaps every place seems grand and perfect when one is 14 and beautiful. Impossibly beautiful, as he had been.

It was his own damned fault, anyway. When the Count had suggested taking him on holiday to Venice, it was he himself who'd insisted on the Hotel des Bains. The place was emblematic, a reminder of a time before the Great War had ravaged Europe. Before cholera killed his mother, before his drunk, despondent father shot himself. Before things fell apart. A time when his beauty had drawn all eyes to him, a time when that beauty had been enough.

But the journey with the Count had been difficult from the first—missed connections, disappointing meals, difficulties with their lodgings. And then Venice, glittering Venice, had been unseasonably warm since their arrival several days ago. Beneath the fine facades that bespoke wealth and power, a fetid smell of garbage rose from the canals; tourist ladies in gondolas held scented handkerchiefs to their delicate noses. Both men's tempers had been short. He'd had an argument with the Count that morning, one of many that had lately punctuated their time together. Jealousy, recrimination, reproach.

But, he reminded himself, if not for the Count, he might well be dead.

The estate Tadzio's father had left had been distressingly meager, most of his father's money having been gambled away or spent on whores. Tadzio, though, quite unsuited for the world of work, soon discovered there was no shortage of older, wealthy gentlemen who would take an interest in him. At first each of the men had been richer and more indulgent than the ones before. But as time went by and he drifted from man to man, his youthful softness hardening, he himself was often the one left behind, replaced by new boys who were younger and perhaps even prettier than he. Slipping toward the demimonde, he took up with a cocaine-sniffing painter. Tadzio himself began to use drugs. His once-shining looks became disheveled and haggard. His health spiraled into decline. He no longer cared for the burden of beauty.

He'd first met the Count at a gallery opening; the painter's druggy canvases had become a minor sensation among Warsaw's cognoscenti. Tadzio was flying on cocaine, invulnerable. The Count, a well-known patron of the arts, had stared at him, as all the others had, but this time there was a difference. The Count's gaze was not merely voracious. It was tinged with pity. "My poor boy," he thought he heard the Count say. Suddenly Tadzio crumbled, tears in his eyes. His mother. He wanted his dead mother, the smell of her perfume, the warmth of her breast. The gleaming, lost purity of her pearls. Sobbing, he threw himself against the immaculately dressed nobleman. "My poor boy," the Count repeated. "Let me help you. Come home with me." Arm-in-arm they left the gallery, past the curious eyes of the crowd.

When Tadzio returned to the painter's atelier the next day, the artist flew into a rage, cutting Tadzio across the cheek with a letter opener, narrowly missing an eye. Bleeding, he'd run away, back to the Count. He and the painter never spoke again. Tadzio still bore the scar.

The Count had brought him to his country estate, locked him in a room where he'd had no access to drugs, and lovingly nursed him back to health, to sanity. When Tadzio regained his weight, the Count rewarded him with an expensive new wardrobe. When Tadzio regained his good manners, the Count took him to parties and dinners at fine restaurants. When Tadzio, at last, had asked the man why he'd done all this for him, the Count replied, "Because everyone must care for something, take care of someone. And I could see beyond your troubles, see how good you truly are." The answer made Tadzio feel guilty, depressed, and strangely triumphant. He'd fooled another one.

As soon as Tadzio had gotten back on his feet, free of cocaine, no longer helpless and half dead, inevitable strains began to show. The aging Count could see as well as anyone that Tadzio, once again so widely desired, might someday slip from his grasp. Gratitude went only so far.

And then came the argument at the Hotel des Bains. He'd sworn to the Count that he'd always been faithful to him, and it had been true, very nearly. In the end, though, he'd run from the room, slamming the door, rushing red-faced down the corridor, past astonished chambermaids, down the stairway to the beach. The Lido was filled with ungainly bathers, noisy children, their stupid, indulgent parents, the rows of stupid little bathing huts. He'd boarded a vaporetto, a noisy public motorboat, not caring where it took him. Its route ran, via Piazza San Marco, up the Grand Canal with its baroque display of riches, past the tourist gondolas, through a welter of floating trinket sellers and a miasma of festering trash.

vaporetto

He'd disembarked near the Ca' d'Oro. Half-blind with anger and remorse, he'd walked farther and farther from the tourists' Venezia. Across the Laguna Morta, the cemetery of San Michele hovered in gray heat. The dead who were buried there, he'd once been told, were soon dug up for lack of space, their bones piled into a charnel house. In this stifling city where nothing changed for the better, only the dead were in motion.

His aimless path brought him at last to the winding, narrow maze of back alleys where the poor people lived. In the old days he'd not even known they were there, the poor people. So pampered had class and beauty kept him that to him the world itself was rich and ever-giving. And Venice was most beneficent of all, that final gilded summer before disease robbed him of his mother, beautiful Mama with her strands of pearls.

Now he came to a little courtyard. On three sides stood laundry-draped tenements, their crumbling plaster peeling away, revealing the brick, crumbling too, beneath. The fourth side, the way he had come, held a little shrine of sorts, a marble memorial stone embedded in a wall, beside it a wooden cabinet that had been painted green a long time ago. Corinthian columns flanked a cross-shaped opening in the weathered wood. Behind the opening's green-painted metal grill hung the crucified Jesus, thin, naked, lovely, head indolently cocked to one shoulder, gilded loincloth draped provocatively low around his thighs.

Three ragged boys were kicking a ball around the courtyard. Sitting down upon a filthy stone bench, heedless of his white summer suit, he watched their innocent play. At one boy's kick, the ball went spiraling crazily toward the shrine. If not for the metal grill-work, the naked god would have been hit in the head. If he were living in a novel, he thought, all this would symbolize something.

"Carlo!" A man was standing in a doorway across the untidy little square, calling to one of the ragged boys. "Carlo! Come here!"

Was the man Carlo's big brother? His father? The shadowy doorway made it hard to tell.

Carlo glanced up briefly, but the boys continued their game. The man walked toward them, into the gray light of the humid afternoon. The man was 30 or so, swarthy, slightly stocky, with glossy black hair, a moustache, an Italian beak of a nose. The dark man noticed the stranger in his neighborhood, stared hard for a moment, then smiled. "Carlo! Come in. Your lunch is ready," the man said, but the man's eyes were not looking at Carlo.

The Italian's gaze did not discomfit Tadzio. Ever since he was a young boy in Poland, he'd been accustomed to the stares of strange men. Young men, old men, shop clerks, nobility--his beauty had drawn them all. And soon enough he'd learned to provoke them, those staring men. To pique their interest, teasing them with some unspoken promise. Long ago, behind his mother's back, his stolid governess beside him, he began to flirt outrageously. But even then he understood that his apparent näiveté made it all seem somehow innocent, as though he were an unsullied thing of nature, quite unconscious of his own allure. There was, he still remembered, an old man in Venice, that long-ago summer at the Hotel des Bains, who would gaze at him across the dining room, or from a chaise longue on the Lido. Tadzio would sweep by the old man, his head held high, his heart beating wildly at the knowledge of the power that physical beauty conferred. He began to seduce, actually seduce, the pathetic old bird. A sidelong glance when he was at the beach playing with his friends. A perfect pose when he waded into the sea, his hip cocked suggestively, just so. The power that this gave him excited him, physically excited him, made him hard beneath his swimsuit. He'd had to plunge into the cold water to disguise his arousal. And still the old man stared, besotted by a purity: the purity of boys, which did not, in reality, exist.

"*Buon giorno,*" Tadzio said to the hawk-nosed man, who now

had little Carlo beside him, gripping the boy around his skinny shoulders.

"That hurts, Papa," the boy said. They were father and son, then. The grip loosened slightly.

"Hello, *signore,*" said the man. "My name is Gianni." His free hand brushed the thigh of his well-worn trousers.

"Tadzio. My name is Tadzio."

What did this Gianni see, staring at him? A hapless stranger who'd lost his way? A rich tourist to be fleeced? An object of desire? All three?

There was an awkward silence. Then the dark man released his grip and said, "Carlo, go inside." The boy skittered off and disappeared into a doorway.

"What brings you here, *signore?*"

"To Venice, you mean?"

"To this part of Venice, sir."

How could he explain? He decided to lie. "My wife is busy shopping. I decided to go for a walk."

"Ah, my wife is dead, *signore.*"

"I'm sorry."

"It happened a long time ago, when Carlo was born." The hawk-nosed man shifted his weight onto one hip, began to rub his palms against his thighs. "There's only the two of us now. And life...life is hard, *signore.* Work is not so easy to find." Ah, there it was!

"Are you hungry, *signore?*" stocky Gianni asked, an unreadable look on his face. "Would you like to share our lunch? It's not much, but..."

Rising from the bench, Tadzio said, "No thank you. My wife will be expecting me." He extended his hand. The man's grip was strong and calloused against Tadzio's smooth white skin.

He had to get out of there. Things had gone too far, lapsed

into uncertainty, the crumbling maze that was Venice.

"*Signore?*" The man's quizzical smile broke through his reverie. Tadzio drew his hand away as if burned and turned to go. He was already in the dark passageway leading from the square when he looked back. The dark, rough man was still standing there, still staring at him. Men's desires had led him to some strange places. And this place was as good as any.

He walked back to the man, stood motionless before him. Gianni smiled and his dark eyes moved down to Tadzio's crotch. "Come this way, *signore.*"

Will you demand money? Tadzio wanted to ask, but the words stuck in his throat. He followed the stocky Italian. Perhaps he was in danger. He didn't really care.

He followed Gianni into his house. He'd never been in a place like it. Even the cocaine-addicted painter's down-at-the-heels studio had an arty, raffish elegance. But this Italian tenement had only an air of desperation and the smell of stale cabbage. Gianni led him upstairs, into a single shabby room. Little Carlo was sitting at an oilcloth-covered table, eating noodles in reddish sauce directly from a battered pot.

"This gentleman has come to visit us," Gianni said. The boy looked up, questioningly, but said nothing. Perhaps this was not the first time this had happened. The hawk-nosed man spooned out the food and handed Tadzio, now sitting uneasily at the table, a bowl. He took a bite. It tasted like poverty.

"Go out to play, *bambino,*" Gianni told his son. The boy ran out, slamming the door behind him. They were alone. Gianni leaned over and ran his fingers over Tadzio's scar. The hawk-nosed man kissed him, tentatively, then fiercely, and dragged him from the table, across the pathetic room. Tadzio felt his cock swelling. He struggled out of his white linen jacket, then tore at the Italian's rough shirt. The man's chest, powerfully built and matted with hair, was so different from his own. They fell onto the room's single rickety bed. Clothes were strewn everywhere. Even erect, Gianni's dark, weighty cock was half-hidden by a long foreskin.

The Italian's piercing smell cut through the room's stale air. Tadzio pinned one muscular arm to the mattress and buried his face in the man's sweaty armpit. The honesty of the odor nearly made him gag. Hairy legs wrapped around Tadzio's waist. For a moment, Tadzio thought that Gianni was like the Count, that he wanted to be entered, but an exploratory touch was pushed away. The strong, hairy man wrestled around till Tadzio was pinned beneath him, legs spread askew. Reflexively, accepting the inevitable, Tadzio raised his legs. A single gob of spit and the Italian forced his way inside. The man's fucking was inexpert but enthusiastic. The bed groaned beneath his thrusts.

Tadzio looked up into the man's sweaty, triumphant face, smelled the garlic and tobacco on his breath. He shut his eyes and imagined the Count lunching at the Hotel des Bains, full of regret. And now Tadzio was so very distant from that once-perfect dining room, from the crisp white table linen, from the vacant velvet chair at the table for two.

It began to hurt. The fucking began to hurt. Tadzio clawed at the man's broad, hairy back, bit the man's lip until blood flowed. The Italian looked furious, then something else altogether, and his thrusts became even more brutal. Gianni's acrid sweat made Tadzio's pale skin gleam. A smell of shit arose. A guttural yell. Another. Gianni pumped one last time into Tadzio. And, as he shot his juices deep within the pale white ass, the leg of the bed shattered, with a sound of splintering wood, and they crashed to the floor. Startled, they stared at one another. And they both began to laugh at their own astonishment. And stared once again, perfect strangers.

Gianni's softening cock had slipped from inside. But Tadzio's was still hard, and he reached down to finish himself off. Gianni brushed the hand aside and, to Tadzio's amazement, bent over and kissed the hard flesh. A calloused hand worked up and down the shaft till climax was near, and then Gianni's soft lips swallowed him whole, and the end came.

Things were suddenly silent between them. Tadzio struggled up from the floor, wiped himself off as best he could. His suit, which the Count had given him, was tangled in a corner, soiled and wrinkled. Gianni still lay on the floor, muscular hand cupped around his genitals for modesty's sake. A cheap crucifix hung on the wall above the bed, a tiny echo of the naked god in the courtyard outside. The sound of children, carefree for the moment, filled the air beyond the open window.

Tadzio was pulling his pants on when Gianni said, "*Signore,* I so much hate to ask this. It's not for myself, you understand, but for Carlo…" It was said gently, but behind the Italian's hard-eyed smile, Tadzio knew, was a threat. He reached into his pocket and pulled out a roll of lire.

Gianni held out his left hand, the one that wasn't on his dick. "For Carlo," he repeated as he took the cash. He looked down at the money in his hand. "So little, *signore?*" he asked. "So little?"

anewpuppy

Okay, I confess—I'd never seen anything as cute as Sean before. When he first contacted me in the online chat room, when I first read his profile, I got more than a little nervous. He was just past 18, his profile said; this made him legal, but this also made him very young. Legal or no, he was more than young enough to be my son.

"hiya," he said, the word appearing in that little onscreen window that holds on occasion so much promise, but more often than not is filled with bullshit.

"How you doing?" I typed back.

"kewl. how r u?"

Not a promising beginning. I spend half my life working with words. Correctly spelled words.

"Fine, thanks."

"watz up?"

"Just cruising." I was looking for an actual fuck-type meeting that night, not a semiliterate conversation with a boy who lived hundreds of miles away. I was in San Francisco, Sean, his profile said, was in Anaheim. Along with Disneyland.

"me 2"

I was beginning to feel like I was chatting up The Artist Formerly Known As Prince.

"im in2," Sean continued, "older dewdz"

At which point my crotch and my brain parted ways. I was getting hard, rapidly.

"And?" I was playing it cagey, in case his parents were watching over his shoulder.

"i want u 2 fuk me"

There it was, then. I was unzipping my pants.

I told him about my writing, my kinks, my open relationship. He said I was kewl.

He told me about living with his parents, his aiming for pre-med, his girlfriend.

"Want to swap pics?" I asked.

When I downloaded his picture, I gasped. I must have. I'd never seen anything as cute as Sean before. He was standing, shirtless, in front of an ocean and a sky, both as blue as a David Hockney pool. His head was cocked, hair jutting wildly from it, his face innocent, smiling, perfectly lovely, perfectly 18. His body was lean, thin even, and hairless. The sunlight molded itself around lean pecs, prominent nipples, impossibly low-fat abs. His pants were riding, as was the fashion, halfway down his hips. A strip of red plaid boxers, then baggy khakis. It looked like he had a nice basket, maybe.

I made myself breathe.

We chatted for a while. Sean was still in the closet, living at home while he finished college. He'd only had sex with a few guys, fellow students, mostly jerking off, and one or two of them had sucked his cock. Lucky boys.

He had a girlfriend. They had sex. But he knew he was queer. Queer*er*: he wanted to be an older man's sex slave. He wanted to be stripped down, collared, tied up, used, fucked. He was so young. So innocent.

He sent me another photo, one of a skinny young guy like him being roped up by two burly men in leather.

"yeah i mean i kno itz not real and posed and all but it getz me off thinkin of bein like that"

"I would do that to you, Sean."

"yeah I kno u would u r so kewl"

I couldn't help it. I shot off messily all over myself.

In the weeks that followed Sean and I chatted often. I was always the one to send the first instant message when he came up on my buddy list, but every time he seemed glad to see me, always had time for me, time to chat.

I was beginning to like him, for all the right reasons and some of the wrong ones. Because he was young and beautiful and still confused and sometimes unhappy. Because I seemed to help him, provide a sympathetic ear, speak from experience, validate his desires. And because I couldn't help imagining him sitting at his computer while we chatted, upstairs in his parents' house, the door locked, his hard dick jutting from his baggy boxers, him spitting on his hand, jacking off. Was this last one a right reason or a wrong reason? Did I have to decide?

He seemed so sweet. But would he have seemed as sweet if his body weren't so perfect, his smile so bright? It didn't really matter anyway. I was his benevolent, more-than-a-little-twisted online gay uncle. He was my teenage fantasy. It was safe. He would never get the permission, the leisure, the balls to fly up to San Francisco and make our imaginings real. We would never really meet. And that was probably for the best.

"I want you to know something, Sean...I mostly go online to actually meet guys, and hardly ever maintain long-term cyber-only relationships. But knowing you gives me a great deal of pleasure...I know you don't think you're special, but you're special to me."

"kewl and do u meet a lot of guyz"

"More than I should. :-)"

"kewl so like how do u do that i mean im askin 4 real how do u meet online that way"

"Depends on the man, Sean. It's usually not that tough, assuming the guy's not playing games."

"kewlness"

"And usually it gets pretty kinky, if that's what he wants."

"hmmm i like the idea of bein ur servant in ALL aspects"

"Yeah, but if we met, do you think you would go through with it, boy?"

"yes sir tho cautiously"

"No problem." How could I be falling so hard for someone I'd never met, whose voice I'd never even heard, whom I'd only seen in one frozen ocean-side moment?

"since trust is a part there would b a start that would b more like a new pup when u get one"

"Yes, but that's not going to happen, at least not for quite a while."

"o yes it iz"

"What?"

"ive decided," Sean typed, "2 tell my parents some story n fly up to see u so is nxt weekend ok?"

I was brought up short. Too fast, too sudden, too scary. "And then what, Sean?"

"ur the writer" Pause. New line. "u make the rest of it up."

I'm in the arrivals lounge at SFO. Sean shows up, baggy clothes, carrying a backpack. Crooked smile on his face. He doesn't look exactly like his e-mailed image. Of course not. In person he's slighter, even thinner than his picture. His face is less perfect, which just makes him sexier.

"Hiya, Dad," he says.

I give him a great big hug. I don't care who sees it; for all anyone knows, we might actually *be* father and son. Then I kiss him directly on his lips. He pulls back, blushing.

"Hey, Sean. Good to see you."

He looks in my eyes, smiles broadly, leans over and kisses my lips. I'm getting a hard-on.

"Let's go back to your place and fuck," Sean says. Hearing

him talk, you wouldn't know that "fuck" is spelled f-u-k.

Sean has never been on a motorcycle before. The ride up 280 goes well enough, but I can tell from his body that he's a little nervous. Still, his arms are wrapped tight around me, his crotch pressing into my butt. All this is new to him. I wonder what he's thinking. We get to my place.

"Dude," he says, "that ride was fun."

"Hella fun," I say.

"Hella fun."

"You hungry?" I ask when we reach my living room.

Looking in my eyes, Sean reaches for my crotch.

"Hey," I say, not believing I'm saying it, "slow down."

"Why? You've got a hard-on."

"Do you?"

"Yeah," says the adorable, thin boy. "Want to see it?"

Without waiting for an answer, he unzips his saggy chinos and pulls out his dick. It is, like the rest of him, impressively cute.

Along about here I'm thinking *What the fuck have I gotten myself into?* And then we're kissing. He kisses well for such a young kid. I hold onto his narrow body and fall in something like love. Everything is just so fucking spectacular. Like the stars.

"Can I suck your cock, Sir?" Sean asks.

The idea of this boy, this boy I've wanted so fiercely, whom I thought I'd never meet, the idea of watching my cock sliding into his mouth, it's almost more than I can bear. But he drops to his knees, unbuttons my jeans, and it's real. Sean from Anaheim is sucking my cock.

You can tell the ones who only *think* they're submissive bottoms; they're supposed to be focusing entirely on the top, but they play with their own dicks without permission or a second thought. Sean, though, has all his attention on me. His hands are on my thighs as he takes my dick down his throat with surprising expertise.

"Enough, boy. Strip," I say. "Then get on your knees. I'll be right back."

I go to the bedroom to fetch a few things; I like the idea that when I get back to the living room, I'll find young Sean there, stripped naked, kneeling on the carpet. My carpet. My boy. My fantasy.

When I walk back into the living room, there he is, his young, thin body stripped bare, his hands gripped behind his back, his eyes cast down. He looks every inch the perfect bottomboy; either he's been reading S/M porn, or his instincts are impeccable.

His cock isn't huge, maybe about 6 inches, but it's standing straight up, and as I walk toward him I see a drop of precum glinting at its tip.

"Welcome to San Francisco, Sean," I say.

"Thanks, Daddy," Sean says, without looking up at me. "Thanks, Sir."

I'm standing inches from him, my prick, still out of my pants, just above his beautiful face. I take the broad leather collar I've brought from the bedroom, position it around his neck, pull the end through the buckle, tighten it down, fasten it. Sean sighs and shivers. My cock is throbbing hard.

I walk behind him. His back is tapered, slender, just this side of bony. His thin wrists are crossed at the small of his back. I'm shaken by a wave of lust, of maybe love. By the need to have power over this cute, cute boy.

I'm still carrying the handcuffs I've brought from the bedroom. Leather restraints are better for long-term bondage, but metal cuffs make for great theater. I kneel behind Sean. At the first touch of cold metal he jumps slightly. I surround a wrist with a cuff, then ratchet it down slowly, each metallic click making it all seem real, final. He's here. He's naked. He's mine. Click. Click. Click.

I tighten the second cuff down. Click. Cold steel against delicate wrists. I touch his ass for the first time. I stroke the smooth, round flesh.

"Thank you, Sir," Sean says. He's still trembling.

I allow myself to wonder just what he's feeling, how much responsibility I bear.

"You doing okay, Sean?"

"Yes, Sir. May I suck your Daddy cock some more, Sir?"

I've got to hand it to the kid, he knows just what to say. I stand up and stick my dick in his face. He opens wide and gobbles it down. I grab the collar and guide my shaft in and out of his wet, hot mouth. Suddenly, like a switch has been turned on, I want to fucking use him for real, just fuck the innocence out of him. Fuckin' boy. I shove deep into his throat. He starts to gag. I keep my cock in there for a second, just to show him who's boss. He tries his best to take it. I pull on the collar. He starts to squirm away. He's drooling. I slap his face. He groans.

What the hell am I doing? I pull out. He gasps for air. His dick is still standing straight up. I stroke his cheek.

Just then his beeper goes off. It's sitting on top of the pile of his clothes in the corner of the room.

"I'd better check that, Sir," Sean from Anaheim says.

I go pick up the pager and show him the readout.

"It's my folks," he says. "I should call them back. They don't know where I am."

I unlock the cuffs; they're biting into his wrists anyway.

"Phone's over there."

He picks it up and dials. "Mom?" he says. "It's Sean. You called?" He's standing there naked, a collar around his neck, his cock still hard, and he's talking to his mother. I've got to give the kid credit; he has guts.

"Yeah, I'm fine," he's saying. "Listen, I think I'm going to be spending the night over here at Brian's, okay?" His naked body is impossibly lithe, his limbs thin but graceful, the angle of his hipbones catching the light. "Bye, Mom," he says, "I love you, too."

"I bet she's younger than I am," I say. He tells me her age; she is.

"I'm sorry," Sean says, "I just didn't want her to worry. And I arranged an alibi with my friend Brian." A lopsided grin. "He's clueless why, though."

"Sean," I say, tucking my softening cock back in my pants, "maybe you should get dressed."

Sean looks puzzled, maybe a little hurt. Or is that my imagination?

"You're a really, really nice boy, and I like you a lot."

"So what's the problem?"

"I'm just worried that you're not, I don't know, *ready* for this." And am I? Some things, I'm thinking, are maybe better left abstract, unfulfilled. In the realm of pure desire.

Sean puts down the phone and walks over to me. He stands up against me, looking into my eyes, and reaches for my belt. He unbuckles it, unbuttons my jeans, and pulls them down to mid thigh. My cock leaps up, intensely interested again.

"Fuck me, Daddy," 18-year-old Sean from Anaheim says. "Fuck me."

"And you've never been fucked before?"

He smiles. "I want you to be the first."

I strip down and sit on the sofa. "There's lube and rubbers over there," I say.

He unrolls a condom onto my cock. I usually find putting on a rubber to be distracting and irritating. Now, with this beautiful boy smoothing the tight latex down over my stiff flesh, it's bliss. He lubes me up.

"Let's grease up your ass as well, boy," I say. I hold out my hand and he squirts it full of lube. I reach around him and finger the crack of his ass, finding the tight, hot hole, loosening it gently with my slippery fingers. "Breathe, Sean," I say. "And want it." My finger is gliding in and out, but he's still tight, very tight. "Are you sure this is what you need?"

"Yes, Daddy."

"Then come sit on Daddy's lap." I think of him talking to his mother on the phone.

Sean climbs on my lap, straddles me, wraps his legs around my waist. We sit face-to-face, our hard dicks rubbing together, our faces inches apart.

"Can I kiss you, Daddy?" he asks.

His tongue enters my mouth, his breath fresh and sweet, a boy's breath. I reach around and grab his ass, lift him upward, positioning his hole just over the tip of my throbbing cock. His tongue still deep in my mouth, he lowers himself onto my dick, his hole tight and resistant. I stroke his face and push myself upward, into his virgin ass. He wriggles around until my cock head is inside him. Our tongues do their wet dance. His mouth opens wide and I shove my tongue into him, as far down his throat as I can. And he slides down on Daddy's cock until it's all the way inside him. It feels great to me, and Dad's hoping the boy likes it too. He pulls his face away and leans back slightly. I look at him, at Sean, my beautiful boy, a man young enough to be my son. In gratitude, astonishment, and fear, I stroke his face, his chest, play with his tits, bend over and take a nipple in my mouth, lick it, flick the tip of my tongue against it, nibble at it, bite down gently, harder, stretch it out with my teeth, bite down until he gasps.

Then we're kissing again, he's riding my cock, my cock that's buried deep inside his firm young butt. And I reach around and slap his ass.

"Ohhh, *yeah*," he says.

I slap harder. I look down; his dick is spewing precum. Our

bellies, mine hairy, his smooth, are soaking wet with it.

He's riding up and down on my dick now, his ass relaxing, accepting, hungry for a man's cock. I spank him with both hands, slapping his ass cheeks with resounding *cracks*.

"Oh, Sir, oh, Daddy Sir, I've needed this, I've wanted you Daddy, oh, Daddy." Sean is speaking in tongues now, a holy roller with a dick up his butt. "Fuck my pussy my pussy my fucking pussy Sir oh Sir."

And I look at him and realize, with all my being, that here is this young, beautiful, hungry queer boy, the young man of my dreams, his half-formed boy's body shiny with sweat, and he's wearing my collar, and he's riding my dick, my mandick planted firmly inside him, his hunger, his innocence, need, and I can't help myself, much as I'd like to, I can't stop myself. "Oh, *shit!*" I scream. And I'm coming and coming, shooting off deep in his rich, warm darkness, and his young sperm is jetting upward, past eye level, landing on him, on me, on our faces, the sofa, everywhere.

A week later, I was online. Sean's screen name came up on my buddy list.

"Hi," I typed out in the instant message window.

"dewd!!! u r awesome watz up"''

"Sean..." I typed out, and then I didn't know what else to say.

untitled

Jared watched the boy across the aisle sway in time to the music. Everyone was on their feet, the concert was reaching its climax, everyone was dancing. Jared was dancing too, after a fashion, but his attention was on the boy across the aisle. The light from the distant stage—they were in the balcony because Jared, and the boy too, he assumed, had waited too long to buy tickets—did a half-assed job of revealing the boy. Particularities were few and far between: the curve of the boy's neck, the rangy body in baggy clothes, a glimpse of profile appearing and then revanishing to the beat. In fact, there were a dozen, a hundred, more, young men in the balcony that night like him, or like as much of him as Jared could see. The boy was midway down the row, a handful of seats next to him vacant, and to his other side several more young guys. Friends, strangers, one--improbably--the boy's lover?

Because Jared had smoked a bowl in the men's room before the concert, and because the music was loud, the bass vibrating through his soles, and because Jared often got horny at times like these, a wave of desire hit him like the wet heat when you walk outside an air-conditioned store in Florida mid-July. He had given up all pretense now, he was half-turned toward the boy, a boy who would never know that Jared was staring. And then Jared realized why his need was so intense, clenching at a crotch that threatened to get hard. Karl. Those scattered signifiers, the little bits of the dimly lit boy that Jared could see, or thought he could see, reminded him of Karl.

It had been almost 10 years ago, he and Karl had been young, still in college, though different schools. They'd been at a poetry reading, fairly tedious stuff, really, and though they'd sat in adjoining folding chairs, they were still strangers. Somewhere along the line, Jared had taken note of the boy to his right: thin, beaklike nose, pale knees sticking out through holes in his jeans. If there is such a thing as love at first sight, and not just a prettying-up of lust, then this was it. As the reader droned on about oceans or imperialism or some damn thing, Jared's young cock got hard; he shifted his shoulder bag onto his lap for discretion's sake. The stranger, aware of the attention, glanced at Jared noncommittally, then away. It didn't make any difference; Jared's dick was still stiff, imagining what the boy looked like beneath his clothes, maybe thinking about what it would feel like to kiss him. He was snapped back to attention by a phrase the poet read: "And I am powerless before great beauty." Under other circumstances that would have sounded pretentious, even laughable. But Jared, too, felt helpless. Silly, really.

There was applause, and Jared realized he should applaud too, and when the boy got up to leave, Jared knew that he would never, ever have the balls to speak to him and that he would walk home from the bookshop feeling like a hopeless, gutless fool. And then the boy turned, looked over his glasses, rolled his eyes upward, and said in a stage whisper, "Christ, wasn't that *awful?* 'Powerless before great beauty'...Clueless is more like it."

A month later, the thin boy—Karl—and Jared were living together. When people are young, they're all on the lookout for The Loves of Their Lives, and when the young people are queer, that search for adoration takes on some extra dimensions of urgency and, sometimes, desperation. Jared had only had sex with three men before Karl, and two of them didn't count. Karl, meanwhile, was an aesthete and a libertine—Jared knew next to nothing about Lord

untitled

Byron, but he thought of Karl as "Byronic" nonetheless. Sure, instead of going to Greece to help in a war of independence, Karl had frequented the men's room in the library at his college, but that, in Jared's semi-repressed eyes, just lent him an outlaw air. Once they were a couple they promised one another fidelity, but Jared found himself imaging Karl in that men's room, perhaps shirtless so his bony white torso caught the fluorescent light, kneeling in a stall, jacking his own veiny, hard cock as he sucked a stranger's hard-on that had been shoved through a hole, the kind of holes that Jared had seen in bathrooms but had never been brave enough to use; instead, he'd stuffed wadded-up toilet paper in them so no one could see him sitting on the toilet as he jerked off between art classes, thinking of the man who'd posed naked for him to draw.

Once Karl entered his life, though, Jared began to indulge his wilder fantasies, at least in a half-assed way. He had never fucked anyone before, but Karl was eager for it. When they woke up, both with morning hard-ons, Karl would skootch under the covers and put his wet mouth on Jared's balls, licking, kissing, then moving up to cock flesh, gulping all of Jared's short, thick dick right down. Sometimes Karl's tongue would move down to his hole and Jared, after initial hesitation, would let it in. When he'd teased his lover into moaning pleasure, Karl would rise, still under the covers, it being winter and their apartment being cold, and straddle Jared's body, rubbing his trim, smooth ass against hard, wet cock, then reaching back and guiding it into himself. Jared was always stupidly amazed at the ease with which Karl took his dick, figuring that he himself would never develop that talent. Karl would lean over to kiss him, a kiss that felt a million times better than he'd imagined back at that bookstore, and then sit up and ride Jared's cock. At first Jared felt a little quiver of disgust at anal sex, but Karl was so at ease with getting fucked, so enthusiastic as he rode up and down on Jared's dick, his own hard-on drooling precum, that Jared would never, ever have dared share his qualms.

His boyfriend was, Jared had to admit, much cooler than he. Karl knew all the latest songs from the hippest rock bands, he wrote poetry himself—disjointed things that Jared never fully understood but always said he liked—and had an attitude like a pot-smoking hipster, which in fact was just what Karl was. Jared couldn't figure out what Karl saw in him but, as he lay there while Karl, impaled on his hefty dick, jacked himself off and came on Jared's belly, Jared was grateful for whatever the fuck it was.

As winter thawed into spring, Jared came to understand that Karl hadn't given up cruising men's rooms, that he even let strangers fuck him while he knelt on the dirty tiles. "But," Karl said, "you know it's you that I love." And Jared did.

After dinner, which too often was ramen or mac and cheese, Karl would load his little brass pipe with grass, fire it up and take a big hit, and pass the pipe over to Jared as he went to put on the latest record by whoever. At moments like that, watching Karl tapping his foot as he tackled writing some new poem, Jared had the wonderful, scary thought that he could never, ever be more happy, more content.

This went on week after week, month after month. They graduated from college. Jared got a job teaching art. Karl worked in a bookstore and continued writing poetry. They loved each other very much.

Then one day in late August, Karl came home and said, "I got the test." Jared didn't have to ask which test. "It was positive."

Jared wondered about himself; he hadn't been tested since he met Karl, and he always figured they were both all right. "Don't worry," he said. "I'm here for you, and there are new treatments. We'll beat this together. I love you." He had a sick feeling in the pit of his stomach, like the moment when a roller coaster goes over the first hill, only worse.

The next few weeks were bad. Jared went in and got tested.

untitled

He was negative, but the doctor told him he'd have to wait half a year to be absolutely sure. It was hard for Karl and Jared to touch each other, and Karl, always subject to depression, became distant and moody.

Then one night Karl didn't come home. He didn't come home the next night either, and Jared began to get seriously worried. Nothing of Karl's was gone, just the clothes he'd been wearing. Jared went through his lover's papers, afraid he'd find a suicide note. He didn't, but he did find a poem Karl had written, scrawled in his hurried, familiar hand. It was dedicated to him. Its title was "Powerless Before Great Beauty" and it closed with the line "Boys come and go; that's what Time is about."

Two days later, unable to eat or sleep, Jared filed a missing persons report with the police. *Karl will be pissed off when he finds out,* Jared thought. *He hates the cops.* But the police could find out nothing, and Karl still was missing.

Jared forced himself to get back to day-to-day life, continuing to hope his boyfriend would return. School started again, and he once again taught children to draw and paint. He began a painting of himself on a big canvas. It started out to be an abstract, but with every stroke Jared felt that he was painting a portrait of Karl. He decided to call it "Untitled."

He felt like shit all the time, dragging himself through his days. The cold space next to him in the bed was almost more than he could bear. One evening he made a decision. He drove to Karl's college, went to the library. It was still open, but Jared almost turned around and went home. He put his hands in his pockets. His dick, he was slightly surprised to find, was hard. He went in, down to the basement, to the men's room Karl had told him about. He was more than a little scared and more than a little ashamed. One of the stalls was already occupied. Jared went into the next one and shut and bolted the door. As he'd both hoped and feared there was a hole in the wall between the stalls. He sat on the toilet fully dressed, his dick achingly hard, and stared at the opening. Within a moment an eye appeared. Jared reached reflexively for his crotch, not so much a gesture of lust as one of self-protection. The eye disappeared and a cock took its place, snaking through the roughly cut hole. It was long and rather thin and veiny, like Karl's dick. Jared hesitated for a moment, but the cock didn't retreat, so he got down on his knees and took it in his mouth. It was like sucking Karl—since he couldn't see who was on the other side, it might almost have *been* him, though of course it wasn't. But Jared felt, unexpectedly, that he himself was Karl, that he was taking his missing boyfriend's place on the bathroom floor. The unseen man was apparently primed to shoot; Jared-Karl got a taste of precum and then the cock started thrusting inside his mouth. Jared-Karl took his mouth away and put his hand on the hard-on and stroked. Four strokes later the dick shot off, big gobs of cum flying every-where, landing on his jeans and on the tiled floor. He grabbed a handful of toilet paper and wiped his pants, but he didn't bother to clean up the floor. It might have been indiscreet to leave evidence, but then, the hole was unmistakable, so it was quite obvious the college must have known what was going on in the library base-ment. Jared whispered "Thanks," and though in fact the other man probably should have been thanking *him,* there was no answer beyond the flushing of a toilet. The man left. Jared pulled out his cock and jacked off, then left the bathroom, queasily sure that any-one who saw him would know what he'd been up to. It was the first time Jared had done anything like that, and, he realized, most peo-ple would have thought he was being compulsive and self-destruc-tive. But that's not how it felt to him: The cock had been warm and reassuring and welcome in his mouth. He drove home and slept well for the first time in a month.

Several days later Jared went back to the library and sucked a beautiful black cock that smelled unpleasantly of cologne. It wasn't as good as the first time, but it was still good, as though he were placing faith in the beneficence of the universe. So he began to extend his range, driving out to the rest rooms on the interstate, where he'd spend a weekend afternoon on his knees, sucking all comers. He knew he could have taken a peek through the glory hole or beneath the partition, but that seemed beside the point. He could always imagine the person behind a proffered cock: the smelly uncut one belonged to a beer-bellied trucker; the perky, friendly-looking one was connected to a guy around his age, cute but in the closet; the hefty one that shot almost immediately was a married guy's, a clean-cut fellow who took off his wedding ring when he fucked face. Or whatever; didn't matter. He was a mouth, Karl's mouth, his own mouth, and the meat that came through the hole was just a gift because cock sucking was the very best thing.

Eventually, Karl finished the big painting. It had taken on the traces of Karl's eyes, his nervous smile, but he left it "Untitled." It had been months since Karl had disappeared, and he decided to accept reality and get rid of his things. Not throw them out, just put them in storage, out of sight. As he packed the clothes, the books, and the poetry-filled notebooks into cardboard cartons, tears rolled down his cheeks. While he was packing, he opened one of the books, poetry by the queer Greek poet Cavafy. He read Karl's favorite. It began hopefully: "You said: 'I'll go to some other place, some other sea, find a place better than this one...'" But it ended glumly, fatalistically: "Just as you've ruined your life here, in this small corner, you've destroyed it now everywhere in the whole world." Jared put the book into the carton and sealed the box with tape.

The years came and the years went and Jared's hope that he'd see Karl again, that he was still somewhere on Earth to be seen, faded steadily. He continued his cock sucking, though when the cops began busting men at the roadside rest stops, he started frequenting the men's rooms of department stores instead, then the video arcades of dirty bookstores, places that stank of Lysol and lust. Improbably, he met a man in a rest room whom he began to date. That lasted almost a year, but sometimes when he was fucking Colin, Jared wished he were fucking Karl instead. They ended the affair by mutual consent; later, it turned out that Colin had also been seeing an older man, an obstetrician. Jared wished them both well.

And now, back at the concert, the band was finishing its set, waving to the audience, walking offstage. There was the usual clamor for an encore, stamping feet that shook the balcony. The band came back on stage, played two of their hits, shambled off again and the lights came up. Jared stared at the boy. It turned out he didn't look much like Karl, not at all. That was a relief, in a way. As the audience headed into the aisle, then down the stairs, Jared maneuvered himself so he was always near the young man he'd been watching. The boy was, it seemed, by himself; the guys next to him had gone off in another direction. The crowd was heading for the door. It was now or never. What the hell.

"Good concert," Jared said.

No response.

"Good concert," he repeated, louder to be heard above the crowd's noise.

"Huh?" the boy said, semi-startled a stranger was talking to him. "Oh, yeah, great."

The boy looked at Jared. Astonishing dark eyes, not blue like Karl's. Jared felt a tightening desire in his belly. He wanted to look into those eyes while the boy and he shot their loads, but how likely was that, really? He realized he was on a fool's errand, that there was no reason to think the boy would be interested in him. Helpless before beauty indeed.

"So what're you up to now?" the boy asked. Oh, my god, those eyes.

untitled

What should he say? Didn't want to scare the boy off, but didn't want to play it too cool either. "Not much." They were out on the sidewalk now, among the stoned and milling crowd. "You want to hang out for a while?" Jared asked.

"Got to get home." Of course. The boy looked straight at him. "You queer?" he asked.

Jared blushed. Christ, was he really that obvious? Had the kid clocked the swelling in his pants? "Yeah," he said, "I am."

"Cool, so am I," said the boy.

Silence.

At last—it must have been all of 20 seconds—Jared, ears still ringing from the concert, said, "Well, I should get going too, I guess."

"Too bad. I thought I might invite you to come home with me." He reached up and stroked Jared's face. "I'd have loved to suck your cock."

Jared, who'd just seen his guilty fantasy come true, was stunned by how easily things had gone. But before he could say anything, the boy blushed, surprisingly and delightfully, and turned away. Jared watched stupidly as the boy made his way through the crowd. *Wait!* he wanted to shout. *I wasn't turning you down!* He could just stand there, or...

It wasn't hard to catch up with him.

And Jared and the boy who was not Karl walked off together into the electric night.

thesweetheartofsigmaqueer

"Suck my cock," I said, and he did. Not the best I've had, but good, very good, and anyway the whole situation kind of excited me. He opened wide and took my dick as far down his throat as he could. I moaned. His tongue did a little dance on the underside of my shaft, and this time I moaned for real.

"That's it," I said. "That's a good, hungry cocksucker." He nursed on my flesh a little more, then pulled away, raised himself up, threw his arms around me, kissed me on the lips. I kissed back.

"Hot," he said when the kiss had ended. "Really hot."

I like to know the guys I have sex with. It's a stupid trait, one that's gotten me into trouble any number of times, but there it is. "How'd you get into..."

"This?"

"Yeah, this," I said.

He lay back, one hand lazily stroking my damp hard-on.

"In high school I always felt like an outsider, and a queer outsider at that. So when I went off to college, I wanted to feel like I belonged. I suppose I still do." He smiled up at me. "My dad had gone to the same university and I really wanted to join the frat he'd been in. So I felt real lucky when, after the bid party, I was invited to pledge. The fraternity brothers were a bunch of straight guys, a lot of them jocks, and though I wasn't exactly that, I guess I passed."

He'd taken his hand off my hard-on. I guided it back and he jacked me off as he continued.

"There'd been a hazing scandal a couple of years before—somebody had nearly died—so the stuff we pledges were put through was more humiliating than anything else. You know the kind of thing: 'Turn around, drop your pants, and bend over.' It's a funny thing about mooning: It can be read as a sign of contempt, but it's also submissive behavior, proffering your ass to an alpha male."

The guy was an intellectual, no fucking doubt about that. I got my fingers wet with spit and reached down to his ass, proffered or not, and began to rub his softly puckered hole.

"Should I stop talking?"

"No, keep going," I said. What the hell.

He smiled and snuggled up to me, his hand still working my cock. "After the trou-dropping the brothers brought out a box of women's lingerie and had us pledges strip down and put them on. We had to walk from the frat house to the quad that way. And back. I can remember what I had to wear, a silky black slip and matching panties.

"I guess I looked good in lingerie; I was accepted into the frat. I moved into a room with my Big Brother, Tony. He was a business major and kind of a jock, but not offensively so, and we got along just fine. In fact, the whole fraternity thing was pretty good. Sure, I was surrounded by straight boys, and sure, some of them could be assholes, but most of them were actually nice. Of course, they didn't know I was queer. I was really closeted then and I wasn't about to let on to the brothers that I wanted to suck their dicks."

"There wasn't a gay frat on campus?" I asked.

"Honey, this was the deep South, okay? Ten years ago?"

"Okay." My fingers were pressing into his moist hole now. I wanted to fuck it. I wanted to fuck *him*.

"Then one night we held a big kegger. I admit it—I was pretty drunk. We all were. Over in one corner, Tony and his girlfriend were having what seemed like a heated argument; it looked like he wasn't going to get laid *that* night. Everybody else was dancing or groping or, like me, just chugging down brews. And a few of the brothers had stripped off their shirts, including this guy named Bret, all muscles and chin. I really had the hots for him. Okay, he was pretty much an unredeemable straight jerk, but with Bret I didn't want discourse, I wanted intercourse. With all that sweaty, liquored-up flesh around, I found myself with a fairly unmanageable hard-on, so I excused myself and went up to my room. I had just gotten down to jacking off when the door opened. Apparently I'd been too blasted to properly lock it. It was my Big, Tony, and he'd caught me with my pants down. Literally. I didn't know what to expect, but I was honestly a bit surprised when he just stood there with a broad, drunken grin. Then he locked the door, unzipped his pants, and slurred, 'Do me instead. I'm so fuckin' goddamn horny.' I'd seen him naked of course, and I knew he had a nice cock, but I'd never seen it hard before. Now his prick was standing up like an open invitation, and it didn't take long for me to accept. Tony stood there for maybe a minute while I knelt, sucking him off, and then he gave a grunt, started pounding into my mouth, and came down my throat. I was still on my knees when he zipped back up, looking down at me with what probably was an appreciative smile—they do say that straight guys are the biggest fans of getting blown. Then he headed back to the party, leaving me and my hard-on to fend for ourselves."

He paused and looked at me uncertainly. I really wanted to put my dick inside him, but I also was a bit curious. "What happened next?" I asked.

"Oh, Tony treated it like one of those 'Boy, was I drunk last night' things. But then I started servicing him on a regular basis. We never discussed it; I just sucked him off when he needed it. I hadn't had much sex before that, so it made me nervous, excited, and a bit ashamed, all rolled up into one. But I sure did like the fact that my roomie wanted to fuck my face.

"Then one night, shortly before Christmas break, when Tony had gone north on a weekend ski trip, there was a knock at my door. It was Bret, smelling like the Heineken brewery. 'Listen, Keith,' he said. And then nothing; the hunky guy was tongue-tied. At last he got it out: 'Don't get the wrong idea, okay? I'm straight, but...well, Tony says you give the best blow jobs he's ever had.'

"I fucking almost fainted. I couldn't believe that my Big had told anyone about me. After all, it seemed like self-preservation would have meant his keeping quiet, right? But then I realized that if I was just a mouth to him, a mouth he could fuck, then he could get his rocks off and still keep his straight credentials intact. He could think of himself as a totally het boy who just liked being sucked off by another guy, and who knows, maybe he was. And now here was Bret, the muscled object of my fevered affections, and he wanted to be serviced too. I know—if I had a shred of self-respect, I probably would have said no. But...well...you know..."

"I think I do," I said, twisting two fingers inside his ass. Just how long was this story, anyway?

"I didn't say anything, so Bret must have figured—rightly, as it turned out—that I'd be happy to suck him off. He held out a gym bag he'd brought. 'Listen, can you put this stuff on? It will make it, um, easier for me,' he said, sounding more like a little boy than I'd have expected. Inside the bag was the black slip I'd worn during hazing. Not the black panties, though. The ones he'd brought were light blue jobbies, very sheer. I couldn't believe it. See, what Bret couldn't have known, what I never would have told anyone, was that I'd found wearing lingerie exciting. Hazing was the first and only time I'd put on women's stuff, but on that walk through campus, I'd barely been able to keep my hard dick from jumping out of those panties. And in the months since I'd pledged, I'd often jacked off to thoughts of being naked except for silky underwear, surrounded by straight guys with hard dicks. So when Bret held out the lingerie I eagerly stripped down, pulled on the slip and powder blue panties, and got down on my knees. 'That's it,' Bret said, 'suck me like you were a girl.' Bret's dick wasn't as prepossessing as the rest of his body, so even with my minimal experience I had no problem deep-throating him. He grabbed my head, muttered, 'Eat it, bitch,' and shot his load in my mouth. And that was that; I'd sucked off the man of my dreams. 'Put the clothes back in the bag,' he said. The slip was light as a cloud in my trembling hands. The crotch of the panties was soaked through. 'And don't tell anybody about this,' he warned. Like I would. After Bret left I jacked off so hard my dick was sore all the next day."

He spit on his hand and went to work on my cock. It felt so damn good that my growing impatience vanished. Almost. But he wasn't finished talking yet.

"That was it. I didn't see Bret again before I left for winter break. I figured that he'd gotten himself some pussy and forgotten about me. But only a few days after I got back to campus, he came over to me, looking a little shy—which on him looked just plain strange—and said, 'Want to go for a pizza or something? My treat.' And so he started using me on a regular basis—in my room when Tony was gone, his room when his roommate was out. Once I even sucked him off in the men's room at the library, but without the lingerie it wasn't as good. Tony kept fucking my face too, I guess when he couldn't get otherwise laid. But it was Bret I really wanted. It wasn't because of who he was, really, it wasn't even his looks. It was because of, well, me. I needed him. I wanted to be pretty for him. I wanted to be pretty so someone would love me."

He looked in my eyes with an expression so pure, so vulnerable that it made me ache. It made me want to come. It made me want to screw him.

"Finally, one night, it happened. Tony was spending the night at his latest girlfriend's house, so I invited Bret over. He brought a fifth of Cuervo and a teddy, garters, and stockings. 'I want you to look like a whore,' he said, taking a big gulp from the bottle.

" 'A pretty whore,' I told Bret, hardly believing I was saying it. '*Your* pretty whore.'

"Bret took out a condom. 'Don't want to catch anything from some faggot, do I, slut?' he said. I couldn't get words out. I just shook my head. And then he pulled his foreskin back, unrolled the rubber, and lubed up. 'Fag, I'm going to fuck you good,' he said. And he did.

"I hadn't been fucked before and it hurt at first, hurt pretty bad when he shoved his way inside me as I lay there on my back, big strong Bret between my stockinged legs. But I managed to take it, threw my arms around him, and his strokes became less brutal. That's when he looked at me blearily and said, 'I love you.' I couldn't believe it. 'I love you, Keith.' Just like that. I felt, well, I felt so damn pretty."

I was beginning to get more than a little annoyed. I wanted to fuck Keith too, just like Bret the frat boy had, but the story obviously meant a lot to him, so I lay there, him in my arms, my fingers up his ass, as he continued.

"That was the only time he said that. In fact, he started to seem more distant, we had sex less frequently. But then, it's hard to have a secret affair with someone who's in the same frat house. I can't say I really loved him, not even a little bit. Even then I didn't think so. But I couldn't shake the feeling that I somehow belonged to him, or at least a part of him. Hell, I don't know, maybe I did love him in a way.

"And then one night I was at the pizza place. I overheard some guys a couple of tables over, talking. I really wasn't eavesdropping; they were loudmouths. 'So ever since that girls' underwear stunt, some guys have been calling your house Sigma Queer,' one of them said. And then the reply, 'Dude, it's not the house that's gay.

Nobody knows that better than me. It's just this one brother, a guy named Keith. He's nice enough, I suppose, but he's a real big faggot.' I recognized the voice; I didn't have to turn and see who was talking, but I did look. It was Bret, his back toward me, and the other guys at the table were all laughing and grinning. I ran out in the street, a slice of pepperoni pizza still in my hand.

"A few days later Bret showed up at my door. I shouldn't have let him in, I guess, but I did. I put on the slip he'd brought. He shoved me down onto the bed, got me on all fours, and pushed the lacy hem up around my waist, and I let him fuck me. I *wanted* him to fuck me, and he used my ass hard. Somewhere in the middle, Tony came back. He sat there watching until Bret shot his load, and then he fucked me too. After it was over I lay there in the dark, wanting someone to love me and crying myself to sleep, but that didn't stop me from jacking off the next day when I remembered being fucked by both Tony and Bret.

"Finally, a week or two after that, I kind of realized I'd had enough. I was having a snack in the kitchen of the house when Bret showed up with another frat brother, a senior, a husky dude who always acted real tough. His name, if you can believe it, was Jimbo. He looked at me and said, 'I'm fucking horny and I hear you'll let anybody fuck your ass.' I couldn't stand the guy's attitude. I told him, 'You heard wrong.' 'Bitch,' Bret said. And then Jimbo spat on me, actually spat on me. And that was it. I decided it was time to move out."

And *I'd* decided it was time for Keith to put out. Enough. I had let him tell his story, and now my reward was past due. I pushed him back on the bed and climbed on top of him.

"All I wanted was to be pretty," he said.

"You *are* pretty, " I said, and I meant it. I ran my hand over his legs, over the black mesh stockings, up to the garter belt. He moaned and spread his legs. My fingers moved to his silky red crotchless panties. My dick was as hard as it gets. I reached over for a rubber.

"You don't have to use that," he said, but I did use it. I didn't want to bring something home, not from a whore like him.

I pushed his legs in the air, my hands against his stockings, his taut muscles beneath. His bigger-than-average dick was stiff against his belly, leaking precum. I slapped some lube on his hole, so wet it was soaking his crotchless panties, then positioned my dick head up against his pussy.

"Pretty," he said. "I want to be pretty for you."

And I slid all the way inside him and started fucking his cunt. His insides felt great, all warm and yielding and wet. I reached under his slip, grabbed one of his little nipples and tweaked it hard. He closed his eyes and licked his lips. Like a slut. Slut. I rammed into his hole, banging him, making him squirm and moan.

"Hurt me with your dick."

"You bet, you little fucking bitch." And I screwed him as hard as I could.

Pretty. He was so pretty. So pretty and fucked up and willing. And good sex, such a good, good fuck.

Much better than my wife.

home

"I think all families are creepy in a way."
—Diane Arbus

Robby looked around, feeling like he was going to choke, like he was going to scream. Everything was perfect, perfect in a perfectly upper-middle-class way. Spotless. Well-furnished. As germ-free as Lysol could make it. His parents' house was a showplace on Heathercote Drive, but all he wanted to do was run through all its tasteful rooms, his hard dick hanging out, and shoot big globs of cum all over the oatmeal-colored sofas, the oriental rugs, the tasteful prints on the wall, the framed pictures of himself from his youth, back when his parents could think they knew who he was and actually come close to the mark. He'd been a beautiful child, and now he was a handsome young man who was, at least for the moment, desperately unhappy. He went into his bedroom, closed the door, and though his parents were at some stupid party, locked it. He reached into what he prayed was a secure hiding place and pulled out his stash of porn magazines.

The pages with his favorite models were easy to find—he'd thumbed through them dozens of times before. He really liked the pictures of muscular men in their 30s, lying on their backs and spreading their legs in the air in order to show off their assholes. Robby arranged a few of the open magazines on the bed, a little parade of tumescent flesh, and pulled off his sweatpants and briefs.

He really hated it in his parents' house. He was in college now, he should leave home, but, but, but... Robby was a smart kid; he knew that as parents went, his weren't all that bad. Didn't matter. He couldn't stand them, and he figured that was his right. He hated his furry blond legs too; someday he would shave them. Someday. He grabbed his limp cock and started jacking off, growing harder as he stared at the puckered holes of the musclemen, soft gateways into the contrived armor of their perfect bodies, a visible admission that they were (presumably) fags who (also presumably) wanted to get fucked.

Looking at one of the models in particular, one with dark curly hair and bright blue eyes, always made Robby feel there was some sort of connection there, that if only he and "Rod Caldwell" could somehow meet, there would be no question of Robby sliding his hard, curved dick into that hole, that puckered invitation, and fucking the hell out of the guy. Robby had never done that, fucked anyone, had never been fucked either, not by anybody. But he figured it would happen someday. Fuck, it had to.

The phone rang. He let it ring. On days like these, when he wanted to escape so hard he could punch the walls, the best thing he could think of to do was jack off. Once, twice, three times a day, till his cock grew red and raw. Oh, fuck, that Caldwell guy was hot. His asshole was hot, the way his big balls hung down, the way how in other photos you could see his foreskin still half-covering his cock head even though he was hard. Rod Caldwell. Rod Caldwell.

He spit in his hand and circled his palm around his own cock head, bringing on waves of intense sensation. Often he'd go on the Internet, talk dirty with older men in chat rooms, download porn pictures. But he'd started his jack-off career with a stack of *Blueboys* he'd fished out of someone's dumpster, and there was still something reassuring about beating off to the printed page.

You weren't supposed to dislike your parents, not unless they did something awful to you. Was being boring, obtuse, and self-absorbed "awful?" The silences *were* awful, but often the talking was worse. Fuck, how could a life so obviously beautiful, so comfortable, an existence most people in this miserable world could not dream of hoping for, be so fucking awful? What an ingrate he was. What an ungrateful closeted faggot son. That's what he was, the kind of boy who'd slip his finger up his asshole, then take it out and sniff it, imagining it was the smell of the muscular butt on page 42 of *Hot Hung Dudes* magazine. Tough. Just tough.

He licked his finger. It tasted like his insides. He knew that some men licked each other's assholes; he'd seen plenty of pictures on the Web. At first it had seemed disgusting, something he'd never do. Now, when he jacked himself off every night before falling sleep in his very expensive bed, he'd fantasize about that, about eating ass. Not clean, not clean like his home, his parents' house. Dirty, funky, out of control. Fuck. Fuck, fuck, fuck.

He had to get out of there. He would. As soon as he had the money, he'd leave. In the meantime, he'd pull another couple of magazines out of their hiding place, the rougher ones, with pictures of men in leather doing unimaginably hot things to each other, and he'd beat off some more. Looking at those images of tough men, the nasty stuff they did, he felt a surge of strength himself. An uninvited image of his parents driving their Lexus off a cliff flashed through his mind, then a pang of guilt, and suddenly he felt not strong, but weak. And tired, as if it were all he could do to keep up stroking his cock while looking at a man shoving a fist up another man's ass. Shove a fist. Yes. Shove a fucking fist, and he'd be free. *Would* be free, someday, someday soon. Why was he such a weak little fuck? Somebody should fuck *his* ass, and if his body wasn't muscular, if it was just ordinary, that didn't mean that no one would ever want to fuck him, did it? Did it?

Once when he'd been very mad and frustrated, he'd smeared a thin film of his own cum on one of the dinner plates, let it dry and

home

put it back, then made sure he wasn't the one to eat off it. Pathetic. Not because it wasn't fun; it had been. But because his rebellion was so...faggotty.

He knew there was a great big world out there, a world where there were men who fucked and fisted each other, and not just when they were being paid to pose for magazines. A life where safety wasn't all, where clean didn't count, where guys did all sorts of crazy things in search of cock. Robby wasn't dumb. He knew all that, and he knew that someday, with luck, it would be his life and if he didn't wipe down the kitchen each and every time he made a fucking sandwich, he—and the world—would survive just fine.

He flipped a page: two men, one standing behind the other, his hand around the shoulders of the man in front, pulling the other's gorgeous body into a backward arc, the man in rear's unseen dick presumably nailing asshole while the guy in front, hand on his own cock, was shooting cum—the camera actually caught the spurt. It was one of Robby's favorite photos, and he decided to beat off to it again. He concentrated on the two men, how they must sound, must smell, must feel to each other, and for a moment he blotted everything else out, he was just lust and anger and lust, so he barely heard the SUV pulling into the drive, though by the time the front door opened and closed, Robby had, well-practiced, shot a load of sperm into a welter of tissues, wiped up, pulled on his pants, stuffed the magazines back in their hiding place, and become, once again, once again, a good son.

bodie,blackeddie,andthefriscoquake

Wintertime in the mountains is always brutal, brutal as hell. You never do get used to it, you never forget it. I left godless Bodie many years back, but those whiteout Januaries still whistle through my bones. There was only one reason to be in that Helldorado, and that was the Standard Mine and the gold it brought up from the cold, hard ground, the gold that we poor-dog diggers brought up, day after backbreaking, perilous day. For every dollar we miners made, the mine owners made 10. But that was just the way of it, and as Texas Joe oft proclaimed, "Gold, boys, is what it's all about."

My last New Year's Eve there was clear and windy, so cold you couldn't hardly stay outside for a minute or thereabouts, lest the wind off the mountains freeze your flesh and steal your life. So we wrapped ourselves up as best we could and hurried on over to the Royal Flush Saloon, our boots crunching through the crusty snow.

At the best of times—even Easter Sunday morning—the Royal Flush was a rough and rowdy place, but on New Year's Eve, every man was raising perdition itself. By the time me and my buddies get there, all and sundry are roaring drunk and the whores are doing turn-away business.

Comes to that, Madame Mustache, one of the gurdy girls, is leaning right up against the bar with her hand down the front of Cal Callahan's pants. And Cal, who's slugging down the panther piss, don't seem to mind at all when Madame Mustache, in front of everyone and God, unbuttons his fly and just pulls out the thing itself and works it hard. As the piano rolls and the whiskey flows, me and my three buddies get hot, hotter, and horny as Christ and the angels.

"Let's get us some cunt," says Lefty.

"Looks like all the cunt is busy," Hiram tells him.

"Well then, fuck 'em, let's dance," Lefty roars, downing another shot.

So we choose up for who's going to be girls, and Hiram and me tie kerchiefs round our arms since we're to be the ladies this time. And off to trip the light we go, Hiram in Lefty's arms and Texas Joe leading me. The dance floor is crowded as a stockyard in June, almost all men excepting for two or three crib girls taking a break from their duties upstairs.

Texas Joe's a nice enough fellow, although always horny and he never takes a bath. And tonight Texas Joe's getting real drunk indeed and while we're awhirl around the jam-packed saloon, he grabs my ass and holds me close and then closer, and tarnation if he doesn't have a big stiff one that he keeps jamming up against me, rubbing that thing on my leg like he's some mangy dog, which in a manner of speaking he is.

"Holy hell," Texas Joe says, "I'm so fucking horny I could fuck a handful of mud. If it wasn't all frozen fucking solid." He laughs like a liquored-up loon. He's got me held tight against him now, and there might be some folks who would mind, prudes and good Christians and suchlike, but on New Year's Eve in Bodie, there's no one awake who could give a fuck. And the truth of it is that I stumbled onto Texas Joe jacking off one summer's night behind the tailings, and he's got a nice big rod that I figure would be mighty fine to fool around with.

So I say, "Hey, Texas Joe, all the whores are busy and I bet nobody's back at the lodging house. So why don't you and me head on back, and I'll give you what you need."

"For real?"

"For real."

"Well, Happy Fucking New Year!"

"Happy Fucking New Year!" some of the other miners yell back as Texas Joe drags me out the door.

By the time we get to in front of the church, Texas Joe's staggering badly, but nonetheless he's got a hot hand down my drawers, working my balls into a lather. For someone who's always loudly proclaiming his love of snatch, Texas Joe sure knows how to give a hand job, but then I reckon he should know how, since he's always practicing on himself. Shit, I'd like to get down on my knees and blow him right there, but his big, frozen prong would most likely snap off in my mouth like an icicle.

So I'm thinking not-unpleasant thoughts about big Texas Joe getting me under his hairy, smelly body, when all of a sudden he gets the heaves and starts puking onto the snow. And then he grunts and passes out, sprawled right across the icy steps of the church.

"C'mon, Texas Joe," says I, "we got to get you inside where it's warm." I struggle to get him to his feet, but my boots keep sliding in the vomit-covered snow, and my poor hands were like to freeze.

"Can I help?" asks a voice, and I look up to see a fine-dressed young gentleman with hair the color of summer wheat. His eyes meet mine, and when they do he gives a little shiver, though whether it's from the cold or something else, I cannot tell.

So then he takes one arm and I take the other and we push and drag Texas Joe till we get him back to the miners' lodging house, which is plumb empty on account of all the boys being out raising hell. When we get him dumped into his filthy cot, my newfound helper smiles and says, "My name is Lars."

"Well, Lars," I say, after offering my name in trade, "thank you most kindly for helping me get Texas Joe back here." At which moment, as though he heard himself mentioned, Joe moans loudly and loses his guts again, all over his bed.

Lars, still smiling, says to me, "Surely you won't want to spend the night here." Sniffing the air, I can only agree. "Why not come back to my room at the Grand Central Hotel?" The Grand Central being the most high-class lodging that Bodie has to offer.

"Thank you kindly, Mr. Lars, but I was figuring I'd go back and carouse at the Royal Flush a while, at least until the stroke of midnight brings in the year."

"Well, I'm not a drinking man myself," says he, "but perhaps you could walk me back to my hotel and then be on your way."

So we set off from the reeking lodging house, and as we hurry over the board sidewalks, my companion tells me how he's come to be in Bodie. He was born in Norway, son of an already wealthy father whose investments in the Standard Mining Company had lately repaid him manyfold. While his father counted his money in his fine new San Francisco mansion, Lars was sent out to oversee the vicissitudes of the family's business. He'd lately spent time in Leadville, and then the Comstock, before making his way to Bodie, which he reached in December just before the Great Storm crashed down, stranding all of us and killing a few.

As we near the Grand Central Hotel, whoops and hollers from the nearby saloons rend the freezing air. In the near distance, two men are fighting in front of the new Bella Union Gambling House, where us miners play faro and Spanish monte until dawn. The next day, I will hear that Tom Dillon stabbed Thomas Travis, and that as Travis was dying, he raised his pistol and shot his assailant clean through the heart.

The Grand Central Hotel is as fine a place as I've ever been in. The lobby's ablaze with light, and the splendid dining hall is filled with well-dressed celebrants. One angelic little girl, no older than 10, is standing on a table, leading the multitude in a chorus of "Take Back the Ring You Gave Me." It certainly is not in no wise the Royal Flush.

The desk clerk, nose in the air, looks at me like we both know perfectly well I don't belong, but changes his tune when Lars says, "He's with me," and slips him a silver dollar.

"So, my friend, can I not invite you up to my room to drink a New Year's toast?" And indeed, when he looks at me with his piercing blue eyes, it seems a fair enough prospect.

Reappearing moments later, a glass of champagne in each hand, he leads me up the sweeping staircase and shows me into his lodgings.

His room is cold, so he feeds the stove before we raise our glasses and toast the year of our Lord 1890. When we've drained our glasses dry, he says, "It still is mighty cold in here. Perhaps we can share the bed until the room is warmer."

Without another word he removes his expensive calfskin boots and I take off my gamier pair, and soon we're lying face-to-face on the starched white sheets of the feather bed, beneath the heaped-up blankets. I can feel his breath upon me as he reaches up to stroke my face. Oh, how my heart does beat!

"There is something I have not yet told you," he says softly to me. "When I was in Leadville, some bandits robbed the mining office whilst I worked there. As they went about their dirty business, they took some rope and tied me firmly to a chair so that I could not interfere. I was frightened, of course, but also strangely excited by the experience."

I did not yet see why he chose this time to tell me this tale.

"And since then..." He hesitates. "Since then I have been wanting to relive that, to be tied up again by a strong, rough man...a man like you."

As he speaks these words, my loins stir to their fullest extent.

"But we haven't the ropes and gear," says I.

"Oh, but I do, in that traveling bag over there. I've tried using them upon myself, but it hasn't been near the same."

Well, sir, as you can imagine, I get up and open the luggage, which contains a large quantity of rope as well as some leather straps and thongs. I have never heard an odder request in all my days, but I surely am game to give it a go.

I tell him, "Sit in that chair over there." Which he does with alacrity. He closes his eyes and is unmoving, breathing nervously. Standing behind him, I roughly pull his hands behind the chair's back, wrapping a rope several times around his trembling wrists, securing it with a square knot. As he makes no complaint, I take one of the straps and draw it around his upper arms, pulling it tight and buckling it so's his chest is thrust forward. At this he begins to softly moan.

"Did I hurt you?" I ask.

"Not at all. Not at all," says he. "I beg you continue."

So I kneel to remove his stockings, rolling up his trouser legs to expose his pale ankles. I grab one naked foot and lift it off the ground, using a rope to secure it to a rung of the chair. I tie the other smooth, bare foot to the chair, leaving his knees spread wide. Already he is pretty damn helpless, but I take another rope and wind it around his thighs, at which I can't help but notice the stiff bulk of his John Thomas pressing up against the fabric of his trousers.

When I've made sure that the rope securing his thighs to the chair is nice and tight, I stand back to admire my handiwork. He seems trussed up pretty good, straining against the ropes and groaning. You can see just by looking in his eyes that he's plumb hungry for it.

"I could do just about anything to you that I wanted, couldn't I?" says I with a growl. "Anything I wanted." And this, rather than frightening him, only seems to excite him all the more. I rip off the buttons of his shirt. His pale white chest exposed to me, I run my hands over the golden hairs till I feel his nipples and give them a fearsome tweaking. He jumps at first, but as I squeeze harder yet he whispers fervently, "Oh, yes!"

Reaching down, I unbuckle his belt and pull open his trousers. The shape of his stiff rod shows plainly through the flannel of his underwear, and when I free it from its constraints, it leaps up quite boldly, a shiny pearl of moisture at its pointy tip.

"Time to truss you up real good, I reckon," I say, which brings a smile to his pretty lips. I use a long piece of rope to fasten his torso to the chair, wrapping it around and around, tightening it so that the rope presses firmly against the bare flesh of his chest.

Then I get a leather thong out of the bag and slowly wind it around the base of his hard rod, going around his balls till the sac is stretched out pretty good, then wrapping it around the shaft till it's all nicely tied up. I then take the end of that long thong and secure it to a coat hook on the wall opposite, so his privates are cruelly stretched out and under constant tension.

"That should hold you," says I, walking out the door.

I go downstairs, past the sniffy clerk, and out into the frozen, moonlit night. Within several minutes I'm back at the Royal Flush, where the party has gotten even wilder. Lefty's sprawled in a corner, a drunken whore on his lap, him working his hand up under her skirts, while Hiram is being whirled round the floor by Big Owen the blacksmith. I go over to Hiram and speak loudly, so as to be heard above the tumult.

"So you haven't had a turn with one of the girls yet, Hiram?"

"No I ain't," says Hiram, voice slurred with whiskey, "and I'm goddamn horny as hell." He reaches down and gives his substantial crotch a squeeze.

"Well, come with me then, for I've a pleasant surprise for you."

We're back at the Grand Central Hotel moments later, and this time the desk clerk doesn't even look our way. When I fling open the door to Lars's room, Hiram is surely surprised. "Well, I'll be damned! What the hell?"

"I've roped this critter, and now I mean to ride him. Care to join me?"

Well, sir, Lars is sitting there with a real dreamy look on his face, softly straining against the ropes that hold him to the chair, and that long prong of his is still hard as a rock.

"Shit, let's get him onto the bed," says Hiram.

So we untie him and, Hiram at his head and me at his feet, carry him over to the four-poster.

"Heads up or face down?" asks Hiram.

"Heads up. At first."

We get him stretched out on the bed and tie his wrists and ankles to the bedposts, tugging now and then to make sure his naked body is good and taut.

"You ready to be ridden, rich boy?"

"Oh, Jesus," moans Lars, "I'm more than ready."

So Hiram and I pull down our britches. I guess I shouldn't be surprised that Hiram's big red cock is stiff and ready for action. "You want him first?" he asks. I tell my pal to go on ahead. With a grunt, he climbs up on the bed, straddles Lars's chest, and slips his big old bone into the Norwegian's open mouth, pumping himself into his throat.

Meantime, I spit into my hand and wet down my fingers real good then reach up between the blond's slender thighs, fingering apart the cheeks of his butt till I feel the heat of his tight hole. He presses down onto my fingers, taking two of them deep inside. As I drive them home, his trussed-up dick jumps and starts oozing juice.

"Tarnation, this feels good," Hiram moans, his hairy buttocks pumping as he slides in and out of the boy's mouth. I lick a finger of my free hand, get it good and wet, and slide it down the crack of Hiram's ass. The muscles resist at first, but soon my finger is deep inside, and it just makes Hiram even lustier.

When he looks over his shoulder, Hiram's all red in the face. "I feel like I'm going to spew any time now. If you want to flip him over, we'd best do it now."

I slide my fingers out of both men's asses, and Hiram pulls his thing out of our host's mouth. We untie Lars from the bedposts and get him onto his belly. Lying face down in the lantern light, his pale naked body looks like drifts of snow.

"Lift up your fucking head," Hiram says, and he sits at the head of the bed, legs spread wide, Lars's head between his big, hairy thighs. "Now suck me some more." Which the blond man does without a bit of hesitation.

I cinch Lars's wrists and ankles back again to the bedposts, then lower myself down between his spread-eagle legs and ease myself into his butt, the red-hot, wet pleasure of it. I pump away into him, enjoying the sight of the coils of rope winding round his wrists, pressing roughly into his smooth, white flesh.

And just then a tremendous ruckus erupts outside, men firing guns into the air and hollering "Happy New Year." Hiram grabs Lars's fine blond head in both his calloused hands, pushes it hard into his crotch, and shoots off into the rich boy's throat. And I, seeing the look on Hiram's face, can hold back no more and plow a jism-filled load deep into that snowy ass.

Well, as you can imagine, it takes a minute for us all to catch our breath, and then Lars looks up, spunk still dripping from the corner of his mouth, and smiles. "Happy New Year, boys," says he with a big ol' wet grin.

At that I suddenly feel kind of melancholy, remembering the folks I'd left behind when I came to Bodie. Here it is New Year's Eve, and here we all are in a lawless, godforsaken hole, colder than hell, far from family and childhood friends. But then Lars claps his hand on my shoulder, and I can't help but grin too. And suddenly Bodie don't seem so cold after all.

bodie,blackeddie,andthefriscoquake

In such a like manner we were to continue, Lars and me and often Hiram and sometimes Cal Callahan as well, once a week or more, until the coming of spring, which brought with it a golden blanket of poppies amid the awful muck of snowmelt. Oh, to be sure, there were those among the men who, divining my time spent with Lars, would grumble, seeing as how he was so rich and our boss, to boot. But I did not tie him up to curry favor. I just know when a man treats me well, and that's a fact. For when all's said and done, rich or poor, our cocks make us equal in the end.

The vernal season brought with it, along with the mud, young Father O'Rourke, who on account of it being the time of the Resurrection, came up from San Francisco to save us miners' souls. He was preaching his Easter sermon to pews full to bursting, being as how it was unseasonably freezing and the church was, aside from the whorehouse, the warmest place in town. But when O'Rourke got to decrying the foul pleasures of the flesh, Texas Joe, who was as drunk as he was ornery, having not slowed down imbibing since Saturday afternoon, stood up and bellowed, "Priest, if you was stuck up here during these goddamn winters, I bet you'd fuck anything that would let you, just like we all do." The ensuing ruckus led to Joe's being vigorously escorted out of the church, while yelling something that sounded like "you fuckhead Bible-spouting cunt" as he went. The service was thereby cut rather short, Father O'Rourke taking quick leave without so much as a final blessing. He headed back to San Francisco the next day, where he eventually rose to be a bishop, but that's a tale that's yet to come.

It was just two weeks after that Easter when the cave-in at the Standard Mine killed Texas Joe and 10 or 12 other fellers as well. And though this made me sad, well, life is full of sorrow and a vale of tears, and there's not much a man can do but lace up his boots and go on living. Life has taught me few enough lessons, but it's taught me that.

So spring turned to summer, and Independence Day rolled around. The mines are shut down for the day, and damn near every man in town is drunk as a hillbilly at a rooster fight, including Sheriff Kowalski. And the talk of the whole damn inebriated town is the arm wrestling contest to be held that night at the New Bella Union Gambling Hall.

Now, men have rode in from miles around for July Fourth in Bodie, amongst them a great grizzly of a man, Josiah Britt by name, who, rumor has it has killed more than one man barehanded by the simple snapping of the poor feller's spine. Well over 6 1/2 feet tall, Britt has been strutting around shirtless all day, the sweat on the matted black hair of his chest and belly sparkling in the warm light of Helios. And unsurprisingly, Cal, already in his cups, has been seen lurking around the big man, hands in his pockets stroking a hard-on that's lasted for nigh on the whole afternoon.

"I figure I can beat any man around," says Britt, cocky as the king of spades. And in demonstration he holds up his right arm and makes a giant muscle, all impressive as fuck, though the smell from his sweat-soaked armpit damn near knocks the bunch of us flat, and we're men who are used to stench.

"I would be most willing to wager," says Lars, "a substantial sum on your doing just that." Lars usually ain't much of a gambling man, but face-to-face with Britt he's got a twinkle in his eye, which gets a mite stronger as his gaze slides south of Britt's belt.

The Bella Union has dug a big barbecue pit out in front, where for a silver dollar a man can eat and drink until he's ready to puke, and many a man has been doing just that. When the blazing sun has set, big blasts of dynamite are touched off in the hills above town, Bodie's own version of patriotic fireworks. The noise gets me to being a tad thoughtful, remembering back to the cave-in that took the life of Texas Joe, cause shit if I don't miss the horny old bastard. But the melancholy passes fast, it being unwise to dwell upon the Big Jump. For we miners all, each and every man of us, know that what puts grub on our table is risky as walking in quicksand over hell, and what happened to Joe could have happened to me, and no hallelujah to that.

I'm painting my tonsils with another drink when Cy Tolliver, the proprietor of the joint, steps to the front door and announces in a booming voice to be heard above the sound of drunken arguments, "Gentlemen, the arm wrassling contest is about to commence."

Over in the alley between the Bella Union and Van Dine's Barber Shop, Callahan looks up from where he's been sucking on the swelled-up penis of Big Owen, which is damn near thick as his blacksmith's arms, and when he sees Josiah Britt heading into the Bella Union, without a word he gets up off his knees and follows him, leaving Big Owen standing there leaning up against the wall, his large, wet prong now unattended to. I, unwilling to let a pretty thing like that go to waste, walk on over and slide Owen's prodigious foreskin back and forth, frigging him faster and faster until Owen's knees sort of buckle and, with a low-pitched moan, he spends his jissom in big, wild spurts. Some of his spunk lands, to my dismay, on my dungarees, which on account of it being a holiday are my best pair and recently laundered at the Wo Fat Laundry. I rub some of the muck off with the palm of my hand, at which Owen grasps my wrist and, pulling my hand to his mouth, licks his own seed down; when he lets me pull my hand away, his bushy beard is smeared with the stuff.

The Bella Union is packed to the rafters with odoriferous, drunken men. Cy Tolliver is standing before a chalkboard on which he's written the names of the contestants, all 16 of them. The combatants themselves are in the center of the room, seated two to a table, mostly stripped down to their waists, it being one hell of a hot night. And while Josiah Britt's barrel chest is maybe the most impressive of the lot, many another fellow has a muscular, well-formed body that holds the promise of a hard-fought contest ahead.

All the men are present, that is excepting Big Owen, who I reckon is still recovering from the pump-draining I've just provided him. "Gentlemen," says Tolliver, "we shall get started now. And it looks as though there's already a forfeit on the part of..." and he looks at the chalkboard, back at the men, back at the board, and calls out Big Owen's name.

"Not so fast!" comes a shout from the doorway. It's Owen, his swagger a trifle undone by the fact he's plumb forgotten to button up his pants.

"Owen," says Tolliver, "it's about fucking time, and that's a fact. You're over there, across from Duncan McCutcheon," and Big Owen goes and sits.

There's a judge standing at each table, for as the prize in the competition is 50 dollars in gold, a certain amount of attempted dishonesty is only to be expected in a hellhole like Bodie.

Tolliver is explaining the rules when another voice is heard.

"Is it too late to join on in?"

We all look around to see who spoke. It's a stranger in town. He's as blond as our friend Lars, but whereas Lars is willowy and handsome, this fellow is quite the opposite, thickly built, with the neck of a mastiff and real big shoulders and chest. He's got the beginnings of a double chin, though he's only maybe 20 years old, and his blue eyes have a slightly crazy, determined look. There is, truth to tell, something about him that draws my excited notice and makes my britches stir.

"Well, sir, it is indeed too late. These other men have signed up days ago for this competition," says Tolliver with a glare.

The big blond looks like he's disappointed enough to smash Cy Tolliver's head in.

"C'mon, Cy," I hear myself saying. "Allow the feller to enter the tournament." A few others say similar as well.

"All right," says Tolliver, "if none of you object, he's in, but as there's now an odd number of men, you—" and he looks straight at me "—can be this man's first match. What's your name, newcomer?"

"Will Shively," says the blond man, stripping off his shirt and heading in my direction. The approach of such a prepossessing man makes, quite naturally, my prong as stiff as a pine tree.

"Only one thing," says Tolliver. "We are short one judge now, being on account of there's an additional matchup." At which Lars speaks up and volunteers to judge our match, and though it's widely known that Lars and I are well-acquainted (and indeed many a man knows that Hiram and I have tied Lars up and plowed him on a schedule near regular as Wells Fargo's) such is the Norwegian's reputation for rectitude that not one man objects. And it does not hurt, neither, that his father owns the mine where we all work.

Shively and I head over to the one empty table amid the throng of spectators, and as we do, additional wagers are being made by the miners, most all of them, I reckon, backing the big, powerful blond.

At the touch of Will Shively's strong, calloused hand, I'm near overcome by desire, and I know then damn-well certain that I shan't be winning the arm wrestling crown. Still, it was at my initiative that the new man was included in the contest, and so I am well-resolved to do my utmost, or at least nearly so.

Lars is standing beside our table, ready to adjudicate our struggle. My muscles tense up, getting nearly as hard as my member. And then Tolliver speaks out, all stentorian, "Gentlemen, the first round of the Bodie Independence Day Arm Wrestling Championships is about to commence." A hush sets over the room. "On your mark...get set...wrassle!"

Well, this Will Shively isn't as strong as he looks. No sir, he's *twice* as strong, and it takes every ounce of my will not to just let him have his powerful way and be done with it. As the crowd cheers their favorites on, Shively applies his considerable leverage against me. I look into his eyes and they, steely blue, gaze implacably back. Then I make my fatal error, that of allowing my eyes to trail downward. The sight of Will Shively's broad chest, nipples erect in a thicket of blond fur, sinews straining, sweat coursing down his bare flesh...Jesus Lord, it's quite disconcerting. For one fraction of a second, all I want is to be overpowered by this handsome man, and in that split second he senses my weakness and slams my arm to the rough tabletop.

"Winner over here," calls out Lars, even-voiced as can be, and that settles that. Only it's with some hesitation that Shively loosens his now-painful grasp on my hand, and the lingering of his strong touch upon me makes my defeat seem of no import whatsoever.

Whatever chagrin I might feel vanishes when I look around me and see that most all the other matches are likewise concluded. Big Owen has beaten McCutcheon, Britt has won his matchup, and only two of the contests are still ongoing. Scrappy Juan Martinez is grunting with agony, his eyes a-pop with the strain of battling Bill Logue, and Easy Averill and liquored-up Penn Cobb are also still in battle, locked in a sweaty standoff. But inch by inch, Martinez pushes Logue's arm to the wood, and then Cobb defeats Averill, and it's the end of round 1.

Cal has come over and he says to me "Good try," but he's looking at Shively while he says it and claps his hand on the victor's muscled shoulder, and I wonder if there's ever a time when Callahan isn't hankering to drop his drawers.

The late addition of Shively to the contest has left an odd number of men to be divvied up for the next round, nine to be exact, but Cy Tolliver's quandary is solved when the inebriated Cobb leans over and hurls his guts onto the floor. It might not be official grounds for disqualification, but Cobb mutters something and makes for the door as one of Tolliver's barbacks sluices the reeking mess away and then pours a pile of sawdust onto the wet floor.

"In Penn Cobb's honor," calls out Tolliver with a grin, "the next round of neck oil is on the house!" And every man cheers loud.

The second round sees Britt pinning Frank O'Rourke in less than a minute flat. Martinez wins his matchup, too, as does Big Owen, and Will Shively damn near busts poor Abel Asch's arm.

Meanwhile, Lars, no longer needed to referee, comes up to me and asks, "Who do you make for the winner?"

"I would have said Britt till this Shively showed up," I reply, "but now I ain't so sure."

"Me neither," says my good friend Lars, "and it has me more than a bit worried, for I've laid a considerable wager on the fortunes of Josiah Britt."

"Lars!" says I, surprised. "I never knew you to be a gambling man!"

"That's usually the case" says he, "but, oh, hell, it's the Fourth of July."

The four remaining contestants, Britt against Martinez and Big Owen paired up with Shively, make ready for their battles.

There's much to be said for the matching up of man against man, testing muscles and mettles one against the other, and not the least of it is the smell that arises from the brutes. As I stand near the two tables that hold the remaining combatants, each and all of them stripped to the waist now and covered with the sheen of sweat, I can discern the animal reek that rises from their bodies, and if my interest had ever flagged, this odor surely serves as a tonic.

At Tolliver's say-so the matches begin.

As Britt bears down on Martinez, it's clear the two are mismatched. Though the Mexican's arm bulges with muscle, Britt's biceps is twice as big, and from the first the advantage is his.

"Sweet Jesus fuck Mary fuck mother of God!" curses Martinez, and then lapses into something Spanish that is no doubt at least as obscene. Martinez does his best to arrest his arm on its downward path, but it's plumb obvious that Josiah Britt has got the upper hand. Britt bares his teeth as he gets Martinez's hand just inches from the table, and though Martinez stalls it there for a bit, the effort takes a terrible toll, and with one final loud "Fuck!" the Mexican lets his arm touch wood.

Meanwhile, Lars is touching wood as well, after a fashion, for his hand is now down the front of my pants, and if anyone anywhere in Bodie might ever have objections, the drunken night of Independence Day is nowhere near the time. The delicate fingers of the mining engineer, well-schooled in the moves that please me and Hiram, is working my crotch into a lather, wherefore my crotch is damn near sopping wet.

In the meantime, Owen and Britt have been struggling mightily. Hand to calloused hand, their hairy forearms bulging with tension, they seem evenly matched, first one gaining advantage, then the other. But then Britt gets a real funny look on his face and steadily forces the blacksmith's hand further and further down till Owen's arm is pinned, and a cheer goes up from the onlooking crowd.

I glance over in the corner, and there's Juan Martinez salving his defeat; he's opened his fly and is stroking on his big brown dick, pulling the long foreskin back and forth over his swelling penis head. And danged if Penn Cobb doesn't weave back into the Bella Union and head over to Juan. They stand there glaring at each other for one long minute, and I figure they're maybe going to fight. But then Cobb reaches out for the Mexican's organ and starts to frig it. Martinez relaxes and grins and leans against the wall, and Penn Cobb drops to his knees and with alacrity takes the other fellow's stiff penis into his mouth.

bodie, blackeddie, andthefriscoquake

It's down to the final contest now, and Will Shively and Josiah Britt, their naked torsos streaked with sweat, are seated across from one another ready to tangle it up. Wagered money's been changing hands throughout, and it's fair to say a quite sizable amount of cash is riding on the result. My buddy Lars, off to take a piss, has withdrawn his expert hand, and danged if my cock doesn't miss him already.

"And now, ladies and gentlemen..." Tolliver looks around and starts again. "And now, gentlemen, commences the final round of the Bella Union's first Independence Day Arm Wrestling Championship. Will Shively here will test his mettle against Josiah Britt, and may the best man win. On your marks, get set..."

Just then the bar room air is rent by a piercing "Ya-hoo!" from Juan Martinez, who's loudly shooting his seed down Penn Cobb's throat. And though Tolliver has yet to officially start the match, Britt jumps the gun and is straining away, forcing Shively's arm, inch by laborious inch, down toward defeat.

Tolliver tries to sputter out his instructions, but the match has started without his say-so, and he realizes it's too late to do any different. Meanwhile, big, blond Will Shively is refusing to let his opponent gain more ground, and their linked arms are stalled midair in an even-matched show of strength.

"Jesus," says my bosom pal Hiram, who's slipped into the Bella Union without me noticing, "I hope to holy hell that this new fellow doesn't win, for at Lars's urging I've laid a sizable sum on Josiah Britt's victory and gave our friend most all my money to lay on the outcome."

Now, this concerns me, for Lars comes from money and can always be bailed out of a jam by his Midas-wealthy father, but Hiram has worked hard for his poke of gold and doesn't have a bit to spare. Meanwhile Shively is gaining the upper hand, having muscled his opponent's arm partway down to the table's surface, and both men's faces are all screwed up from the strain. Just watching the struggle has kept my penis good and hard, and I'm not the only one, it seems, for here and there throughout the Bella Union are half-dressed miners pawing at one another. Indeed, tipsy Penn Cobb, having drunk deep of Martinez's sperm, is now sprawled face down across one of the tables, trousers around his ankles, his fundament spread wide, his hungry hole exposed and up for grabs. Noticing this, Easy Averill lumbers over, his short, fat prong poking out of his fly, and dang if he doesn't spit on Cobb's butt and commence to plugging him right there in the midst of the tumult.

"Fuck! The newcomer's winning, and there goes the two months wages I gave to Lars to bet!" Hiram is sounding frantic now.

Indeed, Will Shively's concentration is nothing short of amazing, his blue eyes drilling into Britt, and it would seem that nothing short of a major distraction will divert him from certain victory.

At which point I get an idea.

Now, it's true that the judge of this contest is the sheriff himself, but I've done him a favor or two in my time, and he's liquored up to boot, so I figure he won't stop me. I elbow my way through the crowd, over to the table where the two men are locked in combat. Then I drop to my knees and scoot under the table, positioning myself between Shively's massive, sturdy legs. I unbutton the fly of his pants and reach inside, pulling out his soft root. Opening wide, I take the thing into my mouth, inhaling the high smell of his crotch, tonguing his foreskin, and hoping like blazes I can distract Shively sufficient for him to flinch.

Within a matter of moments, the fellow's prick has gone from soft to stiff, and I'm sucking away with thorough enthusiasm. I was afraid that Shively would try to kick me off, but he kind of grabs me between his muddy boots instead. So I take him all the way down my throat, till I'm almost gagging as Shively shoves himself into my hungry mouth. Though the shouts of the crowd have gone from a tumult to a full-on ruckus, above it I hear Hiram bellow to me, "That's the ticket! Shiveley's giving way!"

So I suckle on the meaty piece some more, then slide myself back a bit and use a hand to stroke at it, squeezing Shively's copious precum from his big piss-slit. I quickly swallow him down again, wrapping my arms around his tree-trunk legs, and suck so hard I feel his calves tense up and start to quiver. My throat milks his cock head most vigorously, at which point Will Shively can take it no longer. His whole body goes rigid, which bangs my head up against the table, and he shivers and shouts as he pumps load after load of sweet cream onto my tonsils. Which is when I hear the loud thwack of one man's arm pinning the other's—the sound of Shively's defeat, I'm certain—and I feel a flush of pride at having helped my buddy Hiram out of a jam and that's for sure.

It's not till I've gulped down the very last of Shively's jissom that I perceive the roar of the crowd, which is balls-out deafening, a huge human cry of horny, jubilant men. I back off the now-deflating penis and out of sheer politeness stuff it back into Will Shively's pants.

I slide from beneath the table and rise to my feet. And it's then that I see what's happened, for the two men are still sitting there stock-still, a stunned look on Josiah Britt's bearded face. His arm has been pinned to the table by his competitor, and beneath Will Shively's control it remains. It's just the opposite, fuck it all, of that which I labored so mightily to achieve.

"Tarnation!" I say to Hiram. "I'm sure dreadful sorry! What in blazes happened?"

"It was a nice try you gave it," says he, mournfully, "and Britt nearly did have Will Shively pinned. But at the moment he spent his spunk, Shively of a sudden gets all rigid, his arm having a mind of its own, and he just plain rams Britt's hand straight down to the tabletop."

By this time Britt and Shively have relaxed their death grip and stood up from their table. As all the onlookers, winners and losers both, cheer, the two men wrap each other in a big manly hug, bare torso to naked, sweaty chest. Then Shively reaches down to Josiah's crotch and he roars out, "Why the fuck should I be the one who's havin' all the fun?" And he unbuttons Britt's fly and adroitly pulls out the victor's swelling cock.

Which is when Lars comes up to us, and he says to Hiram, "Well, I have a confession. I'm afraid that I just thoroughly forgot to wager that money you gave me. Comes to that, I suppose it all ended up for the best, as you otherwise would have lost it. And if you fellows would come to my hotel room tonight..." and here he smiles that most pretty grin of his, "I'll be most happy to return it to you then."

I have no way of knowing whether Lars is telling the actual fact. For though the handsome young man values the truth, he values friendship more. And if it comes to that, he knows full well that he shan't receive more diligent attention than what Hiram and I have given his naked, tied-up body all those nights at his room at the Grand Central Hotel.

Well now, watching the arm wrestling matches has gotten me all lathered up, and sucking Shively's erection got me even more so, and when I look over, I see that though Averill has finished drilling Penn Cobb's butt, the half-conscious Cobb is still slung over the table, his hairy ass spread, his shiny hole inviting the next visitor. I mosey over before anyone else can get there first, pull out my bone, and slide it up inside Penn Cobb's wide-open aperture.

As I'm pumping away, and a bunch of the boys have commenced singing "The Whorehouse Bells Were Ringing," I feel a hand on my shoulder.

"Thanks," says Hiram, "for tryin' to help me out."

"Shit, buddy," I say, not missing a stroke into Cobb, "ain't that what friends are for?"

And he leans over and kisses me gentle on the cheek. "See you a bit later at the Grand Central," he says, and goes off to get another whiskey.

And I for my part pump ever harder, slipping damn near out of Cobb, then pounding my way back in, all to his groaning delight. Meantime a bellow rises above the crowd, and when I look over, there's Josiah Britt, hands behind his head, sweat pouring from his furry pits, his big hard dick pumping out gob after gob of thick sperm upon Will Shively's grinning face. And after a minute or two more, I myself can hold no longer and shoot off my own spunk like big-city fireworks all over the slick walls of Penn Cobb's guts, a most befitting end to one hot Independence Day in Helldorado, and God bless America.

By then Lars's work as a mining executive was pretty well complete. He'd made a plan to head on back to Frisco as soon as the tracks were clear. Now the snow had long since melted, and just days after the Fourth, he asks me, Cal, and Hiram if we cared to go along with him.

By then the three of us have been tying Lars down and pumping his lily-white butt for many a month. And besides, mining and suchlike has been pretty good to Hiram and me, and it was well past time for us to leave the hellhole of Bodie and head for civilization, where we might avail ourselves of all that gold could buy.

I thought a journey to Frisco was a good idea from the first, but Cal for some reason demurred, and Hiram hesitated until Lars magnanimously offered to take us in the company's private railroad car, pay what costs we incurred along the way, and once in Frisco pay to put us up at the Palace Hotel, a grand joint for sure.

Just a week or so later, Lars, Hiram, and I have said our fond farewells, and though I will for sure miss my comrades, I know as I say goodbye to Bodie that I shan't miss spending another goddamn winter there, and that's a fact. The three of us make our way to Frisco, though not without misadventure and tribulations on the way. Most notably, there was the time up near Sonora Pass when a rockslide brought our train to a halt and forced us to put up in the cabin of a mountain man. I awoke around dawn to find our lusty host's hard meat inside me, which I would not have minded so much had he not left all three of us with a long lasting case of the crab lice. Still, worse things have happened in my life, and I suspect they will again.

We at last made our way to the Golden Gate. I'd never been to Frisco before, and its air of bustle and prosperity was most welcome after our long trek. The pantywaist of a desk clerk at the Palace Hotel gave us a mighty queer look when Lars checked us in, but apparently Lars's rich father's name was known far and wide, for we were soon ensconced in a fancy room with a great big feather bed. And then Lars took us to a haberdasher and fixed us up with brand new duds, and the desk clerk at the Palace never gave us trouble ever again.

Naturally enough, Lars stayed at his "Papa's" mansion on Nob Hill, but every day or two he'd come for a visit to our room, where the three of us would whoop it up and how. One happy night, I recall Hiram and I, become quite adept since New Year's Eve, take great lengths of rope and tie Lars's pale and naked body down to the feather bed. We wind some rope around his stiff, throbbing rod and balls, stretching them out real good, then flip him over face-down and bind his wrists and ankles to the bedposts. I reach underneath him and pull his hard and tied-up manroot out from under, so's it was laying between his thighs. Then I pulled the rope around his organ and cinched it to the foot of the bed, stretching him out most cruelly, till he gasps with pleasure and begs me to relent. Well, sir, relent I did not, and then Hiram jumped in and brought the calloused palm of his big right hand down hard on Lars's smooth rump. At last, when Lars's nether flesh had turned good and hot and red, only then do we service our friend's hole, riding it in turn, first Hiram and then me and then Hiram again, pounding into him bronco-style, until his aperture is good and loose and wet. And then when it seemed he could take no more, me and Hiram take our turns and spew inside him.

When Lars is finally satisfied and all three of us exhausted, we sprawl naked across the bed and feast on trays of oysters and champagne. If any of the bellboys object to our raucous ways, Lars's generous tips keep their lips well-sealed. And one of them, a cute young boy no more than 19, will even join in on one or two occasions, sucking on my John Thomas whilst Hiram pounds his big red pecker into Lars.

And so it might have gone for many months if not for Hiram's profligate ways. Now, I'm not much a gambling man myself, but there was nary a poker game we ran across where Hiram did not join in. And so mighty soon he had been taken by every sharper in town and had run through not only his poke, but also the money that I'd been fool enough to lend him. And so it was that Hiram found himself playing an ebony dandy named Black Eddie for ownership of Lars.

"I'll see you and I will raise you a 20-dollar gold piece," says Black Eddie that fateful night when our friend became the stakes in a game of Seven-toed Pete.

Hiram hems and haws and squints and says at last, "I'll see you."

And Eddie grins, gold-capped teeth gleaming like the sun. His big right hand, encased in a tight leather glove, flips over his three hole cards. Two of them are ladies, to go with one face-up. "Three queens."

"Aw, shit!" says Hiram, his face turning carmine. "I'm near cleaned out, and that's for certain."

I had long since given up losing my money to Black Eddie's poker-playing wiles and was sitting there watching Hiram's downfall chiefly because I was too pie-eyed inebriated drunk to budge. Indeed, the private room at the back of Three Dollar Bill's Saloon would spin crazy-like every time I moved my head, so I was trying my levelest best not to move.

Well, had Hiram been a man of wisdom—or sober—he would have cut his losses and none of what followed would have come to pass.

But Hiram was neither sober nor wise, so he says to Black Eddie, "Ain't there some way I can try and get back on my feet?"

"One last hand, then," says Eddie, and he calls for another bottle. Hiram deals out two hole cards apiece, and his, when he lets me see them, are a seven and a deuce. Eddie has an ace up, and Hiram deals himself another deuce. Eddie bets a sawbuck, and Hiram calls that and deals another round, an eight for Black Eddie and another seven for himself.

About that time the skinny barboy brings a bottle of rotgut into the room, and he's followed in short order by our friend Cal Callahan. Now Cal had come down from Bodie too, arriving a week after we did, his having done whatever he'd needed to do back there—about which he'd say no more than "The bastard had it coming." Callahan had soon sniffed out the pleasures of the Barbary Coast, most notably Three Dollar Bill's. He'd tried out its stable of boys and settled on the skinny kid, who looked mighty unpromising to my eyes. But Cal told me the boy had "an asshole smooth as butter," which made up for his scrawniness, I figure. And it turns out it must be lovesickness, for Callahan hasn't lately joined Hiram, Lars, and me at the Palace Hotel. No on most evenings lately Cal has hung around the saloon like some smitten pup, making sure that none but he would get his favorite's private services after closing time.

"Don't be like that, Johnny T. I only want you to suck it now for just a little while," Callahan moans. "I'll give you a dollar. Hell, I'll give you two."

Well, sir, Johnny T puts the bottle on the table, takes the money from Cal's outstretched hand, and gets on his knees in the corner of the room, whereupon Cal pulls out his big old thing and guides it into the boy's open mouth.

And when I look back at the game again, Hiram has dealt himself a jack and a third seven, and Black Eddie is showing his black ace, a red king, and a trey. And the pot has grown considerable. I figure that Hiram has next to nothing left. And I'm right, for when Eddie raises the stakes another 20 bucks, Hiram moans and says, "I'd see you but I'm damned near busted."

So Eddie says, "I'll tell you what. We won't wager on the next card, and if you don't fold, we'll see if we can come to some kind of...arrangement."

Well, Hiram deals Black Eddie the ace of hearts, but he gives himself another deuce, which makes it sevens full for him.

There's no betting, just some looking back and forth, and then drunken Hiram says, "I guess I ain't wanting to fold. It's just a fucking shame that I'm clean out of money."

Black Eddie grins even wider and says, "Well, there is one wager you can put on the table."

"What's that?" says Hiram, hardly able to focus his eyes.

"That blond slaveboy of yours."

"But Eddie," Hiram says, all reasonable, barely blinking, "our friend Lars has left the city on business and won't return for near-ly a week."

"That's just fine, for otherwise I reckon you'd be running off to him for a stake to get you back in the game. Tell you what, I'll bet you the sum of what you've lost tonight against your surrendering all rights to Lars on his return." Black Eddie is still smiling wide.

Now it is true that Black Eddie's understanding of what's been going on between Lars and us ain't precisely clear. For though it would appear that the blond Norwegian was but the slave of our desires, in truth he could buy and sell us many times over and was never subjected to anything in which he was not willing, not to say anxious, to take part.

And so, though Lars was ours to tie up, tie down, and fuck most heartily, he was not in truth ours to gamble away. But Hiram, deep in his cups, his fortune gone, is not about to admit that. He just nods.

"All right, we play for the Norwegian then. Finish the deal."

The stakes having been decided, there remains nothing more to do than to play out the final hand.

There's a racket over in the corner. "Oh, Jesus!" exclaims Cal, and when I turn to look he's spewed his jissom all over the face of the skinny Johnny T.

I turn back real careful. Hiram, cards in hand, has a strange sort of look on his face. He's dealt himself a facedown ace, which comes as a relief since it won't be Eddie's. But Eddie peeks at his last hole card and grins. "Well now," he says, "I guess there's nothing left for you to bet, unless you want to put up your very own sweet white ass. But I'm a gentleman to my toes, and I reckon the stakes are high enough already. Get ready to hand over your blond fancyman."

Hiram grins right back and says in a real loud voice, "Full house, Eddie."

And Black Eddie, slow and deliberate, turns over his hole cards one by one. A second trey. A third. And a fourth trey. Four threes. Lars is his.

bodie, blackeddie, and the frisco quake

The following days crawl past, me and Hiram doing our best not to ponder what we, or rather he, had done. The night that Lars gets back from Sacramento we're there to meet him at the Embarcadero. Carrying his Gladstone bag, followed by a porter with his trunk, he alights from the ferry, and his face beams

"Well, that's mighty fine of you fellows," says he. "There was no necessity to meet me at the landing."

"Lars, we got something to tell you," Hiram says.

"Not bad news, I trust," Lars says with that pretty smile of his. "Come now, fellows, let's go to your hotel where we might have some privacy." He instructs the porter to send his things on to the Nob Hill mansion, and the three of us are soon in a carriage headed for the Palace Hotel.

As the carriage rattles through the streets of Frisco, Lars, seated to my left, takes his greatcoat and throws it across my lap, then reaches beneath it and grabs hold of my privates. With his right hand he expertly unbuttons my trousers and pulls out my pecker, which is getting mighty hard at his touch. We're in an open coach and I'm scared that despite the cover of night anyone who looks close enough can tell what's going on. I suppose that Lars figures that if he gets into a scrape, his daddy's money will get him out again. As we approach the hotel he strokes faster and squeezes, till I'm nearly fit to burst. Then just as we drive into the hotel's great courtyard, he deftly tucks my hard, leaking meat back in and buttons me up again. Maybe someone who saw us thought it funny how I carried his folded-up coat before me as we ascended to the room.

"Now then," says Lars, "what's this mystery? And let's not converse overmuch, for all these days I've been away I've longed for nothing but to be your slave, to be tied down and used by the both of you."

To our delight, he falls backward upon the bed, stretches his arms above his head as though they were already bound to the headboard, and smiles up at us. Then, most lasciviously, he spreads his legs wide and thrusts his hips upward.

The door to the hotel room, which Hiram has on purpose left unlocked, opens wide and in walks Black Eddie wearing those shiny gloves of his. Lars's eyes open wide in surprise. "And who, may I ask, are you?" says he. But there's no anger in his voice, just a kind of excitement, like he can already somehow tell what's coming.

"Guess your friends didn't have time to tell you yet. Name's Black Eddie. I won you from them in a game of cards."

I'm danged if I know what I expected Lars to do, but I damn never expected the great big smile that spreads across his face.

"Three of you," he muses. "The three of you..."

"No, not three. For I won you fair and square. You're mine alone now."

"And can't they even stay and watch...Sir?"

"Well..." Eddie grins back. "Maybe just this once, just so's they can see what's in store for you."

I look over at Hiram and he nods and we both settle back on the divan against the wall.

"Strip your clothes off, boy," says Eddie, and now there's no grin on his face. And in a matter of a minute Lars is naked, lying back upon the bed, his manhood half erect.

Eddie walks over to the bed, bends over so his face is just inches from Lars's ear, and says real quiet-like, "From this moment on you'll take your orders from me. You got that, boy?"

"Yes."

Black Eddie spits right in Lars's face. "Yes *what?*"

"Yes, Sir," says Lars, saliva rolling down his cheek. His poker is fully stiff now, as is mine and Hiram's too, I reckon.

Eddie takes his big, gloved hand and slaps Lars hard upon the dick, at which Lars gives a jump of surprise, then smiles and reaches up as though he's going to wrap his arms around Black Eddie's neck.

Eddie brings the back of his hand down upon the Scandinavian's cheek. "You're not to touch me unless I give explicit permission. Is that well understood?"

"Yes, Sir," says Lars, atremble with excitement.

Eddie turns to us and says, "You boys didn't know the treasure you had, nor how to train him to do your bidding."

Hiram asks, "Eddie, is it okay if I play with myself while I'm watching what you two're doin'?"

Well, I turn to shush him, but to my surprise Black Eddie replies, "You boys go right ahead, for I am, as I've said, in a generous mood tonight, and now you will see what a real man can do."

And Eddie reaches down and pulls out his cock, which is for certain one of the largest that I've ever seen.

"And now you're going to suck on this big black piece of meat, boy, until your jaws ache and you can't hardly breathe."

Now, Black Eddie is a big, husky fellow strong as an ox. He lifts up Lars bodily and throws him back down on the bed so Lars is crouching on all fours with his face jammed up against Eddie's swollen member. Lars starts licking Eddie's balls like a little blond puppy, but the black man grabs his head, dark leather gloves against pale flesh, and shoves his hard prick into Lars's open mouth. From where I sit I can see the cleft of Lars's buttocks, and I observe that his hot pink hole is twitching in a state of high excitement.

Grabbing Lars hard by the ears and pumping his tremendous manhood into our erstwhile sex slave's throat, Black Eddie says, "Son, I own you. I won you fair and square, and I will train you to serve me just as surely as I would break a wild horse."

At this I feel a surge of jealousy, so I glance over to my buddy

Hiram, but he seems unperturbed. Rather, he's gazing intently at the scene unfolding before us and frigging his dick with vigor. When he notices my glance, he reaches over and grabs my tool as well. It seems passing strange at first, me sitting there watching Lars get used, but soon a strange type of pleasure overtakes me, and I let Hiram continue.

"I'll stand here now while you strip me down," Eddie says to Lars, "and then I'll ride that slim white ass of yours."

And Lars with alacrity undresses his new master and then kneels on the floor at his feet. He gazes up at the burly man standing above him. "May I touch you, Sir?" he asks.

"You may, boy."

Lars reaches up and runs his pale white hands down over Eddie's big chocolate-colored belly, down to his wiry bush and his stiff black pecker.

"You like that thing?"

"I do, Sir."

"Where would you like it, boy?"

"Inside me, Sir. Please, Sir?"

"You think you can take it, boy?"

"I'll try, Black Eddie Sir."

And Lars clambers up on the bed and gets on all fours, his butt in the air. Eddie spits on his ass, pulls off one tight glove, reaches down and fingers Lars's butt hole open, then takes the purplish head of his pecker and rams into his new slave, who screws his face up in discomfort for a moment, then gasps with pleasure, blue eyes open wide.

Now, I'd long ago resolved to be no man's filly, but watching Black Eddie grab Lars's slender hips and pump his way inside his nether parts gets me to thinking some mighty strange thoughts, mighty peculiar. And I can tell by the escalating motion of his hand upon my cock that the spectacle before us has not left Hiram unmoved, neither.

And when Black Eddie starts slapping the Norwegian's ass with his gloved left hand, cowhide against tender flesh, none of us can contain ourselves. Lars himself is the first to blow, screaming as a load arcs out of his pecker onto the sheets. As Hiram shoots his jism, his hand frigs me so hard that I follow suit in seconds. And lastly, Big Eddie, with a mighty grunt of pleasure, rears back and rides Lars's well-used hole till he pumps out his load inside him.

Without another word, Lars wipes off his rider's dick, helps Black Eddie back into his clothes, and gets dressed himself. And he follows his new master out the door, leaving me and Hiram just sitting there like damn fools. Just sitting there.

In the days that follow, me and Hiram don't see anything of Lars, though one day the desk clerk hands us a package from him. Turns out he's sent us a considerable bankroll, for which we're truly grateful.

We figure when Lars ain't at his daddy's mansion, he's underneath Black Eddie, letting that big man stretch him out and use him. And even when I'm poking some boy from Three Dollar Bill's, I find myself wondering what it would be like to belong to that big black gambler.

When we do hear word of Lars, though, it's real tragic and knocks me and Hiram for a loop. For it had come to pass that one day a gang of ruffians attacked a few Chinese on Grant Avenue, and Lars, raised in a country where Christian charity apparently meant more than it does here, went to the Celestials' aid. In the ensuing fracas Lars was struck hard on the head, and after several days in the hospital he joined his Maker.

Though Hiram and I hardly fit in with the nabobs at Lars's funeral, we were wearing the new duds he'd bought us and no one challenged our entry, so we sat in the back of the church while the preacher said whatever it is preachers say. When I filed past the coffin and looked down at Lars's pale, pretty face, all cold and still, and remembered all the good times we had, I swear had I not been a man, a tear would have rolled down my cheek.

Well, sir, the thought of sweet, gentle Lars meeting his Maker in such a violent and untimely fashion makes me mighty inconsolable, so after the services I take a cable car down to Three Dollar Bill's to drown my sorrows in panther piss. And who should be there in the back room but Black Eddie, wearing his elegant gloves, playing seven-card stud with Cal Callahan.

"We didn't see you at the funeral, Black Eddie," says Hiram in a funny, strangled sort of voice.

"When a man is dead," says Eddie, "then he's dead, and that's a fact."

Which makes good sense to me. But Hiram, for his part, makes an odd noise, wheels around, and walks out the door. (And though I had no way of knowing it then, that was about the last I was to see of my friend Hiram for many a year, for by the end of the week, plumb out of cash and despondent at our friend's demise, he'd gathered his things from our hotel room and gone back to the hills.)

"How you doin', Cal?" I ask. Now Cal was one of my greatest pals back up at the mine. When spring came to the Sierra and melting snows had turned the ground to muck, he and me would wrestle in the mud till the stuff squished between our thighs and we was laughing fit to burst. And when I was accused of robbing the cash box at the Standard Mine's commissary, he was the one who came to my defense.

"Not so good," says Cal. "I've been playing on IOUs."

And Eddie smiles, showing those gold teeth of his, and says, "Matter of fact, this was gonna be our last hand." He looks me up and down. "But," he says, "I got me an idea."

"Which is?" says Cal, grasping at straws.

"You throw your friend here in the kitty." And he looks my way and grins even wider.

"What!?"

So Black Eddie tells Callahan the story of Lars, some of which he knows anyway. "And that's my proposition. You put up your friend here and I'll put up everything I've won from you today, and we'll play out the rest of this hand."

Cal turns to me. "And what do you say about it?"

Eddie barks out, "What he has to say don't matter shit."

And sure enough, I can't think of a single word to say. But, mighty strange to relate, my pecker's getting good and hard.

"You'll stand by whatever happens, won't you boy?" Eddie's looking me straight in the eye.

"Yes," I say.

"Yes, *what*?"

"Yes, Sir."

Now Eddie has the 10 of diamonds up, and Cal is showing the four of hearts. Eddie deals Cal the five of spades and himself the eight of clubs. Then the three of hearts to Cal, the 10 of spades for himself. Cal gets dealt the jack of diamonds, Eddie a third 10. I swallow hard.

"Mind if I show my friend my hole cards?" Cal asks Eddie.

"Suit yourself. I'm in a generous mood."

Well, when I take a look my eyes near pop out. Cal is holding the five and seven of hearts, one card away from a straight flush. But he'll be drawing to an inside straight, the odds a million to one. My ass is done for.

Cal knocks back a glass of whiskey.

"No matter what happens," says he to me, "I want you to know you've always been a true friend."

My heart is pounding like a steam hammer.

Eddie deals out the last two cards, face down.

I take a look and can't believe my eyes. Callahan's third hole card is the six of hearts, a friggin' straight flush!

Black Eddie grins his golden grin.

"Okay, Callahan, show me what you're holding."

But I'm whispering into Cal's ear, and as I tell him what I've got to say, he starts to shake his head.

"Do it, Cal," I heatedly whisper, "for I would do the same for you."

He hesitates, and I implore him once more.

So Callahan says, "I fold. The boy is yours."

Well, eventually I earned enough money to pay back Cal what he'd lost on that hand, just as I'd promised that night. So both of us won, in a sense. All three of us won, comes to that.

And so it came to pass that I was to spend the following winter and many a winter thereafter not in the freezing hell of Bodie, but in foggy Frisco instead, under Black Eddie's command. Despite its veneer of civilization, the town in those days was a place where all the lusts known to man ran riot, and, tarnation, maybe it still is. The hilly streets were full of sailors and miners and half-crazy hellions with hard pricks who didn't much care where they put them. Thus, as the months turned to years, I saw my fair share of trouble, and that's a fact. There was many a dissipated night on the Barbary Coast, many days when I did not know what month it was. Hell, what fucking planet I was on.

But time does its work, by Jesus. We all slow down, damn it, every man jack of us who survives long enough and does not die, like the Merced Kid did, half naked in some gutter. I had to face it—the man I was seeing in the mirror was no longer the strapping young miner from Bodie who didn't care fuck-all about fuck-all. Maybe me and my friends remained roaring boys at heart, but Frisco had taught us a thing or two. Which fork to use, for one, and whose palm to grease with money when there were favors to be done. I had to admit it—civilization had done its job.

"And civilization," says Cal Callahan one day, "ain't nearly what it's cracked up to be."

And I surely do know what he's talking about. I look around at our comfortable digs on Hayes Street and think about the good old rough-and-ready days at Bodie, all us miners getting righteous drunk and whooping it up and rolling around naked in the mud on a warm spring day. Now, Frisco has its attractions—decent grub, for one thing, and an almost unlimited supply of hot water—but after spending so much time in town, I'm getting a hankering for something a damn sight wilder.

Just then Black Eddie walks in the room. Now, in the years since Eddie won my ass at Three Dollar Bill's Saloon, the relationship twixt me and him has changed a goodly deal. He's still a mean ol' cuss with a big fat nasty dick. But I'm not no longer his slave as much as a friend and an equal partner. And since Callahan moved in with us, we of habit all three sleep in the same big feather bed, and Black Eddie uses me and Cal in turn as the mood takes him, and sometimes he goes after both of us at once.

"How're you doing, boys?" says Eddie, gold glinting in his smile.

"Pretty damn good," says Cal, "but gettin' a mite bored."

"You always was one to make trouble," says Eddie with a wicked wink, and he makes a grab at Cal's crotch. "And I do believe you're about to get the chance, for Rooster Viguerie's invited all three of us to one of his whoop-de-doos."

Now Viguerie's a man who blew into Frisco from Jesus-only-knows-where with a pile of gold, a passel of ambition, and a dick as big as Texas. He lost no time in busting his way into the ranks of the rich and powerful; even Mayor Schmitz kowtowed when Viguerie snapped his fingers. Rooster's parties, too, were legend, balls-out blowouts at his manse atop Nob Hill.

"And when's the party to be?" I ask.

"In less than two weeks' time, on April 17th," says Eddie. "Hell, given how wild his soirees are, maybe we should be resting up till then. For we're none of us as young as we used to be, and that's a fact."

And I look at Eddie and see the flecks of gray in his hair and think of all the years that have passed since I first made his acquaintance at Three Dollar Bill's. "But Eddie," says I, "you'll always be twice as much man as some young whippersnapper, and *that's* a fact."

And Eddie smiles and takes out his big, dark pecker, which starts to swelling in his hand. "I'm glad you think so, boy," he smiles. He's got on those black gloves he dang near always wears, sometimes even to bed, and when he strokes my face I can smell the smooth leather. He slaps my cheek. "Now get down on your knees and suck this thing." And with the salty hardness of his cock down my throat and the yeasty odor of his crotch in my nostrils, I'm thinking that Frisco's not such a boring place after all.

When April 17th arrived it dawned warm and sunny. I'd just finished being plowed by Black Eddie and stroking Cal until he shot off all over my face. I'm licking the jissom off the sheets when there's a knocking at the door. Eddie pulls on his purple dressing gown and goes to answer it.

"Well, Jesus fucking Christ!" I hear Black Eddie say. "Look who the fuck it is, boys!"

"I ain't dressed!" I call out.

"Don't matter none to me," says a familiar voice. I look up and it's my old mate Hiram, standing grinning at the bedroom door.

"Holy fuck Hiram!" says Cal, pulling on his dungarees. "How the holy hell are you?"

"Not bad at all, boys, though it's been a mighty long time." And indeed it has, for we've not seen hide nor hair of Hiram since Lars's funeral, when Hiram headed back to Bodie to lose himself in mining's hard labors.

Hiram shakes Cal's hand and then grabs up my naked body in a big bear hug. I think back on the long-ago times when we'd shared the task of tying up and fucking Lars, and I hug back.

Two other younger men have followed Hiram into the room. "And who might these fellers be?" I inquire.

"They're my buddies from the mine, both on their first visit to Frisco. Boys, meet Martinez and Hink Rankin." Well, Martinez is a strapping youth who seems to enjoy staring at my half-hard pecker. But Rankin is a crazy-looking coot with a scarred-up face and a glass eye, smelling bad to boot,

"Pleased to meet you boys," I say, but Callahan just smiles, his eyes swooping in vulture-like to the crotch of the young Mexican.

"Martinez, eh?" I say, thinking back to the old days at Bodie. "Any relation to Juan Martinez?"

"He was my papa," says the handsome young man, and his answer makes me feel dreadful old.

"You must have had quite a ride from Bodie," Black Eddie calls from the next room.

"Yes, sir," says Martinez, "for the early thaw has left many a stream swollen and treacherous to cross."

"Ain't the only thing swollen," Cal cracks wise, with a glance at my stiffened member.

"Well," asks Eddie, entering the bedroom, "can I offer you the hospitality of my place here till you've had a chance to settle in and find rooms of your own?"

"That's mighty nice of you, Eddie," smiles Hiram. "Okay with you boys?"

None of us is quite sure whether he's asking his friends or me and Cal, so we all four end up nodding and grinning, though Rankin's grin is lopsided at best.

Black Eddie smiles knowingly, gold tooth shining. "Well, that's decided then. Make yourselves to home." He throws a burly arm around Hink Rankin. "You lads smell like the trail. How would a nice, hot bath sound to you?"

Hink, who *is* smelling more than a trifle ripe, hesitates before accepting. Martinez nods assent. And I'm looking back at Martinez with more than a little interest.

"You take care of these men, get 'em all cleaned up," says Eddie to me, for though our relationship has changed over the years, he still has the right to boss me around, and that's a fact. "After you bathe 'em, give them anything they need. Me and Hiram are going out for a beer." And then he smiles slyly, for I suppose he's noticed my interest in the handsome Mexican. "And take care of Rankin first. That's an order."

By the time the tub is filled with hot water, Rankin is stripped down to his stained and sweaty union suit. Even through the flannel it's easy to see that nature has been generous where Hink Rankin is concerned.

"Are you gonna strip down?" I ask, but Rankin just stands there shyly. *A hell of a time to get bashful,* I'm thinking. So I walk over to him and start unbuttoning his underwear, revealing a lean and hairy chest. When he gives no objection, I continue undoing the buttons, then peel his union suit off him, kneeling so I can get it off over his feet. His feet in particular smell really high, making me quite faint with desire. Unsure of the ugly man's reaction, I kneel and kiss his right foot. But he takes his left foot and presses it down upon the back of my head, and in no time I'm greedily licking his foot clean, tonguing the funk from between his toes. He brings down his left foot and places it before me, and I go to work on that one right away, eventually stretching my mouth around all five toes.

Just when I think I'll perish from delight, he pulls his foot away.

I look up. Even half-hard, Hink Rankin's dick is a dangerous weapon.

"Are you gonna give me a bath or what?" says he, staring down at me with his one good eye.

After he's stepped into the tub, I take a sponge and a bar of soap and begin to clean his wiry body, starting at his neck and working my way down. When I raise his arm to clean his pit the strong smell like to knock me flat, and it is all I can do not to bury my face in it and lick the dark-brown bush.

Well, by and by I get to his crotch and take special care lathering up his John Thomas, which responds to my touch by jerking around and growing to a prodigious size. Even down there, Hink Rankin is an oddity, for his stiff pecker curves downward and not up as most men's do. But it is a fine piece of meat nonetheless, and I soap it up real well and proceed to massage its swollen length.

"Mebbe you'd like to get in here with me," says Hink, eyeing my smaller but noticeable erection.

When I step into the tub with him he throws his powerful arms around me and clutches me to his chest. "It's been a while since I had me a woman," he says, "and I guess you'll have to do." His breath is sour.

And as we stand there dick-to-dick in the warm water, I feel a warmer jet of liquid coursing down my thighs. Though his cock is hard as granite, plug-ugly Hink Rankin is pissing all over me.

"Oh, fuck, oh, fuck," I moan, and sure enough his soaped-up fingers find my asshole, already well-used from Eddie's attentions that morning. Once he gets a few fingers up inside me, he uses that grip to spin me around so's my back is to him. Grabbing me beneath the arms, he shoves his gigantic thing into me, and though I'm loose as could be it still makes me gasp. As I stand there impaled on Hink Rankin's weird cock, I once more think back to the old days, back to when me and Hiram would tie up and abuse sweet Lars. *Nowadays,* I think, *I am the one to be at a man's service, and I surely do not regret it. Times have changed, and that's a fact.*

Rankin thrusts quick and hard, and as he said, he's not had any pussy for a while, and so it doesn't take him long to shoot off inside me, while I for my part spew spunk into the now-cooling bathwater.

"Thank you, Sir," I say when he's extracted his meat from inside me. And I proceed to give him what I'm sure he would agree is the best bath he's ever had.

When I have Rankin all toweled off and attired in one of Eddie's too-big dressing gowns, I go in to fetch Martinez for his bath, but he's otherwise occupied fucking away at Cal Callahan's face. Cal is lying on his back in bed, his dick pointed ceilingward, while the half-naked, muscular Mexican plows into his throat.

I feel mighty disappointed at missing my chance at Martinez, but just then the door opens and Hiram and Black Eddie walk into the room.

"Jesus Christ Almighty!" Eddie bellows with a grin. "You boys better save *something* for the party tonight!"

By the time the six of us alight from the cable car and arrive at Rooster Viguerie's mansion high atop Nob Hill, the party is in full swing. A butler with his nose in the air checks our invite and announces us with a snooty air: "Mr. Edward Washington and party." But nobody can hear, as the band and the big crowd are raising such a ruckus.

It looks like all of San Francisco is jammed into Rooster's mansion, everybody from Mayor Schmitz and his well-heeled bunch to the easy girls from the Barbary Coast. Even the Italian singer Caruso, fresh from a show at the Grand Opera House, is in attendance, talking to a beautiful woman who I know is really a man in a dress. The champagne is flowing freely, and it ain't the cheap stuff, neither.

"Aw, shit!" Cal whispers to me. "Ain't that Gino deLucca?"

I look to where he's pointing, and sure enough it's deLucca, as elegantly turned out as always. "I can't believe," I whisper back, "that squirmy little bastard would dare show his face." For none of us have seen hide nor hair of him for months, ever since he lost his shirt to Black Eddie in a game of five-card stud and disappeared right quick, leaving Eddie with an IOU and a mighty riled feeling. Everybody figured he'd disappeared for good. Some whispered that Eddie had *made* him disappear. And there he is laughing and joking, diamond stickpin aglitter. But then Rooster's parties are like that: They can raise the dead.

"I just hope," I continue, "that Eddie don't catch sight of him." But then, given the size of this shivaree how likely is that?

The boys from Bodie have already found their way to a crystal punch bowl and are knocking back glasses of something pink. "It tastes sweet as puppy pee," says one-eyed Hink, "but it packs a helluva kick." His buddy Martinez looks pretty good in an outfit he's borrowed from Cal, but Rankin's still in his grubby, smelly miner's clothes, and they lend him an air that ain't exactly distinguished, especially among all the genuine Paris gowns. Matter of fact, the sniffy sissy at the door who was checking invites hadn't wanted to let him in, till Rooster Viguerie himself waved him through. And that's the kind of thing that makes Viguerie's parties the jamborees they are.

The band launches into a waltz, and couples take to the dance floor. All kinds of couples, mostly normal, but quite a few girls are dancing with girls, and even men with men. It being Rooster's party, nobody would dare object. Not even Bishop O'Rourke, standing in the corner with a sour look on his face, as full of fire and brimstone as he'd been that Easter back in Bodie. Not even the half-soused Mayor. Not even God himself.

"Want to dance?" Cal asks Martinez, and to my surprise the

Mexican accepts. And he's not a bad dancer, neither. Well, I'm kind of jealous, since I've been hot for Martinez since I first clapped eyes on him. But the best way to deal with disappointment is to get fuck-all laid.

"Eddie, Sir," says I, "do you mind if I go upstairs?"

"Not at all," he smiles. "I still got some catching up to do with Hiram."

And I make my way up the marble staircase, past stained glass windows and crystal chandeliers, up to where the party *really* is.

The upstairs rooms at Rooster's parties are notorious indeed. Once you make your way past the goons standing guard at the top of the stairs, you've got your choice of sins. One room features gurdy girls, willing businessmen, and a mighty peculiar selection of whips and saddles. Then there's the room where women dressed as men smoke cigars and eat each other's pussies. And then there's the room I make a beeline for.

There's naked men everywhere lolling around in the dim light, some of them passing pipes filled with opium straight from the dens of Chinatown, others slugging back shots served by a butler wearing nothing but a hard-on and a smile.

I leave my clothes in a pile in the corner and sink down on one of the big pillows that cover the floor. All around, sweaty men are fucking and sucking each other in twos and threes and fives and in big old tangled piles of Lord-knows-how-many arms and legs. A burly fellow with hair on his shoulders is all over me right off, nursing at my nipples and jamming his stiff little prick against my thigh. He reaches down and starts playing with my hole just the way I like it done. In jig time my legs are over his hairy shoulders and his pecker's prying open my fundament. His prong may not be too big but he sure knows how to use it, just teasing my hole, plunging in and drawing back again and again, and he's got me gasping into his handsome, bearded face. When I fling my arms out for support, someone's dripping-hot prick finds its way into my right hand. I don't know whose it is. Shucks, I don't even *want* to know. I just start jacking away on it as the bearded man lowers his weight down on me and I feel lost in his flesh and his vigorous fucking. Meanwhile, the dick in my hand thrusts faster and harder, then spends cream all over my arm, and some of it hits the side of my face. The bearded man licks it off my cheek, and when he does he groans and explodes inside me.

After he catches his breath, he rolls off me and walks off without a word, leaving me lying there with my still-stiff prick pointed at the moon. Well, sir, a cute, skinny fellow walks on over, nonchalantly straddles me and squats down, and my cock is just plain sucked into his butt. He's bouncing up and down and whooping, when I realize it's none other than Johnny T. Now, Cal has had a hankering after him through all the years since Johnny was peddling his ass at Three Dollar Bill's. They even had a kind of romance going for a while, but the boy wouldn't stop his running around, at least not for Cal, and he left my pal with a well-bruised heart. So I'm hoping that Cal don't walk in and find Johnny fucking himself on my pecker. But mostly I'm just enjoying Johnny T's famously hungry ass.

I'm watching his bright-red dick bouncing stiff against his lean belly when a muscular blond kneels over me and sucks Johnny's cock into his mouth. The blond, his pale skin as smooth as milk, reminds me of Lars. I'm wishing it could be the swarthy Martinez in his place, but I'm in no mood to fuss. So I squirm around till I get my head between the blond's sinewy thighs and start licking his ball sac, and he kind of lowers himself down so I can get his nuts into my mouth. And that's how the three of us shoot our loads, me up Johnny's butt, Johnny T in the blond's pretty mouth, and the blond man spewing all over my chest.

It's not till I've recovered, wiped up, and got my clothes back on that I notice Cal, still fully dressed, standing in a corner talking to just-fucked Johnny T. "Long time, no see," I hear him say kind of sadly, as I go back down to Rooster Viguerie's shivaree.

Things in the ballroom have changed for the wilder while I've been upstairs. It's well past midnight, past four most likely, and all the proper ladies have gone home, leaving the gurdy girls and a pack of horny gentlemen. The band is playing a lively polka, and up on the stage behind them, none other than Hink Rankin is tying up Bishop O'Rourke, who's standing there stark naked but for his socks and his dog collar, his hands suspended from a curtain rod by a red velvet cord.

The band takes a breather, and in the sudden quiet Hink bellows out, "All right, now! Recite the Act of Contrition, fucker!" All eyes turn toward O'Rourke as he shakily begins, "My Lord, I am heartily sorry for having offended thee..." and his Irish prick wakes up and stiffens considerably.

Now Rooster Viguerie himself takes the stage, a bottle of Irish whiskey in his hand, and crows out, "My friends, this is an auspicious occasion, a moment for which many of us have hoped." There's a nasty twinkle in his eye.

He walks over to the bishop. He and Hink spin him round till his back is toward the crowd, and then Rooster Viguerie starts working the neck of the whiskey bottle up into the bishop's ass. O'Rourke meanwhile is going on loudly about not sinning no more, but he sure don't seem to be struggling very hard.

Just then I'm distracted by a nasty snarl. "Gino, you fucking shit-eating rat!" Black Eddie has found his erstwhile friend.

"Eddie," says DeLucca, "let's see if we can settle this in private." And the two of them take off for elsewhere in the house.

Well, Rooster and Rankin are still working over the bishop, and they've been joined by the big, bearded man who fucked me and who, now that he has his clothes on, I recognize as one of the god-almighty-rich Steinfelders, a clan who own most of the banks in the city. But I guess when your dick is hard, how rich you are is plumb irrelevant. Then, out of the corner of my eye, I notice Cal and Johnny T coming down the stairs arm-in-arm, kissing and nuzzling. And damn it's late, for the clock strikes five.

Back on the stage the band has cleared away, and Hink Rankin is pissing all over Bishop O'Rourke, his big dick in his hand and a smile on his ugly face. And Rooster Viguerie is crowing, "They call it *mor*-ti-fi-*ca*-tion of the *flesh*!"

And then Martinez staggers over to me, handsome as hell and drunk as a skunk. Without so much as a how-de-do he grabs my crotch, and damn if my pecker isn't ready for more. So he gets down on his knees right there in that ritzy grand ballroom, undoes my trousers, and takes my peter down his throat.

I'm feeling like I'm ready to bust a load when—bang!— a gunshot rings out somewhere, off in the direction where Black Eddie's gone. Some of the whores scatter, and a few men go to find out what's happened. But right then there's a sudden grinding rumble from deep in the earth itself, and just as I shoot off into the Mexican's mouth the whole room starts to shake. The crystal chandeliers commence to rattle and sway, and one falls to the floor with a tremendous crash. "Earthquake!" somebody shouts, and the walls start to buckle. Words cannot describe the terror of that moment, as the whole fucking mansion begins to dance and give way. Struggling to keep my feet, I make a run toward the door as chunks of the ceiling come crashing down around me.

Not till I've made it out to the street somehow do I notice my thing is still hanging out of my pants. I'm buttoning up when Black Eddie comes to my side. "Sweet fucking Jesus!" he says, and then can speak no more. For when we look out from Nob Hill we can see the whole city of San Francisco swaying and collapsing, and the church bells are making a racket everywhere.

Men and whores, some of them stark naked, are still streaming from Rooster's mansion, joining the neighborhood swells in their nightclothes, and when the shaking finally stops and fires have started blazing, a weird kind of numb panic sets in. Black Eddie and me just stand there feeling lost as we watch the destruction of the city we've long called home. Then Hink Rankin shows up, steady as a rock, and grabs Eddie and me, leading us away from the burning mansion. And there on a street corner Cal and Johnny T are standing, arms wrapped around each other. But we never were to see Martinez again, nor my old friend Hiram. And when, on our way through the rubble-strewn streets, I inquired after DeLucca, Black Eddie looked me square in the eye and said, "That skunk Gino's a goner for sure, crushed beneath the masonry. And I surely do hope they never find the bullet in his brain."

Well, miraculously enough Eddie's house survived the shocks, though it was to be claimed the next day by what became known as the Ham and Eggs Fire. But in the meantime we'd packed our bags, and, discretion being the better part of valor, lit out for parts unknown. Callahan and Johnny T settled into a tent in Golden Gate Park till the city rose from the ashes, then they moved into a flat somewhere, and for all I know they're together still. And the rascally Hink Rankin, well, Rankin...but that's a long story.

It's *all* been a long story, comes to that, the good and the bad of it. And now that most everyone concerned is long gone, I suppose it's high time to tell it; my memories won't let me be. Black Eddie took me back to Bodie last spring when the poppies were bright on the mountains. And as his automobile crested the last hill, it all came back to me, and damned if it didn't. The Standard Mine had shut down years before, and the town was near deserted, for who but a fool would stay in Bodie if there wasn't gold to be mined? As

bodie, black eddie, and the frisco quake

Eddie and I roamed the barren hills hand in gloved hand, there amid the weathered wood of collapsing whorehouses and deserted homes I could see all the ghosts walkin' on their hind legs: the spirit of Tom Dillon, a bullet through his heart, and Texas Joe, his head stove in. Lars, pale, beautiful Lars. And sure enough, the ghost of my own youth. For I soon enough will be joining my buddies from those roaring times. And you know, if I had it to do over again, I don't figure I'd do any of it different, not even if I could.

"Ah, those were the days, and fuck-all if we'll look upon their like again," I said to Black Eddie, there in what's left of Bodie.

"Yes, my friend," Black Eddie replied, "those were interesting times." And he clasped my hand harder and smiled.

safeandsound

Sometimes, maybe always, you can't tell what's going to happen, not really, Danny thought as he slid his hand into Geoff's ass.

He'd first met Geoff by total chance on a crosstown bus. It had been Sunday. Danny'd been heading up to the Metropolitan Museum, Geoff was heading home. But instead of home, Geoff had gone with Danny, the two talking quietly, intensely, as they sat beside the museum's reconstructed Egyptian temple.

Danny had still been feeling raw, though it had been nearly a year since Miguel died. The two of them had met when Danny was making a porn video. Miguel had been playing the part of "the Cameraman" in a little classic titled *Jockboys*. Danny, who'd had the part of "Ryan," always liked to joke that he'd fallen in love while helping to gang-bang his boyfriend-to-be. Miguel had eventually moved cross-country to be with him; they'd stayed together for years. Then, despite unspoken prayers and unpronounceable triple-drug cocktails, they were parted. When he'd called Miguel's mother to offer his sympathy, she'd hung up on him.

Danny had by that time semiretired from his porn career. He'd originally started doing videos to pay for college, and his dark handsomeness and impressively symmetrical cock had bought a lot of textbooks. He'd planned on law school, but the meth he'd been doing to get himself through both studies and work made things more than a little sloppy. By the time he was clean and sober he'd gotten a job as a paralegal, liked it, and had made just one last video—his swan song, *Hard and Wet,* a relatively big-budget production set in a Navy SEALs training camp. Danny's picture had been featured on the box, and he'd made enough money from it to furnish his loft in Tribeca. *Hard and Wet* had just hit the stores when he and Geoff met on that bus, talked for hours beside the ruins of Egypt, talked about life and love and the usual nothing, and had gone back to Geoff's fifth-floor walk-up, where they'd fucked till dawn.

"Oh, fuck *yeah*," Geoff was saying. Geoff said that a lot whenever Danny fisted him, hand swimming up into the soft heat of his guts.

After that night (and a rocky day at work the following Monday), they started dating, falling in love, and at last Danny had asked Geoff to move in. Geoff said yes. The hurt of losing Miguel, the ache of seeing him wither away, would never be entirely gone. For a while Danny had thought that nothing would ever be the same, and it wasn't, not really, but he picked up and moved on because that's what people did, and the touch of Geoff's lips was a powerful painkiller. He let himself, not a bit reluctantly, fall in love again.

Sometimes it came up jokingly in their conversations, but it was nevertheless true: Geoff was not the sort of guy you'd expect to see with a retired porn star. His blond, boyish face was clean-cut, maybe *too* clean-cut, and good looking, but only in a regular-featured, unmemorable way. His body was soft, untouched by Cybex and steroids. He had naturally wide hips, a big ass, and chunky thighs. His uncut dick was just about average, and when it stood up it brushed a poochy little belly.

Danny thought Geoff was the sexiest man he'd ever laid eyes on.

Kinky. That was another surprise. There had been the surprise of meeting a boyfriend on the bus and it not turning out to be some stupid Julia Roberts cliché. The surprise of finding someone who could take Miguel's place without it seeming like a betrayal. And the surprise of finding out that Geoff—bland, blond, and blue eyed—liked to be strapped into a dog collar and harness and slapped around.

Geoff hadn't been living in New York long, so when he wasn't Photoshopping clients' ads and Danny wasn't dealing with legal briefs, they'd do all the perfectly tourist things. They'd climbed the Statue of Liberty, then gone back to Danny's, where he'd tied Geoff's hands behind his back, wound rope around his balls, stretching them way out, then looped it around his hard, oozing dick. They'd taken a hansom cab ride in Central Park, then gone back to Danny's, where Geoff, collared, had worshiped Danny's boots—shiny black boots that pressed against his dick, his balls, that pressed against his face while he moaned and squirmed. They'd gone to the Metropolitan Museum, where they'd spent that first afternoon, and sat in front of a little gold Buddha whose hands were in the "fear not" mudra. And so forth.

Danny's hand was almost in now, his knuckles pressed against the resistance of Geoff's ass—flesh and bone, gateway to his lover's insides. Molten lube was everywhere, little lakes of Crisco.

Danny had never really been into kink before. Sure, he'd made a few videos, *Hazing the Hunks* and the like, that required him to be tied up, paddled, whatever. (Though why he, an actor with a swelling reputation as an anal top, had been cast as an S/M bottom remained something of a mystery.) But when it came to real life, life with Miguel say, he'd pretty much preferred vanilla, give or take a swat on the butt. It wasn't until Geoff, until he'd felt the heat of Geoff's need, that Danny began to see what all the fuss was about. He started turning into a committed and—he hoped—talented and nasty S/M top. That was another surprise, one that required a bit of self-acceptance on his part. He could tell himself, especially at the start, that he was only doing it because it made Geoff happy, but he knew damn well that wasn't true. He enjoyed the power, the sheer nastiness of it, making that handsomely ordinary face of

Geoff's break apart in pain, revealing what lay beneath the clean-cut exterior: the crouching darkness that lived, Danny figured, inside every human animal.

Geoff, moaning, pushed his asshole out, then sucked Danny's hand right in. A guy's insides, Danny mused, weren't quite what you'd expect, more of a maze than you'd think. It *all* was a maze, a complex firing—*bing bing bing*—of the synapses of desire. Sometimes, though less and less often, he'd remember Miguel, how much simpler things had been before the multiple losses, loss of boyfriend and surprising loss of innocence. Now that he was no longer just a vanilla slut, part of him could watch himself abusing his boyfriend—like others had watched him on porn tapes—while another part of him gleefully hammered away.

But if life was hard, Geoff was soft, inside and out, and yet paradoxically tough. He could take a fucking hell of a lot, and Danny loved him for that. Because Danny chose to believe what Geoff said: that Geoff was doing it, taking it—the pain, the humiliation, the fist—out of love.

And now Danny's hand was all the way inside, and Geoff was way the fuck out there, eyes rolled up, thin stream of drool trickling from his beautiful lips, precum dripping from his piss hole.

They'd almost broken up, months before, shortly after the sex had gotten rough. There was already enough cruelty in the world, Danny had said one tearful night, without bringing it into their bed. It was then that Geoff finally had confessed: "I knew who you were when we first met. I knew you'd done porn before you told me. I'd owned your stuff, had a few of your tapes. I couldn't believe it, that you'd actually want to have sex with *me*. And now...God, Danny, please don't leave me."

"Stop crying. Please."

"I love you, Danny. You don't have to do anything you don't want to. Just don't leave me."

And Danny stayed.

He looked over at the bedside clock. Two in the morning, and it was a workday, damn it. Music filtered from the CD player in the corner, an old Lou Reed song. *It's such a perfect day...*

"Geoff?"

"Huh?" Floating.

"I think it's time to wrap this up...I'm getting tired."

"Mm," Geoff said, reaching down for his pretty, semihard cock. Danny started punching his fist softly back and forth, into his boyfriend's guts. His other hand reached down to his own dick.

"Fucking faggot. Take it, faggot," Danny said, because that's what Geoff liked to hear. The stretched-out hole tightened over his wrist. If Danny was playing a part, it was a part he enjoyed, one he was learning to play well, one that made his dick hard. *...I'm glad I spent it with you.*

When they came, Geoff climaxed in a long, seeping orgasm— endless, thick cum oozing over his belly, trickling down his wide hips. Danny pumped hard into his own hand—short, sharp thrusts, gushers pounding out wildly.

After they'd gotten their breath back, disentangled, and cleaned up, they fell asleep in each other's arms, sheltered from the vagaries of fate. *Oh, such a perfect day. I thought I was someone else, someone good...*

The alarm dragged Danny into the morning. Not enough sleep. Geoff would be working from home today so Danny let him snooze on.

When he was ready to leave, he walked over to the bed, softly pulled back the blankets, and looked down at the fleshy, beautiful body of the man he loved so damn much. He bent over, kissed Geoff's forehead, whispered, "Bye, sweetie. See you soon."

It was just a short subway ride to the office, but he was a bit early and surprisingly full of energy, so he decided to walk the dozen blocks to work instead, something he rarely did. He felt so good. It was indeed a perfect day, a beautiful September morning. The sun shone down, round and honeyed as the Buddha's compassion, as Geoff's asshole. And as the two towers got larger and larger, a thought arose. He could call in sick, head back home, talk Geoff into fucking off too, spend the day with him in bed. Or he could walk on, spend the day in his cubicle high up in those twin towers. It's what he was supposed to do, what he'd committed to. It's what responsible adults did. Still...He hesitated, breathing in the fresh diesel of the city air.

It was a beautiful day.

publicationcredits